Christmas CRISIS

Coleman Creek Christmas Book Three

Rory London

Five Hearts PRESS

Presents belong in boxes.
People don't.
This book is for anyone who has ever struggled with that.

Christmas CRISIS

Playlist

"The Christmas Blues"
Dean Martin

"I'll Be Home for Christmas"
Michael Bublé

"Good King Wenceslas"
Bing Crosby

"Across the Universe"
Fiona Apple

"At Last"
Etta James

"Never My Love"
The Association

"Sweet Gingerbread Man"
Sammy Davis Jr.

"Santa Tell Me"
Ariana Grande

"God Rest Ye Merry Gentlemen"
Bad Religion

Chapter One

Miranda

NOW

Liar, Liar Pants on Fire

Slimy Little F*ckb*y

Stone is the Absolute Worst

Scrolling through my Instagram feed, dread clawed at my stomach. The app's incomprehensible algorithm knew my habits, that I always slowed down at mentions of Stone. And now it had plenty of material to show me. I lay in my bed and swiped through post after post of vitriol. The online haters had found their latest outrage.

Be Honest, You Always Suspected Stone was a Creep

Top Three Reasons to Hate on Stone Caseman

Stone Caseman Bites the Hand that Feeds Him

This was not good. And the worst part was, it was all my fault.

I slammed my phone down on the bedside table and sat up against the headboard, running my fingers through my hair. The knot in my chest tightened. I'd already texted Stone, but he hadn't replied. I decided to give him a few more minutes before calling. Holding a pillow to my nose, I huffed my frustration into the cotton. Should I delete the photo? Or would that look like an admission of guilt?

Picking my phone back up, I opened the app and forced myself to assess the potential damage.

The image itself was open to interpretation. A selfie of me and Stone squeezed together on a couch. His arm hung around my shoulders, fingers splayed over my bare biceps. My head tilted toward his neck. I remembered the day. We'd gone body surfing off the coast of Maui before retreating to our secluded rental. We certainly looked cozy. Still, one picture could be explained away.

The problem was that internet sleuths had gone through every photo in my feed, looking for clues to prove their more salacious theories.

Look in the background, it's obvious she's at Stone's house! That picture is from the coffee shop Stone goes to. I'm pretty certain there are pics of Stone with that jacket she's got on. The woman she's with is Stone Caseman's personal assistant.

Just as I finished reading the last one, the woman herself messaged.

SHOSHANNA (STONE'S PA): Are you up? I'm calling in five minutes.

SHOSHANNA (STONE'S PA): I'm assuming you've seen? What were you thinking?

SHOSHANNA (STONE'S PA): Never mind. You can tell me when I have you on the line.

I groaned and fell back against the mattress. It wasn't even seven o'clock. My plan had been to sleep in for the first time in months. Then my phone started pinging. And pinging.

And pinging.

Last night, I'd been feeling sorry for myself. Everything was jacked. Stone. Work. *Leo.* I'd spent the late evening hours with cheap vodka, Hulu, and french fries before falling into bed.

Part of my pity party was in response to the fact that today was the first Thanksgiving in years I wouldn't spend with my sisters. Maureen and Marley had left for an off-the-grid trip with their partners. They were staying at a friend's cabin and planned to do the big turkey dinner there and then hang out for ten days to relax and go snowshoeing.

Our entire lives, I'd been the *outdoorsy* one, so the irony wasn't lost on me that the first time my sisters wanted to do something sideways of a city or beach retreat, I was stuck in the office and couldn't get away. Then again, as much as I hated being on my own for the holiday, I had no desire to be the fifth wheel on their romantic trip.

Because they hadn't invited my boyfriend.

To be fair, they also didn't know he existed.

Scratch that. They definitely knew he existed. They just didn't know he was my boyfriend.

Also, Leo might be there.

But even without those deterrents, the possibility of my going was a non-starter. I'd only been hired on at my new job in September. It was too soon to ask for time off. Luckily, the office closed for the week between Christmas and New Year's, so at least I'd be able to go home to Coleman Creek then. That left me four weeks to feel sorry for myself.

I was stuck in Los Angeles. With no family. A still-unfamiliar job. In a standoff with my best friend.

And no boyfriend.

Stone was filming in Vancouver. We'd talked on FaceTime last night before I'd settled in with the vodka bottle and *The Bear*. I knew he felt bad that I was spending the holiday alone, but he also had an early shoot. Canadian film crews didn't care about American Thanksgiving.

He was probably on set at this very moment.

Or maybe he wasn't. Perhaps he was busy finding out that I'd accidentally ruined his life and made him a target of social media vultures. Maybe he was hiding in his dressing room doomscrolling and reading all the terrible things people were saying about him.

I barely had time to go to the bathroom before my phone rang. Shoshanna's taskmaster voice came through immediately.

"Hey, Miranda, you know that photo was completely unacceptable. Totally in violation of your agreement."

Alrighty, then. So not even a "hello." Also, I was unclear which "agreement" she referred to, other than the imaginary one in her head. She'd spent the past year pestering Stone to make me sign an NDA, but I'd never been comfortable with that, and he hadn't pushed the issue—although he had brought it up again recently. Fame had come so quickly and furiously for him that it always seemed like he was playing catch-up to learn the rules. I imagined he would have insisted on the legal document eventually, but he'd accepted my word until now.

Which made me feel doubly bad. He'd put that faith in me, and I'd repaid him by being careless.

I sighed, flexing my jaw. "Hi, Shoshanna. Yeah, I know I messed up. I promise I didn't do it on purpose."

"What were you thinking? After all this time, to be so remiss?"

I'd been thinking it sucked balls to be home alone on the couch the day before Thanksgiving. I'd been thinking I had important things to say to Stone, but as soon as his face popped up on my screen, I knew it was the right call to save them until we were in person. I'd been thinking about how I'd finally started my new corporate job, but the rest of my life was stuck in limbo.

And I'd been thinking about Leo.

But sulking wasn't in my DNA. I was a firm believer that a lot of true happiness began with playacted happiness. Keeping my chin up was my comfort zone. So I'd been consoling myself by going through old photos on my phone, trying to capture better energy by posting some favorites under the caption "Good vibes dump."

Ten photos. And I could have sworn the Maui pic I chose was of me solo in the surf. But clearly, the evil vodka and greasy fries had lulled me into inattention. Because the picture I'd actually included was the incriminating couch selfie.

My profile was public, my account less me and more nature-loving doppelgänger, and I'd amassed a decent following after seven years of posting my travel and outdoor adventure photos.

Closing out of the app last night, I had no idea that I'd unleashed a storm. But someone had recognized Stone. And then the sharing began.

And now—here we were.

"Have you heard from Stone?" I asked Shoshanna, rather than answering her question. "I'm surprised he hasn't called me. Or even texted."

"I told him not to," she answered matter-of-factly. "I'm worried his texts are being stolen, frankly, which is a fucked-up thing to have to worry about. He called me on my landline at home this morning. I guess one of the guys on set woke him up. I'm working on a plan with the publicist. Stone's going to get a burner and said to tell you he'll call you as soon as he can. I'm assuming your phone is safe for now since people are just figuring out who you are. As far as I can tell, no one has connected your Instagram account to Miranda Davis. At least not yet. I suppose that's lucky."

"I need to talk to him, Shoshanna."

"And you will. But first, let's get him the temporary line. It might be overkill, it probably is, but it'll make us all feel better to be careful."

"Seriously? Can you please expedite that process? He's my boyfriend. And this is on me. I need to explain." I was a little annoyed that Stone had called Shoshanna but not me. Except that was on-brand. I might be his girlfriend, but he relied on his PA to tell him what to do, where to go, and who to talk to.

"Like I said, you will," Shoshanna repeated. "But let's make a plan first."

Her voice sounded frustrated, but I didn't sense genuine anger behind it. She was a professional.

Like everyone given the label of "famous for being famous," Stone had his detractors. No doubt Shoshanna had been preparing for something like this for a while.

"I'm really sorry," I offered. "I had too much to drink last night and posted the wrong picture." Thumbing through my albums, I saw the shot I'd intended to put up directly beneath the one I'd posted. Just a slip of the finger.

A slip of the finger that ended more than a year of successful subterfuge.

"I know you are," Shoshanna said resignedly. "And this plan with Naomi was always risky. If I could go back in time, I don't think I would have done it. I knew people would take an interest in them, but not to this degree."

Yeah, hard same, girl.

When Stone and I began dating fourteen months ago, he'd been a somewhat well-known internet personality. His profile rose significantly after he was cast in an indie movie co-starring Naomi Butler, who'd been in the public eye since childhood with a role in a popular family drama.

Halfway through filming their movie, a few months after Stone and I became exclusive, Shoshanna and Naomi's assistant hatched a scheme to drum up interest in the movie by having Stone and Naomi "date." Up to that point, he and I had kept our relationship private. His friends didn't know. I hadn't even told my sisters. So the plan wouldn't even require Stone and me to stage a breakup.

The prospect of watching my boyfriend go into public places with "America's Sweetheart," not to mention the physical affection they would need to engage in to perpetuate the ruse, hadn't been my favorite thing. But since our relationship was so new, and with both their publicists convinced it was a prime opportunity, I hadn't felt right vetoing the idea when Stone asked me.

To his credit, he made genuine efforts to ensure my comfort with the situation—short of not doing it, of course. He let me know exactly what was going on, detailing their plans at every turn.

I got texts at all hours that said things like:

STONE: Just warning you I need to kiss Naomi outside the restaurant when we leave. Shoshanna said it has to be on the lips. Sorry. *sad face emoji*

STONE: Shoshanna gave me a gold chain to wear with an infinity symbol on it. I have to tell people Naomi gave it to me and then always wear it. Sorry. *head smack emoji*

STONE: There's an article coming out where Naomi got asked if I have a big *eggplant emoji* and she didn't reply yes or no. (Shoshanna told her to just smile if someone ever asked her that question). Sorry. *green nausea face emoji*

That last one stung. At least no reporter had been gross enough to ask Stone whether he'd compare Naomi's breasts to grapefruits or melons.

In truth, I got used to the situation quicker than I thought I would. It helped that when their deception began, I had a busy life of my own. My MBA program kept me plenty occupied, not to mention my family and friends, part-time job, and planning for a post-graduation career. In a lot of ways, having what amounted to an incognito boyfriend, someone I didn't have to account to my friends and family about, worked for me. Most of the time.

And while Stone and Naomi dined at the trendiest restaurants and strutted across red carpets all over the country, he and I enjoyed cozy nights in and trips to private destinations.

Stone and Naomi had been pretend-dating for eleven months, and we'd achieved a stasis that worked for all of us. Stone got a girlfriend who grounded him in his non-celebrity life. Naomi got to date an up-and-coming bad-boy type who helped modify her image. And I got a relationship with someone fun that required minimal effort or accountability.

But even though I'd settled into the arrangement, that didn't mean I'd never questioned it.

Because a year was a long time for no one to know the truth about us. No one except me, Stone, Naomi, and their handlers.

And Leo.

"Honestly, I don't think I would have agreed to it either," I told Shoshanna.

She caught the undercurrent of my words, the implication that it was the PR teams who'd made things harder when they moved the finish line midway through the race.

Instead of honoring the original plan to have Stone and Naomi end their "relationship" amicably after the movie's premiere, they'd insisted on maintaining the deception, arguing that the positive publicity was worth it.

I was usually a cool cucumber, but it wears on a gal after a while when the entire world thinks your boyfriend is in love with someone else.

Which was why I'd planned to bring the situation to a head sooner than later.

But not like this.

"Well, I guess it makes no difference what we would have done in hindsight." Shoshanna exhaled noisily, drawing me from my thoughts. "The only thing that matters now is that every troll on the internet thinks Stone cheated on Naomi with @theadventurousmiranda, and they're out for blood."

"Should I delete the post? Turn off comments?"

"I'll get us on a video call with the publicist within the hour. Let's see what she says. The damage is done. I'm not sure if it makes you look more guilty."

Exactly my thoughts from earlier.

A call from an unknown number interrupted us.

"Gotta go, Shoshanna. I'm guessing that's Stone."

Five seconds later, I picked up with a sheepish, "Hello?"

"Hey, darlin'." Stone's slow drawl came through the phone. "Happy Thanksgiving... Soooo, I'm guessing you hit that vodka pretty hard after we closed out last night?" He chuckled low, and I could picture him shaking his head. "How are you doing with all this?"

I might have just ruined his career, and he was worried about me. Damn.

It strengthened my resolve. No matter what happened between us, I needed to fix this.

DURING OUR CALL, THE PUBLICIST, Lauren, told me to leave the post up but turn off the comments. Then we brainstormed ways to convince people that something true wasn't (Stone and me) and something that wasn't true was (Stone and Naomi). My head swam just thinking about it.

They asked me how Stone seemed, and I replied that he thought things would blow over soon. Shoshanna and the rest of his team had guided his career to extreme heights practically overnight, so he had a lot of faith in them. Also, he was a mellow guy in general. His amiability was something that had drawn me to him initially—the most authentic part of his otherwise curated image.

Shoshanna and Lauren spoke with Naomi's people, and they decided the first order of business was to make sure the world saw Stone and Naomi together. Then we'd convince the public that Stone and I were just friends. Naomi would back us up, saying she knew me and had met me many times, and that would be that.

Then another photo showed up online.

Someone else had been on the beach in Maui. They'd caught me and Stone in the background. In that picture, he held me in his arms, wrapped in a towel. I remembered the moment. We'd been sitting outside, waiting for the sunset. I couldn't recall seeing anyone near us. The cabins were a quarter mile apart. But that was definitely my towel, and that was definitely the outside of our cabana.

In the photo, we gazed into one another's eyes. Like lovers. Harder to explain away than the couch selfie.

Shoshanna, Lauren, and I got on another call.

"We could say it was manipulated," Lauren suggested.

Shoshanna shook her head. "That would work for a while, but since we know the picture is authentic, it's too risky a strategy."

"Why isn't it enough for Naomi to say she doesn't think Stone cheated on her? Like, if she knows me and all, shouldn't that be adequate?" I asked.

Lauren tsked sadly. "When Naomi was a kid, her handlers did her dirty. They leaned into this bubbly, perpetually innocent version of her, so even as she aged, everyone assumed she could be taken advantage of. Being with Stone was working in terms of rehabbing that persona. She was finally being perceived as more of a grown-up. But if she goes on record as trusting Stone despite the photo evidence, they'll assume she's being manipulated. The public tends to be cynical. It's easy to buy the narrative that an upstart social media star used sweet little Naomi for his own gain."

"That doesn't seem fair. I've met Naomi. She's no dummy."

"Welcome to being a young woman in the public eye."

I grimaced.

Lauren pinched the bridge of her nose, adjusting the camera to display less of her nostrils. "We need the public to believe you and Stone are just friends. The pictures are just so damning."

A thought occurred to me. I almost didn't want to voice it out loud, but it refused to go away.

"Would it help if the public discovered that I've been involved with someone else for the past few years? If pictures are what it takes to persuade people, what if there were a bunch of me being cuddled up to a guy who isn't Stone? Going places and hanging out with him?"

"You want us to stage photos with another man?" Shoshanna hummed. "I feel like it might backfire. Nowadays, folks are pretty good at sussing that out."

"I wasn't suggesting that. I'm asking what would happen if those pictures actually existed."

Shoshanna glared menacingly at her camera. "Have you been cheating on Stone?"

I pffted. "No. Keeping things quiet with him has been a big enough pain in my ass. Trust me when I say I don't have the capacity to maintain more than one secret relationship at a time."

"Fair enough," Lauren said, lips twitching. "Then what do you mean?"

"Stone may be my boyfriend. But he's not the only man in my life. And I have plenty of photos to prove it."

Chapter Two

Leo

NOW

I stretched my arms above my head, rolling out the shoulder kinks from tiling for the past hour. My crew had agreed to work on Thanksgiving morning since the homeowners said they'd pay us double to keep the project moving. I still planned to make it to my parents' house tonight for turkey and pie, but otherwise, I'd be spending most of the long holiday weekend at the jobsite.

Gathering up my tools at the end of the shift, my world tilted on its axis when I overheard a conversation between two of my crew members.

"Who do you think @theadventurousmiranda is?" Amala asked.

I halted at the mention of Miranda's Instagram handle.

"I dunno," Lisa replied. "But that Hawaii pic was from March, so whoever she is, she's been in Stone's pants a long time."

Placing my toolbox on an empty pallet, I tried to act casual as I walked closer to the bench where they sat looking at their phones. "Hey. What are you talking about?"

"Oh, hi, Leo," Amala said. "Just some hot celebrity goss." She laughed lightly. "Not your thing, I know."

"You never can tell," I said with a shrug. Clearing my throat, I added, "You're talking about Stone Caseman, right? ... I, um, I'm a fan."

Amala eyed me skeptically. "Really?"

"Mm-hmm." I hung my thumbs on my belt loops.

She didn't look convinced but answered gamely. "Well, you might be less of a fan when you find out he apparently cheated on Naomi Butler—you know they're dating, right?—with some random hoochie mid-wannabe-influencer."

"Oh, wow." The shocked face I conjured wasn't entirely contrived. Miranda had been so careful. "Do they know who the, uh, random hoochie is?"

"Nuh-uh," Lisa replied. "Just her Insta handle. And the only thing you can tell from the profile is that she's an action-adventure type. She doesn't give away anything personal in the captions."

"Her bio says she's based in Los Angeles," Amala put in.

I was familiar with Miranda's Instagram feed. I looked at it more often than I probably should. In addition to amazing sunsets and lush landscapes, there were plenty of selfies. It didn't sound like her identity was public yet, but obviously, it would be soon.

"Maybe it's a misunderstanding," I offered.

"Or maybe Stone is a rat bastard cheating bitch," Amala said forcefully. "And this adventurous Miranda person is a ho."

Ouch.

I wanted to ask more questions, but my coworkers were already looking at me like I'd been body-snatched.

After waving a quick goodbye to the crew, I hurried to my truck and pulled out my phone. I found several Reddit forums synthesizing what happened. Luckily, next to politics, crime, and news about bigger celebrities, the story of Stone and Miranda seemed to be a relatively niche topic. That it wasn't dominating my social feeds was a good sign.

But even without dominating, it was still there.

I let out a groan. I'd known something like this would happen.

As soon as Miranda started dating that dipshit, a ticking clock began. Eventually, being with someone who got famous by drinking hot sauce and cannonballing off rooftops into backyard pools was going to blow up in her face.

Especially when that someone insisted on keeping their relationship hidden.

I'd only known Miranda for two years, but our bond was already truer and deeper than any other relationship in my life. From the beginning, she'd understood me like no one else. Her sister Maureen joked that our closeness stemmed from the fact that Miranda and I were essentially the same person, except I was the massive thirty-six-year-old male version, and she was the spritely twenty-seven-year-old female version. Miranda's approach to the world mirrored my own—drink deeply from life, be happy, and express gratitude for whatever good you encounter. Don't sweat the small stuff.

Stone coming into Miranda's life nine months after she and I met had been a hiccup, further complicated when he started fake dating Naomi Butler, but mostly, we'd weathered it.

But ever since Miranda graduated from her MBA program and started working her first career job at a big marketing firm, something had been off. With both of us.

Things really came unglued a month ago, on Halloween.

The memory of our call that night still sat in my stomach like lead. We were as honest as we'd ever been, and we'd paid a hefty price for it. I'd clumsily said too many things she hadn't been ready to hear.

The next day, I called her, hoping twelve hours to cool off had put us back on level ground.

Her phone rang three times before it picked up.

"Hey, man. I saw it was you, so I answered. Mir's in the shower."

"Stone?"

"Yeah. Is it urgent? I can grab her if it is. Or you can call back and leave a voicemail if it's private."

I hated it when Stone was considerate. He'd been cool with me ever since I stumbled onto his and Miranda's relationship, trusting me to keep their secret. And to the best of my knowledge, he was respectful of our friendship. It annoyed me sometimes to realize he wasn't a bad guy. Just a thoughtless one. But I'd never apologize for wanting better than thoughtless for Miranda.

His presence in Miranda's apartment—with her in the shower—hit me like a bitter dose of reality. After everything I'd said, she'd gone to him.

"No. No message. I'll shoot her a text later."

I hadn't texted.

And neither had she.

Now it looked like I had no choice but to break the stalemate. I thought about my coworkers unknowingly calling my best friend a ho. I couldn't sit idly by while Miranda became a target of internet trolls.

Even though I lived in Tacoma and she lived in Los Angeles, we'd been good at making that distance disappear. I wanted her to know that no matter what was going on between us right now, I would always be in her corner. Especially since I knew her sisters were currently out of reach, at a cabin in the middle of nowhere.

I cradled my phone in my palm. If it was awkward, so be it. She needed me.

But before I could press the dial button, it buzzed.

MIRANDA: Hey Leo. I know things are weird with us ATM. But can I call you in a sec?

ME: Of course. Weirdness can take a back seat for now. I saw what happened. Are you ok?

MIRANDA: Glad you saw. I didn't want to have to explain. And honestly, dude, I could be having a better day *winky side-eye emoji*

At least she seemed to have a sense of humor about it.

ME: I'm really sorry. Anything I can do?

MIRANDA: That's why I want to talk. I think I might have come up with a way to do damage control and clean this up. But I'm gonna need your help. And I want to ask in person. If it's okay with you, I'd like to fly up for a couple days.

She needed to come here? To have a conversation? It wasn't unlike her to travel spontaneously, but still.

ME: I'm supposed to work but I can see about getting a sub.

MIRANDA: Working Thanksgiving weekend? Shoot. I thought it would be okay.

ME: Special job. But let me check. You're more important.

MIRANDA: Thanks L. I needed to hear that.

ME: Anytime

MIRANDA: I'll call you in a few minutes. I'm still waiting to hear back from Stone's PA on some things.

I took a deep breath. Just seeing his name on my screen irritated me.

ME: Is Stone with you?
MIRANDA: In Vancouver on a shoot. Closer to you than me *smiley emoji* But he and I talked this morning.
ME: Okay. Well I'm done working for the day. Just call me when you can.
MIRANDA: Thank you again. And Happy Thanksgiving.
ME: You too

The phone stayed warm in my hand as I watched the three dots appear and disappear for long minutes. I wondered what other things she'd written and erased before a message finally came through.

MIRANDA: I've missed you, Leo-Bear. Talk soon.

Chapter Three

Miranda

NOW

The drive from the airport to Leo's apartment in Tacoma was less than half an hour. The whole way there, I kept waiting to feel nervous, but it never materialized. Not during the flight. Not when I walked through the terminal. Not when I hauled myself into the rideshare at 11 p.m. After the way we'd left things on Halloween, I should have felt some trepidation about seeing him face-to-face, but I didn't. Only relief that we were talking again.

Even if the circumstances were less than ideal.

When I first heard his voice a few hours ago, I almost cried into the phone. Until the moment he'd picked up—his "Hi Miranda," followed quickly by "How can I help?"—I hadn't realized how much his absence from my life over the past four weeks had affected me. I'd masked it with work and Stone and other forgettable nonsense, nearly convincing myself it was okay. But hearing his deep baritone offering comfort broke a dam inside me.

I'd missed my best friend.

As much as I'd wanted to cry and apologize and give in to my emotions, I forced myself to focus on the disaster at hand. Leo would do Thanksgiving with his parents as planned, while I drove to LAX and caught the first flight to Seattle. He offered me his second bedroom for the weekend. For a hot minute, I thought about getting a hotel, but if he was willing to put Halloween behind us, I was going to take that gift. Besides, I'd stayed at his place so many times it would have been strange not to.

And now that we'd hashed out those logistics, I steeled myself to make a big ask of him.

Shoshanna and Lauren had agreed to my plan after I showed them the cache of photos on my phone. Contrary to what my forty thousand Instagram followers believed, I was actually a pretty private person—hence the reason my socials contained only pics of my adventures, not my friends, family, school (now work), or home life. As far as the internet was concerned, I was an extrovert who liked to travel and do outdoorsy things. Still, I'd maintained an air of mystery, not hinting at my identity. I didn't even caption most of the images.

But the albums on my phone told a different story.

There were pictures of Stone and me. But since we spent most of our time together at our homes, other than a few secluded vacations, there weren't many. You could only pose for so many living room selfies before you got bored with it.

Most of my personal pics were disorganized and banal. PowerPoints taken during classes, screen grabs of QR codes, evidence of cooking fails and makeup tutorials gone wrong, weekend hiking trips with friends, an unreasonable amount of adorable dogs I met on the street, bookstore shelf shots reminding me what I wanted to check out from the library, and candids of me with my sisters.

And Leo. Beautiful, warm, Viking-statured Leo. Starting two Christmases ago, when his brother James fell in love with my sister Marley, he'd been a constant presence in my life. And my camera roll.

Even though he lived in Washington state and I lived in California, we'd been able to get together somewhat frequently and stayed omnipresent in each other's lives thanks to the twin miracles of texting and FaceTime.

There were pictures of us at Disneyland and the Grand Canyon. Dancing at Marley and James's wedding. Holding hands before doing a Polar Plunge. For the first time, I was thankful Marley had made Leo and me wear matching footie pajamas for Christmas last year.

I'd only had to show Shoshanna and Lauren a few to make them enthusiastic about my idea. The many screenshots I'd taken of Leo and me video chatting especially excited them. Leo was terrible with phone angles and therefore often unintentionally hilarious, prompting me to preserve close-up shots of his inner ear and forehead pores for my amusement, including the timestamps.

We would still be accused of faking the photos, of course, but since none of them were faked, it was our best hope.

As long as I could get Leo on board.

He opened the door to his apartment before I even knocked. "Miranda, I know I said this on the phone, but I'm so sorry for how we left things after Hallo—"

I barreled into his arms. "You don't need to apologize, Leo. We both let it get out of hand. I know you only questioned things because you care about me."

The tears I'd been holding back since that morning fell onto his shirt.

He wrapped me tightly in his arms, resting his chin on the top of my head. "Hey, you're okay. You're okay... Ssshhh." His hands ran circles over my back. "And you're right. I do care. I'm just glad our stupid argument didn't keep you from calling when you needed me."

Sniffling, I breathed in the familiar scent of him. Sandalwood from his soap combined with the vaguely fruity smell of his shampoo.

I closed my eyes, pushing my cheek into his broad chest as I mumbled, "I hope you still feel that way when I explain."

He pulled away and set me back from him, handing me a tissue. Picking up the duffel I dropped, he slung it onto his shoulder before tipping my chin up with one finger to meet my gaze. "You know I'll do whatever you need."

Meeting his eyes, I swallowed. He held my stare for a few seconds before dipping his chin.

I followed him into the living room. It hadn't changed since the last time I'd been here in August.

After Marley and James's wedding in July, I spent most of the summer in Coleman Creek, the little town in north central Washington where I'd grown up and where my sisters still lived, but I'd stayed a few days with Leo before heading back to Los Angeles. I hadn't seen him in person since then.

Since the incident in the bed, my brain reminded me, before I quickly shoved the thought away.

A certain rightness settled over me whenever I returned to the Pacific Northwest. Even though I'd lived in California for nine years, it had never truly felt like home. Looking around Leo's familiar apartment, I realized it was as much a home base for me in this state as my childhood house in Coleman Creek.

I loved Leo's place. Always had. It was oversized and quirky. Just like him.

Dove-gray walls surrounded the open-concept kitchen and living room. An overstuffed brown leather sectional held center stage in front of the large flatscreen, covered in an array of mismatched throw pillows. An enormous charcoal drawing—a Dalíesque surrealist interpretation of the London skyline—took up almost an entire wall above the small dining table. I'd once asked Leo why he had this weird, dark, pseudo-goth, not-at-all-subtle piece of art in his home as it didn't seem to align with his personality.

"I didn't buy it because it spoke to my soul or anything like that," he'd replied matter-of-factly. "Mostly, it's because it reminds me of the conversation I had with the artist." Then he told me about a flea market he'd been to in a little nowhere town in Oregon, where he'd met an elderly painter who had amazing stories about growing up in Castro's Cuba.

A piece by the same artist hung in the hallway, a bowl of fruit with the apocalypse in the background, and another in the guest bedroom, a sinister vision of a sunrise over a desolate landscape, with a nuclear cloud visible. The first time I stayed over, I put my stuff down on the bedspread and stared at the painting before turning to Leo. "I get you had a moment with the artist, but that looks like a bad metal band's album cover. If I have nightmares…"

He'd chuckled. "If you have nightmares, I'll protect you."

Nearly two years later, I still recalled the way those words made me shudder.

Leo carried my duffel into the guest bedroom while I sat down on the couch. I'd only been awake since my phone started going off that morning, but it felt like weeks.

"You hungry?" Leo asked, walking into the kitchen. "I brought a bunch of leftovers back from my parents' place. It was only the three of us, but Mom made a huge spread."

"That would be amazing, Leo-Bear." Without thinking, I added, "It's bizarre that I resigned myself to skipping Thanksgiving and now I'm having turkey dinner with one of my favorite people in the world."

He sucked in his bottom lip, nodding. "I'll heat up a little of everything."

"Thanks. Not too much, though. My stomach's been in limbo all day."

"Understandable. But you're here until Sunday, right? We have time to make a dent in these leftovers."

"Yeah."

I needed to be back at my desk on Monday morning. Prepared to be an exemplary employee. Shoshanna and Lauren were certain my identity would be revealed by tomorrow, and I didn't want my bosses to be upset with me once they realized their new marketing assistant was involved in a celebrity gossip scandal. I already felt like I was stumbling at work, still getting my feet wet at the company. The last thing I needed was for this to make things more uncomfortable.

"Were you able to get the weekend off?" I asked Leo.

"I compromised," he answered, pulling plastic containers from the fridge. "Tomorrow morning, I'm going to work a half day, then I got a sub in for Saturday, so you'll have me most of the time."

Emotion welled in my throat. Despite our spending the past month at odds, he wasn't missing a beat stepping up for me now. I twisted my hands together in my lap.

"Listen, Leo. I really appreciate you having me and feeding me, so I think I ought to lay out the reason I'm here."

He paused in the act of spooning green bean casserole onto a plate. "Alright."

"Before I explain, I want to be very clear that you can say no. And there won't be any hard feelings between us. We'll still be best friends."

Putting the plate in the microwave, he turned in my direction with a sigh. "I didn't want to push. But obviously I'm curious." He sat down next to me.

I straightened my spine even as my right knee bobbed against his. "You get the gist of everything going on with Stone, right? How the part of the internet that cares about these sorts of things thinks he's cheating on Naomi Butler with a mystery girl who is, in fact, me?" Leo bobbed his head. "Well, Shoshanna—you remember that's Stone's assistant—doesn't think a simple denial is going to cut it. Once they figure out who I am, and they will, it will be even more real. Stone and I have done a decent job keeping our relationship private. You're the only person in my life who knows about him and me, and he's been guarded too, so our friends and family will have plausible deniability. But Stone and I haven't been total mole people, either. There are resort staff and other guests who might have seen us on vacation, and not just on that Hawaii trip. I've accepted food deliveries at his house and driven his car to the mall—little things that didn't matter when no one was paying attention. But now those details might add up."

"I see," Leo said thoughtfully. "I suppose there's no possibility of just telling the truth? Admitting the relationship with Naomi was for publicity?"

"Not that I'm an expert, but that would probably be just as bad as his being a cheater. Either way, the fans would feel duped."

His mouth turned down. "What's your solution?"

"To explain to the public that Stone and I are just friends, that there's no way he and I could be in a romantic relationship because I'm already in one with someone else." I eyed him.

"Me?"

"Uh-huh. There are so many pictures of us together, and we look so relationship-y."

"Relationship-y." With his flat delivery, I couldn't tell what he was thinking. He pressed back into the couch cushions.

At his lack of response, I continued rapidly. "The idea is that Stone's people release a bunch of photos of you and me from the past few years, proving we've been a couple. And even though I don't have personal stuff on social media, both my sisters do. There are enough pictures of us on Maureen's and Marley's public profiles to prove our case. If it came to that."

Leo stood and began pacing. "So you want to tell people we're in a relationship and have been for a while?"

"Yes. We say that we're both friends with Stone, maybe Naomi too, but that it's you and me who have been dating."

"What if people think you and Stone are cheating on me and Naomi with each other? Why does our being in a relationship prove different?"

In my conversation with the PR team earlier, we'd addressed this possibility. "Shoshanna thinks that as long as you and Naomi confirm the story of us all being friends, it shouldn't be an issue. Once the public knows about you, it'll be easier to believe this was all a misunderstanding. Even if they were ready to turn on him this morning, people want to believe Stone and Naomi are in love."

His lips pursed. "What about our family? Our friends? What do we tell them?"

I drew in a breath. "This is the part I think you're gonna like least." *The part Shoshanna and I argued over the most.* "It's best if we do everything we can to truly...sell the story."

Leo's eyes widened. "Wait... You want to tell them we've been dating? Like, this whole time? And kept it from them? My brother and my parents?"

"Yes." I fixed my gaze on him. "It's believable. Everyone always says how close we are, and as far as they know, I've been free to date you."

Leo resumed pacing. "And what reason would we give them for hiding our relationship? I'm fairly certain my parents have been a pinch away from asking me directly why we aren't a couple. What am I supposed to say?"

Unlike Leo, I'd had hours to answer all these questions in my mind.

"We tell them we were only dating casually at first, maybe since James and Marley got engaged. They would understand why we wanted to be careful and not risk our friendship. Plus the family dynamics. After that, we didn't tell them because we didn't want to steal any thunder from the wedding. And we worried about disappointing them if things didn't work out, so we kept it to ourselves. I know that explanation might hurt them a little, but it's plausible enough that they'll accept it. I've been quiet about my love life for years, so that'll track. And you don't talk about dating either, so they won't question it."

"You know why I don't talk about it, Miranda."

My breath caught. Of course I knew. I was one of only a handful of people who did. "I think they'll be so happy for us they won't dig too deep. They'll see why we chose to do it at this moment once I'm linked to Stone in the media."

"And when they find out the truth?"

"We'll cross that bridge when we come to it. But we're grown adults, Leo. As much as I love my sisters, they're not my primary consideration here."

"No. That would be Stone." A rare bitterness crossed his features before he turned away.

I stood, hovering a hand above his shoulder from behind. "Stone is important to me. You know that. But that's not entirely the reason. I'm the one who made this mess. Now I feel obligated to fix it. I realize none of this is on you, and I'm asking you to help me clean up a problem I created. But I am asking... Please help me make this better."

Leo spun to face me. His features appeared heavy with resignation but also, thankfully, affection. "Of course I'll do it. You know I'll always be there when you need me." After a beat, he opened his arms, and I stepped gratefully into his embrace. "If the reverse were happening, I know you'd do the same for me."

"Absolutely, I would."

"Okay. Then how about you eat some of this food before it gets cold, and we can go over specifics tomorrow? Get our stories straight."

"We're doing this?" I needed the extra confirmation.

"Yeah, Miranda. I will be your pretend boyfriend so you can help your dumbass real boyfriend out of a PR problem he's having with his fake girlfriend."

I laughed. "Okay. I think it's going to be easier for us to create this illusion than it would be for a lot of people. Between our matching timelines, photos, and how often we're together, it shouldn't be hard to convince anyone, friend or stranger, that we're a happy couple."

23 MONTHS AGO - DECEMBER

THE BOXES AND FURNITURE FIT NEATLY on one-half of the carport. The last of Mom's things, ready to go to charity. I put my hands on my hips, contemplating the piles. It didn't seem real sometimes that she'd been gone for over a year, but I was glad Marley was finally moving into her old room. No use for the biggest one in the house to sit empty.

Still, seeing the scarred oak bed frame in pieces cut deep. I'd spent so many nights in it as a child, huddled with my mom and sisters watching movies. I didn't regret moving to California for college, but each time I came back to Coleman Creek, everything felt a little different. A little less like home.

I heard shoes shuffling on the concrete floor. James's brother, Leo, walked in carrying my mom's old dresser. I'd met him the day before at the Coleman Creek High School Talent Show. James sang a holiday song to Marley, declaring his undying love for my sister with a sappy slideshow backing him up. They were both teachers, so I supposed nothing said "I love you" like a well-executed PowerPoint presentation.

There was no doubt in my mind that Marley and James were in it for the long haul, so I figured Leo would be a part of my life too. Good thing he seemed like a nice guy. We'd exchanged small talk over the past twenty-four hours, and he'd been nothing but friendly and approachable—all smiles, which was how people often described me.

He placed the heavy dresser down carefully on the concrete. "Hi, Miranda." Puffing out a breath, he straightened. "Everything okay? Can I help you carry anything?"

"No, thanks. I'm just sort of taking a minute to...sit with all of this."

His eyes softened as he wiped an arm across his brow. "Gotcha. Sorry for intruding."

"Oh, no. Don't even worry about it. You're not intruding. Truly. I'm not feeling sad...only being mindful of the moment."

He dipped his chin. "I'm sure your sisters appreciate that you're here for this. I'm glad to help as well. Marley's told me some great stories about your mom."

I hummed. "She was really something special. And as much as I agree with donating her things so Marley can move into the big bedroom—it is her house now, after all—it's still hard." I ran my palm over the dresser. "When I'm away at school, I can almost convince myself Mom's still here, waiting for me. Then I come home, and each time, it's like she's slightly more...gone."

Leo put his hand over mine, patting it gently. "You're still grieving, and it's okay to take it slow. The fact that you're helping Marley move into your mom's old room tells me you're probably doing okay, even if it's a lot to take in."

The acceptance in his eyes settled me. My sisters and I talked about our mom all the time, and of course we'd mourned together, but it was nice to hear from an outside source that it wasn't an overnight process.

Or a linear one.

The sinews of Leo's forearms rippled as he picked up the dresser again to wedge it closer to the boxes, tightening the space. Impressive. That thing was solid wood and weighed a ton. But I assumed he possessed the strength to match his size. He stood at least six foot four without shoes and appeared to be made of bulky muscle. With his longish blond hair and beard, my mind immediately conjured an image of Thor. I bet he got that a lot, with the likeness so uncanny. The thought made me snort.

"What?" he asked.

"Honestly? I was wondering how often people compared you to Thor."

His right cheek lifted. "It's happened once or twice."

I guffawed. "I suppose there are worse things."

He stacked a plastic bin on top of another and exhaled. "I'm girding my loins to bring your mom's old mattress down here. The junk company won't pick it up until after Christmas, but I think Marley wants it out of the house so she can set the room up."

"Girding my loins" with a straight face? I liked this guy more by the minute.

"It's really nice of you and your family to help move everything." Leo and James's parents, Chris and Deanna, were upstairs sorting clothing.

"James is crazy about Marley. We all are. Feels like helping family."

He meant it. Leo was obviously kind, like his brother.

"Who do people compare you to?" he asked.

"Huh?"

"You know, like I get Thor a lot. I'm guessing with your blond hair and how beautiful and outgoing you are, you get...Barbie?"

I cracked a smile. "It's happened once or twice."

"I'll bet."

With any other person, I would have interpreted his words as flirting, but his delivery was so neutral, I didn't think that was the case.

"For the longest, it was Elle Woods," I said, "but lately, it's been almost exclusively Barbie. Probably because of the movie."

"Elle Woods?"

"*Legally Blonde*?" He stared blankly, and I shook my head with a laugh. "Never mind."

We stood across from one another, our poses mirror images as we each bent one knee to rest a boot against the carport's support posts.

"Do you like the comparison?" he asked.

I blew air into my cupped hands before answering. "It's not that I mind it, since Barbie is sort of a feminist icon. It's just that people have been calling me 'Outdoor Barbie' at school for a few years now, because I travel and hike and climb and raft and stuff. But I'm also getting my MBA and graduated summa cum laude with my bachelor's. They mean it as a compliment, but it feels a little reductive, being narrowed down to my hair color and the fact that I can get a decent campfire going." I shrugged affably. "I dunno. Maybe it's the plight of every blond to be taken seriously. That's the stereotype, anyway."

"Believe me, I understand, working in construction. The God of Thunder is cool and all, but it gets old being asked where my magic hammer is at every jobsite."

His eyes danced, but I knew he'd grasped my point. Commiserated with it.

People assumed I was always a warm, bubbly ray of sunshine. Perpetually cheerful. I'd perfected the art of keeping my cloudy days to myself. And while I considered myself an overall happy and contented person, it was nice to have a more nuanced thought and not feel like I was busting apart someone's image of me. I could be optimistic and playful and exuberant and still not be Barbie. Leo seemed to understand that.

"How about I think up a more generalized nickname for you?" he offered. "And you could do the same for me. Nothing narrow. Just boring and simple. Like how James's friend William is Will."

"You know you can just call me Miranda?"

"I like a challenge."

A laugh escaped me. "You sound like you might already have some ideas?"

"How about Mir?"

I smiled. "My sisters call me that sometimes. You can call me 'Mir' if you want to."

Leo shook his head. "Nope. I want one just for me." He waggled his eyebrows.

That definitely seemed like flirting. But looking at his face, I could just tell that it...wasn't. Strange.

"Do you need a nickname for your brother's girlfriend's little sister?" I asked, amused.

"No. But since they're dating, I'd like to get to know you better. If that's okay. When James gave us the rundown of Marley's family, he told us Maureen was the 'intimidating' sister, and you were the 'sweet' one. I get the shorthand, but there's obviously more there. With both of you."

"I am sweet," I said wryly.

"You're other things too."

"How are you so sure?"

"I have a sixth sense about these things. You're someone worth knowing."

I caught the subtext. It was like recognizing like. Not as in, *I'm also worth knowing*, but rather, *I also want to be known.*

My heart thumped a few extra beats.

Marley had mentioned that James's brother was nice, but she hadn't gone far enough. Between his moving heavy furniture, asking thoughtful questions, and giving genuine compliments while expecting nothing in return, Leo was impossible not to like.

I felt compelled to know him too.

Over the next two days, Christmas Eve and Christmas, we spent a lot of time together. He interacted with Marley and Maureen, and was very solicitous of his parents, but we kept winding up in each other's vicinity. Sitting next to one another at dinner. Opening presents side by side in the living room. Playing with Marley and James's dogs outside.

I learned that Leo was a contractor in the Seattle area, working for a company specializing in renovations and remodels for luxury homes. He was thirty-four, nine years older than me. He rented an apartment in Tacoma because he was saving up to buy a house and drove an older model truck for the same reason. Although he never said so directly, I gleaned from context clues that he wasn't currently dating anyone. He loved plain pasta with red sauce and listening to memoirs on audiobook. The most embarrassing moment of his life was farting during the one and only yoga class he ever tried. He lifted weights at the gym, but other than that, his job kept him fit.

Leo and his parents had driven separately to Coleman Creek because Chris and Deanna were staying until after New Year's, while Leo needed to return to the city for work. I decided to save my sisters the long drive and hitched a ride to Seattle with him. He offered me his second bedroom for a few days until my flight to Los Angeles.

Even though we'd just met, I felt comfortable enough to agree. The plan didn't faze our families either. They'd all noticed how well we got along.

"It's like you and Leo are two peas in the same nauseatingly chipper pod," Maureen declared.

I'd happily take that descriptor. I'd never felt such an instant connection to someone the way I had with Leo, and the prospect of spending the next few days with him had my senses buzzing.

Chapter Four

Leo

NOW

I told my crew chief that I would stay until noon. We were making good progress on remodeling the lakefront home for a wealthy older couple. The clients seemed like good people. Besides paying us double time for working over the holiday weekend, they'd provided lunch for the team as well.

"Cutting out?" Charlie asked as I gathered my tools, grabbing one of the delivered sandwiches to eat during my drive home.

"Yeah. Thanks for the save getting the sub. I'll miss the overtime pay, but it couldn't be helped."

"Unplanned visitor, you said?"

"Yeah, my...friend...from California showed up." I almost said girlfriend because I wanted to try out the word, but it got stuck on my tongue.

"Miranda?" Of course he knew who I was talking about. I'd introduced them several times over the past few years when she'd visited.

"Yep. She, uh, thought she had to work but was able to get off last minute."

"Cool. Tell her I said hi."

"Sure thing."

As Charlie went to sit with Amala, I recalled he'd asked me a year ago if Miranda and I were dating. I'd told him no. I wondered what he'd think when he saw pictures of *my girlfriend* and me online over the next few days.

Because the project was well ahead of schedule, my company was giving everyone time off until after the New Year once it was complete. My guess was we'd finish the punch list around December 5. Even adding in another day or two for paperwork, I'd have almost a month off.

Funny enough, last week I'd contemplated how I should use that time, and I'd put going to California to set things right with Miranda at the top of the list. After that, I'd planned to spend the Christmas season with James and Marley in Coleman Creek. I was almost as fond of my brother's adopted town as he was. But I guessed this new arrangement with Miranda might require some flexibility there.

And that was fine with me. From the moment she'd launched herself into my arms last night, I'd been filled with overwhelming gratitude that our connection was not irreparably damaged. Our fight on Halloween had been awful, and I wouldn't have blamed her for doubting whether she should come to me. As annoying as it was to watch her berate herself for potentially harming Stone, I would have hated it more if she'd thought I wouldn't help her and hadn't reached out. But she had. Despite everything, she knew I had her back.

I wasn't completely sold on her assertion that she'd caused this problem, though. While it was true that she'd accidentally posted a photo she shouldn't have, Stone could have avoided the PR nightmare by not beginning his deception with Naomi in the first place. But we'd already had that argument, and it had only caused hurt between us. At least with this plan, I had something to do. A way to be proactive instead of just watching from the sidelines while Miranda wrung her hands over Stone.

It felt like I'd been gritting my teeth for a year.

Charlie reappeared at my side as I latched my toolbox. "It's probably a good thing you're leaving early today," he said, reaching into the cooler for a soda. "Amala told me her whole family is visiting for the holiday. All the sisters."

I smile-grimaced. Amala had three younger sisters, all single, and all looking for boyfriends. The joke on our crew was that whenever her siblings were in town, our colleague turned from a badass construction worker into a scheming matchmaker. And it wasn't like the sisters were bridge trolls or had terrible personalities or anything. It was just that none of the guys wanted Amala involved in their love lives. Not that it stopped her. The last time her sisters visited, she introduced them to me several times and orchestrated a few *accidental* run-ins at the food truck near the jobsite.

"Good thing you're happily married," I said to Charlie.

"No doubt."

It occurred to me that one upside of being in a fake relationship with Miranda would be relieving the pressure of having to answer to anyone about my single status or general lack of dates. I didn't have close friends other than Miranda, only acquaintances and coworkers good for the occasional hang. Still, after they'd asked enough awkward questions to figure out I wasn't gay, they pretty much all offered to introduce me to women they thought I might be interested in.

On the surface, I understood. I was thirty-six and single, never married, with decent enough looks, a good job, not a weirdo or a psychopath, and could hold my own in conversation. I enjoyed gaming, but not to excess, ditto with alcohol, and I treated women with respect. Not in a creepy manosphere vlogger way, but genuine respect.

I liked women. I did. I just didn't want to date them.

But fake dating, I could do. For Miranda.

"Alright," I said. "I'll make my escape before Amala can tell me how much her little sisters want to see the inside of my truck."

Charlie burst out laughing. "Don't forget to tell *your friend* I said hello."

WHEN I LEFT MY APARTMENT around six that morning, Miranda had been sleeping off the events of the day before. When I got back, she was still in bed. Only now she was crying.

I heard her sniffles from the living room as soon as I opened the front door. I was on my way to find out what was wrong when another voice came through loud and clear.

Nasally and annoying.

"Darlin', it's gonna be okay. I like the plan. With Leo. He's a good dude, keeping our secret this whole time. This is gonna work."

Stone. Ugh. Video chatting with Miranda. At least he hadn't manifested in my apartment. But it made me queasy to hear him say nice things about me. All of this would be less complicated if he were a mustache-twirling supervillain instead of just a thoughtless little twerp. I resented that I—somewhat—sympathized with Miranda's desire not to destroy his career.

Not wanting to eavesdrop, I rapped on the hallway wall.

"Come in."

Miranda scooted up against the headboard when I entered, patting the space beside her on the unmade bed. She was still in a T-shirt and pajama bottoms, and her hair didn't look brushed. Her computer sat open on her lap. Stone appeared to be sitting in a set trailer, with a rack of clothes behind him. He'd be unrecognizable to most of his fans, who were used to his wild hair and the beachy, shirtless vibe of his videos. The loveable himbo. The Stone on screen had slicked-back hair and wore a well-fitting black suit with a black button-down underneath, open to mid-chest. His hair had been darkened, and he sported three days of beard growth.

"Hey, Leo!" Stone waved enthusiastically. "Do you like the threads?" Leaning away from the camera, he pulled out his lapels. "I'm playing a Mafia enforcer. Pretty cool, right? It's only for one season because—spoiler alert—my character gets blown up in the last episode. Man, I'm really looking forward to filming that—"

"Focus, Stone," Miranda admonished gently. "Unless you want the general population to wish your blown-up character is actually you, we need to make sure we're on the same page here."

"You're right. Sorry." He gave an *aw-shucks* smile. "I get excited talking about this gig." Stone stared straight at the camera. "Leo, my dude, I want to tell you how much we appreciate you doing this. Shoshanna thinks it should all be smooth soon. Miranda is still upset by her oopsy, though, even though I keep telling her I know it was an honest mistake."

Miranda pressed against my side. "I'm not really crying anymore. Stone just woke me up with a call request—Shoshanna finally got a new laptop to him—and I think it made me emotional seeing his face, after everything that happened yesterday. I'm good now."

"You're more than good, babes. You're beautiful. I'm just sorry we've done so much of our relationship this way, over screens, and I wish I could be there in person to tell you it's gonna be okay."

I could tell Stone's remorse was sincere. As much as moments like this helped me understand why Miranda started dating him in the first place, and perhaps why she'd stayed in it as long as she had, his lack of urgency got under my skin. He seemed perfectly content to let Shoshanna—and Miranda—solve this problem for him.

On the bed, Miranda burrowed into me, pulling my arm around her shoulders. Stone remained unfazed. I supposed the people in our lives were so used to our affectionate behavior that it no longer merited a second glance. Even from her boyfriend.

To me, she said, "Stone was telling me that Naomi is all-in with the plan. But they also agreed that they're going to wait to end things until after Valentine's Day—it would be too suspicious to do it now—so no one freaks out again. Shoshanna will send out her statement about us within the hour. By some miracle—or maybe because of the holiday—no one's revealed my identity yet. Lauren thinks it looks better that they're releasing my name now, to show we're not trying to hide anything."

"Which means if there's anyone you want to give the heads-up to, this is the time," Stone chimed in.

"Are you going to tell anyone?" I asked Miranda.

"Since my sisters are unreachable until next week, I only need to warn my supervisors. I'm going to shoot them an email in a few minutes, letting them know my fifteen minutes of fame are starting."

I thought about my work situation. "My crew doesn't need a heads-up. They already assume Miranda and I are secretly together."

"Really?" Miranda sounded intrigued.

"Mm-hmm. It's easier for them to wrap their minds around, since they don't know why I don't date."

"You really don't, then?" Stone asked. "I've never seen you with anyone, but I always figured you were just, like, discreet." He chuckled. "I bet you'd kill the game on dating apps. You could lean into the whole magical hammer thing."

Oh, that's right. Stone is still Stone.

I pushed the mute button on Miranda's side of the call. "You didn't...tell him about me?" I questioned, avoiding moving my lips so Stone couldn't make out the words.

"Of course not," she answered the same way.

Pushing my fingers against my forehead, I breathed out. "Sorry. That was stupid. I shouldn't have asked."

I unmuted the computer. "My bad, Stone. Technical issues." Scooting a few inches away from Miranda, I said, "The reason I don't date is complicated... And private."

He raised his palms. "Hey, no worries, dude. Your hammer is your business."

Miranda covered her giggle with a cough.

Muffled shouts sounded from behind Stone. "Dang. Gotta get back on set." He stood. "Thanks again, Leo. Babes, we'll talk soon."

"Talk soon," Miranda replied to the already-black screen. Facing me, she asked, "Seriously, who do you need to tell?"

"Right now? Just my parents. And as soon as your sisters, James, and Will get back, them too."

Miranda rose from the bed and stretched her arms above her head. The move displayed a ribbon of toned stomach and pushed her breasts against her thin tee. A twinge of electricity zipped down my spine at the sight of her pebbled nipples. I forced myself to ignore it.

"You can call your parents while I take a shower. I smell like an armpit." She sniffed her shoulder.

"You do not smell like an armpit. I'm the one who's been sweating at a jobsite all morning. I'll call my folks and then shower when you're done."

"Hopefully they aren't pissed at us."

"I doubt they'll be upset."

Miranda grabbed a towel from the linen closet before hesitating outside the hall bathroom. "Leo?"

"Yeah?"

"It's oddly okay, isn't it? This thing we've set in motion. Once we've told everybody in our lives, all we have to do is *date*. It seems too easy."

"Miranda, you of all people know it's not going to be that easy for me. I can stand next to you, take you out, hold your hand, and even put my lips on yours if you think it's necessary. But I don't know how to make it look real. Being with someone."

Anchoring the towel over her shoulder, she approached and looped her arms around my neck. As my hands raised instinctively to grab her hips, she lifted on her tiptoes to kiss me on the cheek. "I'll help you, Bear."

I felt it again. The twinge. It raced through me, hiding and dipping and diving between the usual nothingness. I'd held Miranda in my arms like this dozens of times. But now, as she stepped away and sauntered into the bathroom, it was there. Not just a twinge. A lingering awareness.

Not so long ago, that feeling had been a revelation.

Now it taunted me.

Yesterday, Miranda worried things might be awkward between us because of leftover tension from our fight. She didn't know it, but she was only half right.

23 MONTHS AGO - DECEMBER

Miranda and I didn't stop talking the entire way back to Seattle. She hooked a playlist up to my truck, but we'd barely made it out of Coleman Creek before we turned the volume down to hear each other talk.

Getting to know her had been the highlight of my holiday, which was saying something, considering my brother James had just made it official with the love of his life. But no one could blame me for falling under Miranda's spell. By the time she told me her three all-time favorite TV shows, *Game of Thrones*, *Mad Men*, and *Stranger Things*—of which I'd seen all and included *Mad Men* in my top three—I realized how long it had been since I'd felt so relaxed and open with anyone.

I kept my acquaintances and work relationships surface-level. A quick coffee. The occasional movie or ball game. Things were just easier that way. An effective strategy for avoiding questions.

Being with Miranda reminded me that sometimes it was worth the discomfort of getting past the surface to forge a closer connection with someone. I'd missed having that in my life since James moved to Coleman Creek.

Unfortunately, a tight bond wasn't likely to happen with Miranda either, considering she was twenty-five and lived in California. But the thought of playacting at it with her for a few days lit a spark inside me.

Truthfully, it didn't feel like playacting at all.

More importantly, by the time I turned my truck onto I-90, I had solved the question of the nickname.

"*Panda*?" she said incredulously, making a face. "Four days to think about it, and that's what you come up with?"

"What? It *rhymes*," I declared, as though that settled the matter. "Plus, it's generic enough to be meaningless."

"Other than the rhyming?"

"Other than that. Obviously."

"It makes zero sense."

"Miranda-Panda, or just Panda to keep it simple. Because you're cuddly and sweet, but you are also rare and exotic and precious."

She stuck a finger in her mouth and made a gagging noise.

"It's decided," I said, grinning at the windshield.

She puffed up her cheeks. "Alright, then. How about I return the favor?"

"A nickname?"

"Uh-huh."

"My very own nickname? From my very own Panda. I'm honored."

Miranda's lips twitched as she rolled her eyes. "Thor is a god, right? Larger than life? Kind of like you?"

"You think I'm godlike? Wow. Thanks."

She flicked my arm. "Just large. With much more of a mouth on you than I thought when we first met, clearly."

"It takes me a minute, but I'm warmed up now."

"I gathered," she replied, her tone so low and rich it drew my eyes to her briefly as she continued. "You need a nickname appropriate for your general"—her hand waved at me in a circle—"largeness. But you also have to atone for *Panda*."

A huff worked its way from my throat. "I'm listening."

She paused dramatically. "From this moment forthwith, I dub you 'Bear,' or when we are in formal settings, 'Leo-Bear.'"

"*Leo-Bear*?"

"Yep. Turnabout is fair play. If I'm a bear, then you are too. And not a cool one, either. Just a plain old boring one. You don't get to be a Kodiak or a polar or a grizzly."

"Generic 'Bear' is not the insult you think it is. I can live with it."

"We'll see." She smiled and crossed her arms.

"Panda?"

"Yes, Bear?"

I smiled. "Just checking."

I carried Miranda's suitcase into the guest room, pointing out where I kept the extra towels in case she wanted to shower. But she said she was tired after the long drive, so we both retreated to our beds almost immediately.

It wasn't until I woke up in the morning and heard Miranda moving around that it struck me how unusual this situation was. Not bad, just unfamiliar. I'd never had a woman stay over during the six years I'd lived in this apartment. James had crashed in the guest room plenty of times, but having Miranda in my space felt different.

As I pulled on joggers and a sweatshirt, the sound of water running in the hallway bathroom startled me. When was the last time I even turned on that shower?

From our time in Coleman Creek, I knew Miranda was a coffee drinker, and I'd seen her eat all kinds of breakfast foods. I had six near-expired eggs in the fridge. Before whisking them up to scramble, I put four slices of sourdough in the toaster.

I was scrolling through options on the TV when the water turned off. A moment later, Miranda appeared in the hallway wrapped in a towel, directly in my line of sight.

Our gazes caught and held. I took in her long hair, which she'd brushed away from her face. Wet tendrils strayed across the apples of her pink-flushed cheeks. I registered the curve of her shoulder, as perfect as a painting. Just like the rest of her. The towel hitting at mid-thigh emphasized the sculpted muscles of her long legs. The slender fingers of her hand trembled slightly where she held the knotted towel between her breasts.

I knew it was impolite to stare, that I should cast my eyes away so she could retreat. But I couldn't. I felt compelled to study the striking woman before me, drawn to her in a way I couldn't articulate.

As our silent conversation stretched into seconds, she bit her lip, peering at me from beneath her lashes. A visible swallow worked its way down her throat. Looking at her eyes again, I saw her pupils widen. In her expression, a question lingered. *Hopefully, she didn't think…?*

Shit! What the fuck was I doing? Staring at her like a creep.

I smiled in a way I wanted to seem friendly without being dismissive as I turned back to the TV.

"Hope you're hungry," I said. "I'm making breakfast."

"Oh, yeah, sure." Her voice stuttered. There was confusion there, but no detectable anger or embarrassment. I heard her damp footsteps as she entered the guest bedroom, then the *snick* of the door shutting.

I exhaled.

When Miranda emerged five minutes later dressed in jeans and a snowflake sweater, she appeared unperturbed. She sat at the high bar attached to my kitchen counter. I handed her a plate and a cup of coffee, pointing at the creamer in case she wanted to doctor it. Instead of seating myself on the other barstool, I stood across from her and leaned over my plate on the counter.

I piled my eggs onto my toast, sandwich-style, before glancing over to see Miranda had done the same thing.

"There's a tomato on its last legs," I said. "Want me to slice it up for these?"

"Yes, please."

We ate our egg-and-tomato sandwiches in easy silence while the news played on the muted TV. This piece of a relationship—this quiet, not-laced-with-expectations companionship—was the piece I sometimes thought I could do. The piece I sort of wanted.

"You're working today?" she asked.

"Today and tomorrow, although only half tomorrow since it's Saturday. I'm off Sunday for New Year's Eve." Miranda's return flight was on New Year's Day. I wished I didn't have to work so much for these few days she'd be with me. "Do you have plans?"

"I have friends from Coleman Creek who live in Seattle now, so I'm going to see them. But I'll be back by tonight."

"Wanna grab dinner? Order in?" Hopefully, I didn't sound too eager. But I wanted to spend time with her and have more of these moments before she flew away.

"Sure. I assume my friends will want to grab lunch, so let's order in. Two restaurants in a day is a bit much."

"Thai okay? I have a go-to place."

"Love it."

That night, we shared pad Thai, massaman curry, and fresh spring rolls, and watched *It's a Wonderful Life*. I hadn't bothered with a Christmas tree in my apartment, but Miranda produced a cinnamon-scented candle from her bag that Marley had gifted her. We lit it so at least my living room smelled somewhat festive.

Miranda moved closer to me on the couch as the night wore on, bending her knees to nestle her leggings and wool socks against my thigh. I slung my arm around her shoulders. She looked up when I did that, studying my face. After a few seconds, she turned back to the movie.

The night was...cozy. Peaceful.

I didn't take it for granted.

We drank hot chocolate and played Scrabble before heading to bed around eleven.

"Good night, Leo," she called from the guest room as I put our mugs in the dishwasher. "Thank you for today. And for letting me crash here." Happiness warmed my chest as she added, "You know, when my sister fell in love with James, I wasn't expecting...this. But it's been a pleasant surprise. Hanging out this week."

The fullness in my heart intensified. "You're welcome here anytime. I mean that."

She nodded and slipped behind the door.

Sleep proved elusive. My mind churned, knowing that Miranda was in my home. I didn't hate the feeling. Although I didn't consider myself a lonely person, I did spend most of my non-working hours alone.

For most of my adulthood, I'd avoided certain situations and attachments because I worried about disappointing people. And up until Miranda nicknamed me 'Bear' and sang along to Nick Drake in my truck, holding myself apart hadn't felt like a sacrifice.

Now I wasn't so sure.

I closed my eyes. Behind my eyelids, pictures flashed. Miranda's grief-tinged smile as she spoke about her mother. Miranda wrinkling her nose at being "Outdoor Barbie." Miranda cheating at Scrabble, insisting GOODZY counted. ("It is a word! Like, this hot chocolate is super goodzy." Of course I'd given it to her.)

More images rolled through my mind. The heartiness of her laughter. The kindness of her words. The perfect slope of her neck.

For the first time in forever, I recognized something foreign in myself.

Curiosity.

It was a pinch, a flicker, a blink-and-you'd-miss-it specter, but it was there.

With a start, my eyes flew open.

A dart of excitement went through me.

I didn't want this week to be a fun one-off with my brother's girlfriend's little sister. I wanted more days like this. A real friendship with Miranda.

SUNDAY NIGHT, WE GRABBED DRINKS with my coworkers, and Miranda charmed them all. I introduced her as my friend, which earned a few puzzled stares from my crew. They'd never seen me with anyone, but the explanation that our siblings were dating seemed to make sense to people.

"You sure there's nothing there?" Charlie asked me, gesturing to Miranda, who was playing pool with Lisa.

I shook my head. "We get along great. But that's all."

We stayed at the bar until eleven, deciding to watch the New Year's Eve fireworks on TV at my apartment. I'd offered to drive us into Seattle to see them live at the Space Needle, but Miranda said she'd done it a few times as a kid and that was enough for her. I wasn't about to complain about another night on the couch.

Close to midnight, I was still trying to figure out how to ask if she wanted to be intentional about staying in touch. With James and Marley partnered up, we'd certainly see each other occasionally, but if we were going to be real friends, we'd need to be more deliberate than that, since we lived in different states.

In my thirty-four years, I'd never had this conversation. I'd grown used to falling into shallow friendships with coworkers or guys at the gym, and I didn't know how to broach the subject.

As the fireworks played on TV, the pink and blue lights reflected in her eyes. She was getting on a plane the next day. I needed to do something.

"Miranda?" When the show ended, I turned off the TV.

"Hmm?" She moved her head sleepily from my shoulder to lie against the armrest on the other side of the couch.

"I have a New Year's resolution."

One of her eyes opened. "Am I supposed to guess?"

I chuckled. "That wasn't where I was going, but out of curiosity, what would you say?"

She opened the other eye and raked a calculating gaze over me. "Let's see. We've already discussed your exercise habits, and you eat pretty healthy. You don't smoke. Or drink too much. Or spend too many hours on social media. And nothing about this apartment or your job situation shows money issues or, like, a gambling problem. You don't strike me as a porn addict or secret internet troll. I also haven't noticed any hoarding tendencies. You're a good son and brother, and your main hobbies are reading and lifting weights at the gym—"

"Was there a guess in there, or were you just going to keep extolling my virtues?"

"Shhh, Bear. I'm thinking. Mesmerizing you with my superior deductive reasoning skills." She snapped her fingers. "Travel more? Maybe listening to all my dumb stories gave you the bug... Oh, no, wait, speaking of bugs, is your resolution to get a pet?" She tapped her foot against my thigh.

I laughed. "No pets allowed in the building, unfortunately. And the travel thing is a good guess, but you were closer when you talked about me listening to your stories, which are not even the least bit dumb, by the way."

"Huh?"

"I'd like to hear more of your stories. Actually..." I smiled. "My resolution is that I want to stay friends with you. I mean, if that's something you're up for."

She pffted. "Um… That's it? Not much of a reveal. Of course we're going to be friends. I doubt James and Marley are breaking up anytime soon. You haven't seen the last of me by a long shot."

"True." I chose my words carefully. "But what I meant was, I want to make a go at being real friends, not just the kind that get thrown in each other's path every once in a while." I shifted my body to face her on the couch. "Hopefully, you know me well enough after this week to get that I'm being upfront, and not some kind of crazy stalker—"

"I would never think that."

"Then I guess what I'm saying is that I've loved hanging out with you, and I'm willing to put in some effort to make that happen more often."

"What do you mean?"

"I mean that if we try, we can see each other more than just when you're in town to visit your sisters. There's texting and FaceTime, and if I hard-drive it, I can make it to LA in a day. Plus, flights are quick and fairly cheap. You're in school, so you have natural breaks, and my work schedule has some flexibility too."

Miranda tilted her head. "You want to come to LA and see me so we can be friends?"

"Not all the time. But…yes?" I scraped a hand through my hair. "Look, I know it sounds odd. I *can* hear myself. But I don't know how else to say it. We had a lot of fun this week. I felt so relaxed with you… And not to sound like a total loser, but I don't make friends easily." At her considering expression, I plowed on, "You can say no, of course. Maybe this is all me, and you have loads of friends and don't need to hang out with a random mid-thirties construction worker…" I dropped my hands in my lap, lacing my fingers until the knuckles turned white. "But I didn't want to let you fly away tomorrow without…putting it out there."

She pushed her foot against my thigh again. "You're definitely not a loser." Her warm blue eyes settled on mine. "I don't think anyone has ever proposed something like this to me before. Friends have always just sort of come in and out of my life by chance."

"I realize that's the usual path, but I guess I didn't want to risk it. Not with us." Now that I'd let her in on my thoughts, certainty made me bold. "I know we just met, but it feels like I've known you for years. Like we're meant to be in each other's lives. Not just on the edges."

After a few beats, she murmured, "I feel the same way."

It was hard to tell if the barely audible sentiment was for me or for herself.

I whooshed out a breath.

"You thought I'd say no?" she asked.

I shrugged. "Fifty-fifty likelihood you'd flee my apartment in horror."

Her jaw ticked. "You're not getting rid of me that easily, Bear." She shifted to hug her knees.

The weight dissolved from my chest. "Glad that's settled." Standing, I stretched a hand to her. "I guess we should get to bed, then, since we need to wake up at five to go to the airport."

She nodded, placing her palm in mine. "And Leo?"

"Hmm?"

"I'm glad it's settled too. As in, I'm happy you asked me." After rising and giving me an inscrutable look, she turned toward the hallway. "Night."

"Night, Panda."

The next day, I dropped her off for her flight. I felt her absence immediately, letting myself sit with the unfamiliar ache. A moment later, my phone buzzed.

MIRANDA: I admire you. That conversation was a risk. But you were right. Not having it would have been a bigger one.
MIRANDA: See you soon, pal.

It couldn't be soon enough for me.

Chapter Five

Miranda

NOW

Shoshanna and Lauren sent the story of my "relationship" with Leo to an independent entertainment journalist they trusted. By early afternoon, pictures of me and Leo, along with our names, basic information, and a rough timeline of our involvement, were in the public sphere.

I made my account accessible to Lauren so she could help keep track of comments, grateful I'd never expanded to other platforms. We hid some comments that came in on the first day and turned off the ability to add new ones to older posts. It wasn't a total scrub, but it made the trolls' job harder.

Together, we crafted a statement that I posted alongside a carousel of ten pictures of Leo and me.

"You know me as @theadventurousmiranda, but my given name is Miranda Davis. I'm outing my identity because I feel the need to defend my friend, Stone Caseman. I met Stone by chance during a

*trip I took with some friends last fall. At the time, his videos were just starting to take off. I'm not interested in being a more well-known public figure (hence why this is the first time I've put my name on this page), so I asked him to make sure I didn't appear in his videos or on his socials. While I value Stone's friendship, the main man in my life is Leo Wymack. Leo and I met two years ago. Technically, we're family since his brother is married to my sister, even though we live in different states. Our relationship has been mostly long-distance, like my friendship with Stone, but it is quite serious. I'm asking my followers, other commenters, and members of the media to please stop insinuating that I am anything other than Stone's friend. I wish the best for him and Naomi. Thank you for reading, and I hope you will excuse me while I return to my life as a person with no desire to be in the public eye. *heart emoji*"*

The good thing about the statement was that it was worded to be somewhat true. I had met Stone camping near Laguna Beach, and I had requested we keep our relationship private from the beginning. And since meeting, we'd spent significantly more time apart than together.

Leo looked over my shoulder as I posted it.

"Can I veto that picture of me in the car?" he complained. "I have, like, twelve chins."

I tittered. "You're not usually self-conscious."

"I'm golden until eight chins."

"Shoshanna thought it would be a good one to use because it's so candid."

He spread his arms wide. "Oh, well then. Pardon me. I suppose if the wise and all-knowing Shoshanna said it…"

"Stop being difficult."

In the picture, Leo slept in the back seat of his truck. I remembered the day. During one of our long drives, we pulled over at a rest area. I'd reclined the front passenger seat and leaned back so the frame captured both of us. With my head practically in his lap, I held the camera above us, making a peace sign and duck face while Leo dozed in the background. I understood why the PR team thought it was a good choice to prove our closeness. It certainly looked intimate. But Leo made a fair point that he'd been sleeping in a funny position, and multiple chins could be counted.

"I suppose it's fine," he grunted.

"The one of us at Marley and James's wedding counterbalances it," I argued. "You always look amazing in a suit."

He blushed—just a little. "Thank you." Picking up his phone, he sat down next to me on the couch. "I have an account, but I don't post on it. I only use it to follow people. Do I need to?"

"I talked to Lauren about that. She said no. If anyone asks, we'll just say you're not on social media. With your obscure handle and profile pic, no one would guess it's you following me."

Leo's profile picture was the fruit-bowl-apocalypse painting in his hallway.

"Out of curiosity, what do you plan to say if anyone asks about the Hawaii picture?"

"The idea is to not address it directly. I'm not going to answer any questions. No need for me to linger as part of the story. We want to keep reminding people that Stone and Naomi are the famous ones here. If Stone gets asked, he's supposed to just say we were in Hawaii at the same time and watched the sunset together. Basically, say as little as possible and hope that all the other stuff makes his holding me look less sus. My feed during that time is shots of me body surfing and hiking in the jungle, so it's easy enough to make the argument that it wasn't some romantic watch-the-sunset trip."

"It's not a perfect plan, but I think you're right. It'll fade."

"Definitely not perfect. But probably easier to manage than trying to pretend the people in the picture aren't us, or that someone manipulated the photo."

"It's crazy how we can't trust pictures anymore."

"No idea what you're talking about, Leo-Bear. Sabrina Carpenter definitely has six fingers on her left hand and wanted to be the face of the cannabis shop on the corner."

Chuckling, he opened the app on his phone to confirm that my statement popped up on his feed. "Is Stone going to repost this?"

"Hopefully, he won't have to. He's releasing his own version, essentially confirming what I say here."

Leo rubbed his thighs. "So what do we do now?"

"Lauren will monitor the responses. She suggested I stay off the internet for at least a day, and I think that's good advice. Until this blows over, Shoshanna wants us to be seen together as often as possible. Now that the public is watching, we should go places and hopefully get noticed."

"I'm assuming that means you want to go out tonight?"

I nodded. "I'm in town until Sunday afternoon. Since you're doing me the favor, you can decide what we do. As long as it's somewhere people might see us."

"Great. Because I have an idea."

My cheeks lifted. "That was fast."

"Because it's obvious. Early birthday celebration for you."

I startled. I'd practically forgotten my twenty-seventh birthday was on Monday. But of course Leo remembered. He grinned, and I wondered what he had up his sleeve.

Whatever it was, I didn't care. He'd already given me the greatest birthday gift by sharing this burden with me.

"What should I wear?" I asked.

His expression brightened. "You know Seattle embraces the full hoodie-to-tuxedo range of acceptable attire pretty much anyplace. And you look beautiful no matter what. Just put on whatever you'd normally wear on a date."

"Date, huh? Really committing to the role?"

"I'm really trying to."

20 MONTHS AGO - MARCH

LEO WAS VISITING LOS ANGELES during the break between school quarters. It would be the first time I'd seen him in person since New Year's. My apartment didn't have a second bedroom, but I'd bought a pull-out couch for the living room and some cozy blankets so he could stay with me. He'd offered to get a hotel, but with our time already limited, I wanted to spend as much of it together as possible.

Over the past three months, I'd tucked away bits of intel about what Leo liked. I'd stocked the pantry with spicy wasabi peas and Hawaiian coffee. There were extra-large towels in the bathroom. A basket of paperbacks I'd finished that I knew he'd enjoy sat on the coffee table. He could take those back to his apartment.

We'd texted every day, and video called once or twice a week. Sometimes our conversations were ridiculous, with stupid GIFs or me complaining about my classes. Other times, they felt like therapy.

For a long while, I'd been toying with the idea of being more insistent that the true me wasn't the outdoorsy, thrill-seeking person my friends assumed I was. Even if it upset them or changed their opinion of me. Verbalizing my frustration about that to Leo over Christmas had intensified the urge.

As I slipped cases on the new pillows I'd bought for the sofa bed, I realized how much I was looking forward to being the Miranda only Leo knew for the next few days. Adventurous Miranda could sit the heck down for a minute.

In fairness, it was my fault I'd fallen into the habit of hiding my authentic self.

When I arrived at college my freshman year, I immediately fell in with a friend group of exuberant, kind-hearted students who viewed Southern California as a playground for all things active.

I went with it, telling myself I'd purposely chosen a college far from home to face new challenges and make discoveries. And what was more challenging than being around folks who spoke casually about the hedonistic joys of zip-lining through clouds or conquering class 5 rapids? Excited to be so readily adopted into a tribe, I didn't put a lot of thought into whether it was the right fit. Instead, I leaned into that identity.

To the rest of the student body, our group was fun and chill—"hippies" and "granolas." We were the good-vibe people who got invited to every party, but offended no one when we didn't show up. It was easy.

It helped that my mom and sisters seemed proud. They'd been worried I'd use my newfound freedom and distance from home to experiment with more nefarious activities, so my stories about running a Halloween 5k in a vampire costume or falling off a surfboard fifteen times before finally being able to stand amused them. I reveled in their approval, in being seen as strong and capable, and not just the happy baby of the family.

Also, I wasn't a total noob. Growing up, I'd engaged in plenty of outdoor activities. Hiking and river tubing in the summer and snowshoeing in the winter were part of the Coleman Creek culture. But my new friends introduced me to experiences on a whole new level. Canoeing and paddleboarding. Off-trail skiing. Multiday rafting expeditions. It was exciting and novel enough that I could ignore the hollowness of my connection to them. I wanted deeper friendships, but I didn't click easily with people in that way. Superficial good times I could do. The consequential stuff rarely materialized.

At least no one seemed to find me *objectionable*. I leaned into that. If they couldn't truly know me, at least they could like me.

But as the months and years passed, I wearied of never being fully myself, unable to escape the feeling that I was putting on a performance.

A few years into earning my bachelor's, I finally admitted to myself that my tendency to *go along to get along* wasn't serving me. Despite being surrounded by people, I was lonely. Wanting to see what the rest of the world had to offer, I strategized ways to make more friends. I still wanted to spend time with my current group, but I'd done enough kayaking for a lifetime. My future would include more lazy couch days, nights out dancing, and binge-watching trash TV.

At least, that was my plan.

Then my mom got diagnosed with Parkinson's Disease.

She insisted I stay in school and continue my activities, telling me how happy my "adventure tales" made her. Without hesitation, I put all thoughts of changing things on the back burner. I kept having adventures. Fresh stories for her.

My activities and travels became grander. My tales more epic.

Mountain climbing in South America and Cambodia. Six weeks of volunteer tourism building homes in Mexico, cliff diving on the side. A safari in Kenya and beach days in Croatia, taking odd jobs to fund my excursions.

But even as Mom *oohed* and *aahed* over photos of me and my friends hiking through jungles in Costa Rica, I didn't mention her slow deterioration to a single one of them.

And when she died a year and a half ago, they said, "I'm sorry," but none of them came home with me to attend the funeral.

Before and especially during the years of my mom's illness, my Instagram page provided an outlet for the artificial existence I'd created for myself. It was still shallow, but I had control of the narrative. I invented the persona there. The part I enjoyed most was thinking of it as a business venture—an application of the skills I learned in my classes.

Building up @theadventurousmiranda as a brand sparked my imagination. Trying to game the platform's algorithm, dreaming up reels that gained me hundreds of new followers. I received DMs from start-ups who thought I'd be perfect to hawk their protein powder or hiking boot inserts. I never tried to make money off my page, but its success helped me feel confident in that marketing skill set, something I'd need to sell myself in a crowded job market after graduation.

After Leo and I began talking, I explained the evolution of the character I'd built online to him, emphasizing that she was far from the real me.

"I sort of got that, Panda," he'd said. "From our first conversation at Christmas. It's okay to want to manage how people perceive you as you change and grow, especially when you're in college."

"Did you?"

He scoffed. "Definitely."

"So what were you like back then? Was it hard navigating around all the dinosaurs?"

"Watch it." He laughed. "I was your basic know-it-all little shit. I'd been an athlete in high school and played rec sports during college. Did the frat thing. My bachelor's is in communications, which has been surprisingly helpful in the construction business." His tone sobered. "I had a lot to figure out about myself in my early twenties. Same as anybody."

I didn't press him to elaborate, knowing he'd tell me when he was ready.

Since my mom died, I'd been pulling away more deliberately from my friends, finding excuses not to hang out. The result of six years spent in one another's orbits had turned my group into running buddies and movie dates, but not people I implicitly trusted. Not people I revealed myself to. The more I got to know Leo, the more I understood the difference.

The shift was already beginning. After finally earning my undergraduate degree—traveling had necessitated stretching it out to six years—I'd rented my own apartment for graduate school. Thankfully, my mom left us a nice inheritance, giving me the flexibility to navigate Los Angeles's insane rental market. After downloading some apps, I'd gone on a few first dates and friend dates. I hadn't experienced an instant connection with anyone the way I had with Leo, but making the effort felt like progress.

I looked forward to completing my MBA, holding a stable nine-to-five, and establishing myself on a more traditional path. While I'd still take part in outdoor activities as hobbies, I wouldn't allow anyone to assume it was my entire identity ever again.

When I detailed this vision of my future to Leo, he'd listened with no judgment and, to my great pleasure, no surprise.

"You don't have to sell me on the idea that you're multidimensional," he said. "I know there's a lot more to you than meets the eye. But you need to extend some grace. You're impossible not to love immediately, so you have to forgive people if they neglect to dig deeper." He winked.

"You did," I challenged.

"That's because I know what it's like to have people decide they know you at a glance."

Another enigmatic statement. I didn't push him to break it down because I felt sure I'd get the whole Leo eventually. He'd been giving himself to me in chunks, and I knew the missing pieces would come.

On New Year's, his urgency in asking to be friends had surprised me. I'd been feeling the same pull toward him, although I hadn't articulated it quite as clearly in my mind. He'd done us both a favor by putting it on the table the way he had.

When he'd offered to let me stay with him, I'd thought maybe he felt something romantic between us. I'd certainly been drawn to him. But in his apartment that first day, when I stood in my towel and our eyes met, he hadn't crooked a finger or leered. Nope. He'd simply admired me, the way someone would with a painting or a fancy restaurant meal.

Leo sent classic mixed signals over those initial days. But he seemed so oblivious to his own behavior that I couldn't fault him. I'd tried to figure out where his head was at by throwing out a few feelers—lingering glances, snuggling into him, letting him wrap his arm around my shoulders—but his responses were never more than friendly.

Yet he also wasn't pushing me away or discouraging those touches. He appeared to revel in our closeness. Where most guys would interpret my knees bent into their thighs or my head on their shoulder as an invitation, Leo seemed to stop processing beyond, *man, I really like having your head on my shoulder,* or *it's so cool how comfortable I am with my arm around you.*

He said he didn't have many friends. Maybe he was just bad at knowing where typical boundaries lined up? Or maybe I was wrong, questioning whether exchanging cutesy nicknames and being so touchy-feely signaled something more than platonic vibes?

I'd spent those days in his apartment wondering and was grateful that his ultimate request had been definitive.

We should be better friends.

Just friends.

Now, over two months later, our relationship was more intimate than any other friendship I'd had. I'd even told him things I'd never told Maureen and Marley.

And I felt certain it was the same for him. He texted me about his job, how he sometimes experienced moral panic over renovating homes in wealthy neighborhoods when unhoused people lived in tents blocks away. He watched a lot of cable news, listened to a ton of podcasts, and worried about the state of the world. I reassured him that he had the right to earn a living, that his concern was a sign of decency, that he wasn't alone in his worries, and that he shouldn't feel guilty about enjoying life.

As I dusted my already spotless shelves, I thought about how Leo radiated light and goodness, despite his fears and misgivings. We had that in common. The difference was that when we were together, neither of us had to pretend to be cheerful.

We fit together naturally. Made each other better.

Because I wasn't a plastic doll. And he wasn't a superhero.

LEO ARRIVED LATE AT NIGHT. He'd driven straight through from Tacoma, his truck rumbling in after one in the morning. Before I'd even had a chance to show him around my small apartment, he took one look at the pull-out and barely kicked off his boots before crashing out. He would be here for three days, and we'd be able to spend all that time together since I'd taken the time off from my part-time job at a retail shop near campus.

He was still sleeping when I checked on him before taking a shower the following morning, but I came out of my bedroom after getting dressed to find him sitting up, rubbing his eyes. The blanket pooled around his waist. He'd taken his shirt off during the night, and I felt a very not-platonic stirring in my belly at the sight of his pecs flexing as he groaned and stretched his arms above his head. His pink nipples were quarter-sized, covered with a mat of hair that matched the dirty blond on his head. I peeked lower to see he still wore his jeans, top button undone.

I gulped down my reaction. He wasn't trying to be sexy. He really wasn't. There was only one of us in this room who realized how hot it was for a built guy with bed head and hooded eyes to stretch and roll his shoulders, forcing all that toned, tanned muscle to bunch and ripple.

Jesus. I needed to stop.

"Mornin'," he said, scratching his stomach lazily before following it up with, "Disneyland?"

Huh? "Disneyland?"

"Mm-hmm." He smiled.

"As in, that's what you want to do today?"

"Yep. If you want to, of course."

"I mean, you're the out-of-town guest. Therefore, you get to run the show." I leaned against the archway to the kitchen, folding my arms. "You've never been?"

"When I was a kid, but I've always wanted to go again. I know you live here, so maybe it's old news, but I thought it might be fun."

I tapped my lips thoughtfully. "I think it's still early enough to make it worth our while. Let's go see Mickey."

"As long as you're really okay with it. I got the idea in my head around hour sixteen of my drive, so it's possibly just a crazy thought fueled by gas station donuts and sleep deprivation."

The more he hedged, the more I warmed to the plan. I hadn't been to Disneyland in ages. Partly because it wasn't an on-brand thing for @theadventurousmiranda. I'd spent too many days in service to that version of myself. This was for Leo and me.

"I actually haven't been in a long time," I told him. "Now that you've suggested it, I'm excited."

"Cool." He stood and walked nonchalantly to the hall bathroom, his button still undone.

As I got down two bowls for cereal and downloaded the Disneyland app to my phone, it occurred to me that Leo and I had completely skipped past any awkwardness that might have been expected considering we hadn't seen each other in person for months. Nope. He fell asleep on my couch and woke up asking to go to Disneyland. No stops in between.

I chuckled, pouring the Strawberry Shredded Wheat I'd stocked up on for him.

Chapter Six

Leo

NOW

I meant what I'd said to Miranda earlier. I didn't know how to date someone. All my attempts were in the distant past, and all had been varying degrees of terrible.

My first thought was to just act the way we always had. Then I realized it wasn't possible. Because everything had changed. What we'd said on Halloween—we couldn't unsay it. What I knew about Miranda and myself—I couldn't unknow it.

But that didn't mean I couldn't shove it down into a corner of my brain and forget about it. For now.

The twitchy awareness of her I felt under my skin would have been there with or without this latest disaster with Stone, but I appreciated being able to blame any strange behavior I might exhibit on nerves caused by our fake relationship.

As we drove up I-5 from Tacoma, I tried not to think about all the things I hadn't told her.

About how, after our fight, I'd called, planning to lay myself bare and make amends.

But when Stone picked up her phone, I'd swallowed my confession.

I shook off the bitter memory. For now, I focused on our date. Letting myself have a taste of what it might be like to be with someone.

To be with her.

"Are we going into the city?" she asked, fidgeting with the zipper on her North Face jacket.

Her date-night outfit consisted of a casual coat, jeans, a flannel, and boots. She'd put on more makeup than usual, and her hair was down instead of in a bun or ponytail. When she'd come out of the second bedroom, she'd sheepishly explained that Shoshanna advised her to look as much like her Instagram persona as possible when we went out together, to further our chances of being recognized. The makeup and hair were her attempts to show that she cared enough to get a little fussy for her "boyfriend." I'd rolled my eyes at the calculation involved in what clothes to wear, but she looked fantastic. She always did.

"Not quite that far."

I pulled into the parking lot of a mall south of Seattle city limits. At first, Miranda looked confused. Then I circled the main building, and she saw our destination.

"Here?" she asked, staring up at the massive arcade and bowling alley.

"Why not? I'm guessing you're in the mood to hit something, and they've got Whac-A-Mole and Skee Ball and air hockey to choose from, not to mention a ton of shooter games. We can also bowl if you want." At her continued silence, I wondered if I'd miscalculated. "We can leave if it's not okay. I figured you could use the noise and the distraction. But if you'd rather do something else, I'm totally down for a change of plans."

"It's perfect, Leo." She looked around as we strode in, almost losing her balance when a group of rowdy preteens raced by, shoving each other and laughing. "A birthday fit for a ten-year-old...and also this twenty-seven-year-old."

I breathed a sigh of relief as I bought cards to use for the games. No matter what weirdness existed between us at the moment, I knew my friend. She needed a break from being the Instagram version of herself. @theadventurousmiranda would probably spend her birthday taking long walks on the beach or having a candlelit dinner in an exotic locale. And there was a world where the Miranda I knew wanted that too. But right now, she needed to be reminded that I saw the other side of her—the part that loved the colorful lights and loud noises. She didn't need a beautiful sunset. She needed buzzing neon, plastic cheese nachos, and the discordant *ding ding ding* of someone winning a prize at the claw machine.

Miranda cackled as I embarrassed myself on the ancient *Dance Dance Revolution* platform and clapped maniacally whenever one of my Skee balls landed in the ten-point circle. I got my revenge by demolishing her in a dinosaur-themed shooting game. As we played and got sweaty, she ditched her fleece, revealing a T-shirt underneath that read *I'll Wait While You Overthink This*. The hair she'd styled before we left my apartment got twisted into a knot on top of her head.

After two hours of games, we moved to the bowling alley. I'd just picked up a spare when I noticed a group of teenagers attempting to take covert pictures of us on their phones. Both Miranda's and Stone's statements had been in the world for a few hours, and it was obvious we'd been recognized.

My back stiffened as I sat down in the hard plastic chair across from the ball return.

Miranda took the seat next to me, resting her head on my shoulder. "Don't mind them," she said. "I know it's weird. But hopefully, it means the plan is working." She patted my thigh. "Besides, you have more important things to worry about right now."

"Such as?"

"I know you just got a spare, but you rolled gutter balls in the fourth and fifth frames. I'm kicking your butt right now."

"Consider those gutter balls a birthday gift."

At her answering grin, the teenagers snapped more pics. I ignored them.

We decided to play one more game of air hockey before leaving. After winning, she came around to my side of the table and circled her arms around my neck.

"Thank you so much for today, Bear. This is exactly what I needed." She stood on her toes to make sure I could hear her through the din of the games. "I haven't totally forgotten about what's going on, but being here with you makes it feel more manageable."

Holding her close, I anchored my hands on her hips. "I'm glad. And we'll manage together."

"I know we will." She angled in, resting her cheek against my chest. Could she feel my heart beat faster? "Who would have thought that one of my best dates ever would be a pretend one?"

I tipped her chin up. "I got you. It doesn't matter what you call it. It's just us having fun. Nothing new there. And nothing pretend about it."

We stared at one another. "Just us," she whispered.

I leaned forward and kissed her forehead, feeling the now-familiar shiver travel down my spine.

Without thought, my mouth moved sideways, and I placed another soft kiss on the hollow of her cheek, inhaling the scent of her skin. Her audible sigh of contentment hit my chest like an arrow. Instinctively, my lips trailed lower, then lower, until I pressed them softly against hers.

I'd never kissed her on the mouth. Never tasted her before. And although the kiss was chaste, my fingers still squeezed at her waist, pulsing with heat.

Letting my lips linger, I closed my eyes and trembled, my mind completely blocking out the beeps and flashing lights. It was just Miranda and me, and I let myself have it.

When I finally pulled back after ten seconds, her expression clouded with the last thing I wanted to see.

Confusion.

I stumbled back a step. *Shit!*

I'd kissed her. Forgotten myself for a moment. Forgotten Stone, and this situation.

Not what she needed right now.

"I noticed someone taking a picture," I lied. "Thought I'd give him a show."

She exhaled with obvious relief, letting out a nervous giggle before gazing fondly at me. "Jeez, Leo, when you worried you wouldn't know how to date someone and make it seem real—"

"Yeah?"

"You really shouldn't have worried."

WE HAD AN AMAZING TIME at the arcade. And she'd been stoked when I suggested an early birthday dinner at the kitschy Mexican place nearby. Between Miranda's good mood and the success of being recognized and photographed on our "date," I felt pretty encouraged.

So naturally, there had to be a bump.

After a dinner of chicken fajitas, chips and salsa, and two margaritas apiece, we were contemplating dessert when Miranda's phone rattled. She'd looked tipsy a few minutes ago, but her face sobered when she glanced at the display.

"I need to get this," she said, holding up a finger.

I nodded, motioning to ask if I should leave the table. She shook her head.

In deference to being in the middle of a restaurant—where at least one other couple had taken our picture—her voice remained low. Across the table, I caught most of her replies to what was a very one-sided conversation.

"Hello... Yes... Yes... No, I flew up to Seattle... Yes... No... I'm not sure because we're still trying to figure out—... That was never my intention... Yes... I understand... No... It makes sense..." She pinched the bridge of her nose, squeezing her eyes together as she listened to whoever was on the other end of the line speak for a minute straight. "I'll let you know as soon as I can... No, I'm aware. I un—... Right. That's a good question... I know. We haven't talked about it, but I can connect you... I agree, that's probably best for everyone at this point... after New Year's at the latest...

Yes... Thank you. I will on Monday." She laughed half-heartedly. "Twenty-seven. Definitely my strangest yet... I appreciate that... I'll keep an eye on my inbox... Thanks."

Punching the red button on her phone screen, she slumped back against the booth before reaching for her margarita glass, slurping the last dregs aggressively. "Pretty sure I'm gonna need flan and a tres leches cake, maybe churros too."

At least her sense of humor remained intact. "Do you want to tell me who that was?"

"My supervisor, Walt. Technically, my boss's boss. Head of our division. He got my email but said he already knew because one of my coworkers recognized me from the earlier pics."

"Why didn't he contact you then?"

"Didn't say. I assume he was taking a wait-and-see approach." She straightened. "He's old-school. Not the type of man to spend time online. Or even go to the movies. I doubt he knows who Stone is. But now that my statement is up and he's clear that this might cause gossip online for a few days, he's worried about the company."

"I'm not sure why he cares. I know you emailed them in the name of transparency, but it's not like this will affect your work."

"It's a fairly conservative business. I think he's being cautious because he doesn't want any undue attention. Our clients are, for the most part, serious, circumspect people. Legacy companies and politicians. He mentioned that an entertainment journalist already contacted the general line—and to paint a picture, he said 'entertainment journalist' the way most people would say 'explosive diarrhea.' He's worried someone will try to take my picture coming and going from the office, and he doesn't want the company connected to any media circus. As much as the business is about PR and marketing, its goal is always to stay in the background."

"Alright, I get what you're saying. But it's not like you asked for any of this. Assuming people believe your statement, it's all a big misunderstanding."

She frowned. "True. And he's not threatening to fire me or anything. He just doesn't want a bunch of eyes on them. Like I said, it's a real *put your head down and get your work done* kind of office. That was one reason I wanted to work there."

As much as I understood that, respected it even, I hated that Stone and his dumbfuckery had brought trouble for her at work. Especially since she was still worried about finding her footing there. "Did Walt say what he wants you to do?"

"He told me to work remotely for the month. December is a dead time anyway. Fewer meetings. I can still get my work done, but if I'm not in the office, there's no reason for photogs to hover."

It seemed like overkill to me, especially since celebrity stories always came and went quickly. From the look on Miranda's face, she agreed. "You okay?" I asked.

"I guess I have to be, but it still sucks. It's not a remote work office, and I'm sure plenty of my coworkers would love the option of being at home. I know Walt's doing what he deems necessary, but it feels like I'm getting special treatment. Not a great look for the new kid."

"You don't think your coworkers will understand?"

"It's not that. Remember when we talked about how I haven't gotten to know them? It's cool that my birthday made it onto the office calendar and all, but I've been keeping my distance, doing this whole subterfuge with Stone. I doubt anyone there has my back yet."

With everything happening, I'd almost forgotten that she'd been hiding her relationship with Stone for over a year. And all the implications of that.

Reaching across the table to take her hand, I ran my thumb across her knuckles. "I have your back. And we can get all the desserts if it will make you feel better."

"Thanks, Leo-Bear. It does make me feel—"

Plop!

We both looked up as someone smooshed a massive violet sombrero on Miranda's head and placed a pastry with a candle in it on the table in front of her. I pulled out my phone to record as every server in the restaurant magically appeared to sing "Feliz Cumpleaños."

The employees' faces displayed a range of emotions, from overtly enthusiastic to seething. I grinned at the young guy mouthing the words and felt a pang of sympathy for the woman in back, the only one who could carry a tune. The rest of the team simply leaned into their grumpy bulldog vocals. I'd let our server know about Miranda's birthday before our margaritas came out, and this ritual was even more delightfully tacky than I'd hoped for.

Miranda obviously thought so too. She laughed, and I thought I saw tears in her eyes, though it was hard to know for sure with the sombrero covering the top half of her face.

After they finished and whisked the sombrero away, we sat alone again at the table.

"I loved that," Miranda said. She closed her eyes and blew out the candle. Opening them again, she studied me across the table. "Leo?"

"Hmm?"

"I bet there will be plenty of pictures of us to satisfy the wolves after today. That sombrero was really a gift from the universe. Not to mention *everything* at the arcade."

Our kiss. She meant our kiss. "You're probably right."

"It's going to blow over. I can feel it. And I'm pretty sure I could get through the rest of this on my own if I had to."

"Of course you could," I replied. "But I'd never let you do that."

"I know. That's what I'm saying. I *could* handle it myself. Especially after the good start we got this afternoon... But I don't want to. It helps me so much being near you."

There were countless things I could say in reply, but I settled on, "Me too."

She clasped our hands together again, and it felt like my entire body centered on the place where her soft palms rested in mine.

With a glint in her eyes, she asked, "How do you feel about a long-term houseguest?"

20 MONTHS AGO - MARCH

AFTER MONTHS OF BEING ALMOST PERFECTLY in sync, Miranda and I discovered an area where our life philosophies diverged.

And it happened to be at the "happiest place on Earth."

My approach to Disneyland was laid-back. I figured we could explore one area at a time, get in line for whatever rides seemed interesting, and not stress too much along the way.

Miranda had a decidedly different methodology.

"We can't do it that way, Bear," she insisted. "It's bad enough that we got here two hours after it opened, so we missed some prime beat-the-crowd time. If we want to get on all the good rides *and* watch the parades, we need to be strategic and game it out in the app and follow the plan."

"What if I want to stop and get a churro?"

"What if ten minutes waiting for breaded cinnamon sugary goodness costs us an hour in line for Space Mountain?" she retorted. "Seriously, there are *systems*."

"For walking around Disneyland?"

"Of course. We can't go at this like rank amateurs."

"Aren't we amateurs? You said yourself you haven't been here in years."

"Just because we aren't experts doesn't mean we need to surrender to stupidity."

I lifted my hands with a grin. "Alright. I'm honestly fine with anything, so I'll follow your lead."

She spared a moment to pretend that wasn't the only acceptable response before offering, "I'll make sure you get a churro at some point."

I laughed. "Sounds good."

Miranda's plan of attack had my smartwatch chirping. I hit ten thousand steps before eleven a.m. It seemed counterintuitive to traipse from Tomorrowland to Adventureland instead of just moving to whatever was nearby, but she knew what she was doing. She purchased an add-on in the app that let us get in quicker lines for certain rides, and by the end of the day, we'd managed to hit all the premier attractions and watch a parade. Also, we got churros and a turkey leg to share, which we ate standing up while waiting in line for the Indiana Jones ride. According to Miranda, sitting down to enjoy your food was for suckers.

It was a great day, and exactly what I'd driven a straight eighteen hours to experience—spending time with another person and feeling totally in tune with them. Nothing forced. Nothing to hide.

By the end of the day, I knew I could trust her with the full truth about myself.

After my disastrous experience with Ilona, I'd learned my lesson. Keep it to myself and everything stayed copacetic.

But I knew with Miranda it would be okay. She wouldn't judge me for who I was. Just like I didn't judge her for not being @theadventurousmiranda.

One of the Disney photographers snapped pictures of us in front of the castle.

"They'll show up in my app," Miranda said. "I'll send them to you."

We stayed in the park until close, squeezing in one last ride on Pirates of the Caribbean to finish our day.

"Should we do California Adventure tomorrow?" she asked, looking at the entry to the park across from the Disneyland exit.

"Next time," I said. "I'm so beat from all the walking we did today—thanks to your *methods*—I think I need a breather."

"You love my methods."

"I do."

When we got back to Miranda's apartment, we wound down on the couch for half an hour, eating a late-night pizza and watching TV before she headed into the bedroom.

It was such a perfect day. Not the right time to have a heavy conversation about me. I wanted to share that part of myself with her, but there was also no urgency about it. The moment would present itself soon enough.

Once I told her, she'd know all of me. That thought filled me with an intense longing.

Only Miranda made me feel that way.

Chapter Seven

Miranda

NOW

I settled into Leo's spare bedroom with a weird feeling in my gut. So much had happened, but now that the initial frenzy of problem-solving had passed and I felt calmer, I could reflect on just how mind-bending the past forty-eight hours had been. I'd gone to sleep the day before Thanksgiving expecting to wake up to a hangover. Instead, I'd woken up to a mess.

Less than two days later, I felt sane again.

Because of Leo.

It stung that my boss had essentially exiled me for a month over something that would likely blow over in a few days, but it helped to have someone to commiserate with.

When the grumpy server had pushed the oversized sombrero onto my head tonight, it was like he'd hit me with a bolt of clarity. This initial crisis with Stone would pass. The collective internet wasn't known for its long-term memory. The issue was whether

Stone would still have a career once the gossip died down. He was easy to dismiss, too new in the public eye to survive being a pariah—even if everyone forgot the specifics after a few days. Audiences could be vicious that way. They wouldn't remember exactly what he'd done. He'd simply be canceled and forgotten except for the occasional trivia question about the influencer guy who cheated on Naomi Butler.

But I wouldn't let the worst happen. A few more photo ops with the natural affection between Leo and me on full display, and Stone should be in the clear.

And with our urgent fire cooled to embers, I could focus on the nagging loose thread in the back of my mind, the one I'd been compartmentalizing like a champ since Halloween. The dystopic painting mocked me from its familiar place on the wall. I needed to confront my sombrero-inspired epiphany.

Leo.

My best friend, my confidant, my partner in crime, and now, my pretend boyfriend.

After our fight, we couldn't return to exactly what we had before. Where did we go from here?

Leo, not Stone, was the most pressing question mark in my future.

Was his ability to soothe my soul and make me feel safe a good thing? Or something I needed to learn to do for myself? For both our sakes.

I'd run to him, knowing he'd help me. It scared me how quickly I'd surrendered to the relief of letting him. But maybe this should be the last time. Because after he'd invited me to stay with him for as long as I needed to, as he'd patted my thigh and offered me assurances that he'd help me see this thing through, I didn't know where role-playing ended, and reality began. Everything felt real.

Reaching up, I touched the places on my forehead and cheek where he'd kissed me at the arcade.

My fingers drifted to my lips.

He'd always been clear that the connection between us was, in fact, real. But it could never be everything.

He could never give me everything.

Leo's presence in my life had been an anchor for two years. But it was time to reevaluate. This mess had brought us back together, and after the magical day we had, I was grateful for the chance to cleanse away the bitterness of our argument. But it shouldn't create a path to go back to what we were before those hurled words.

Back to wishing for something from Leo that he could never give me.

Brushing my fingers along my cheek again, I recalled the last time I'd been in this apartment, in August. I shut my eyes against the memory of what had happened in Leo's bed.

A soft tapping at the door was followed by Leo poking his head into the room.

"Hey, Panda," he said, rubbing a hand over his face. My breath stuttered at the sight of his shirtless torso over the waistband of his pajama bottoms, his tall body silhouetted in the doorframe. I eyed his chest hair, remembering running my fingers through it the night of Marley and James's wedding. "I got up to grab some water and heard you moving around... Can't sleep?"

Shaking my head, I sat up in bed and flipped the switch on the nightstand lamp. "Too wired after everything."

"Same." He folded his arms across his chest. "But you didn't get much sleep last night either. You need to rest before you totally crash out."

One side of my mouth tipped up. "Gonna offer me a Xanny or something?"

He laughed lightly. But instead of responding, he simply gestured to the bedroom door and beckoned me through it. "C'mon."

I couldn't fight it. And he was right. It would help me sleep. Even though I knew something between us needed to change, there was no reason to push that issue right this minute. For now, it had been a shitty couple of days, and I wanted this.

Wordlessly, I walked past him into his room. He stepped ahead of me to pull back the covers on the bed.

Slipping in, I rolled onto my side, facing away. He crawled in behind me and lined up our bodies. One of his arms draped over my waist, and he pulled me back against his bent legs. His other arm slipped beneath my neck until I used his biceps as a pillow.

I felt every place our bodies met. His rough chest hair against my T-shirt between my shoulder blades. The soft cotton of his pajamas on the backs of my knees. His warm breath on my neck. His soft cock nestled in the cradle of my ass.

"Sleep," he murmured, pressing a blink of a kiss to my earlobe. "I've got you."

"I know."

20 MONTHS AGO - MARCH

THE DAY AFTER WE WENT TO DISNEYLAND, I woke up refreshed and ready for whatever else Leo wanted to do. I was no stranger to a heavy walking day. But my houseguest, not so much.

He declared his feet were killing him, and a low-key beach day was in order.

"You know how the beaches are in Washington," he explained, dragging a plain white T-shirt over his head as he sat on the couch. "Rocky. And the water is so cold. I just want to lie on the sand and have it be warm for a change."

The California ocean would be cold in March, but the sun was out, and he'd at least be able to stick a foot in and feel the waves.

"Let's go to Santa Monica. We can walk on the pier and the promenade and visit some of the touristy spots once you're done being a lazy bum."

I yelped in surprise as he dragged me onto his lap, proceeding to rub his knuckle into the crown of my head. "Don't call me lazy. Not when you made me walk miles and miles yesterday just to get in a few extra rides on Big Thunder Mountain."

I shoved away from him, laughing as I retreated to the other side of the couch. "Did you just give me a noogie?"

"Not my fault. You deserved one. Besides, it's better than a wet willy." He grinned.

We stayed at the beach for hours. I napped and played word games on my phone while Leo kept his nose in one of my old paperbacks.

Accustomed to our flirtations-that-weren't, it didn't faze me when he ran his hands over my back putting on sunscreen, when he looked appreciatively at the fit of my one-piece while also appearing completely unmoved by it, and when he lay back against the towel and slung one arm around me while the other held the book above his face.

Sometimes I wished Leo wanted more, that he was at least a tiny bit open to the possibility of a romantic relationship between us. I certainly wasn't unmoved when he removed his shirt, clad in only a pair of medium-length navy blue board shorts. Half the women on the beach turned his way when he dipped his whole body in the icy waves, returning to our towels with water dripping over his muscles.

He was a man in his prime. Yet he seemed completely unaware of the effect he had on people.

The effect he had on me.

Welp, life wasn't always roses. So he wasn't interested. Big deal. I could more than live with being just friends. Especially since Leo hadn't talked about bringing wetsuits to the beach so we could surf. He was fine with a day spent lounging and reading. I'd needed that energy in my life for so long. Maybe an amazing friendship was better than a love affair that could go to shit.

We ate dinner at a seafood restaurant near the pier. Leo ordered a tuna steak, and I ordered shrimp pasta, requesting extra plates to split our entrées.

For dessert, we shared a chocolate lava cake. As Leo held a fork to my mouth, encouraging me to take the last bite, an older woman walked over to our table.

"Hello. Aren't you—" she began to ask me, until I peered up and she got a better look at my face. "Oh dear, my apologies."

"Is everything okay?" Leo asked.

The woman spoke to him. "Yes. I'm so sorry. From the side, I thought your girlfriend was one of the young ladies who work in the salon where I get my hair done, so I came over to say hello. Apologies again for interrupting."

"I'm not his—"

"No apologies needed," Leo said, winking at her. "I suppose that means the ladies at the salon are very beautiful."

The woman paused. "They certainly are." She glanced my way before smiling. "Sorry again for the intrusion."

Leo dipped his chin at her. "Have a nice night."

As she walked away, I grinned. "She thought I was your girlfriend."

"Of course she did." He chuckled. "I was feeding you chocolate cake."

"You told her I was beautiful."

"You are."

I blinked. "Sometimes I don't understand you, Leo."

"Hey, Panda?"

"Hmm?"

"Because you're one of my favorite people on the planet, and also probably my best friend, I'm not going to pretend I don't know what you mean. You're trying to call out that there are times I do *boyfriend-y* things, but I've been clear that I'm not interested in a relationship."

I snorted. "Did anyone ever tell you that you're incredibly subtle and indecipherable? Seriously, total brick wall."

He barked a laugh. "I owe you an explanation. But can it wait until we get back to your place? I'd rather have this talk in private."

"Yeah, Leo-Bear. I have a feeling it will be worth the suspense."

Chapter Eight

Leo

NOW

My main thought as I pulled Miranda against me was that it was a good thing I'd had a rare jerk-off session in the shower before bed. At least I wouldn't need to worry about my dick misbehaving.

When I'd gotten up to fill my water bottle, I heard her stirring in the guest room. I debated not saying anything—not wanting to push my luck after the fantastic day we'd had—but ultimately, I couldn't resist.

I'd always offered her comfort, and we'd shared a bed more times than I could count. Enough for me to know that it helped her sleep. At least it had in the past.

She didn't know that my thinking had evolved. That the bed we shared was less neutral than she might believe.

But if I could play the role of fake boyfriend in public to save Stone, then I could play the role of unaffected platonic best friend behind closed doors to make Miranda feel better.

That was why, as I drifted off to sleep, I reminded myself for the millionth time that it wasn't just Miranda I held in my arms.

It was Stone Caseman's girlfriend.

20 MONTHS AGO - MARCH

THE DRIVE FROM THE RESTAURANT to Miranda's apartment probably should have been tense. Except it was us, and we weren't that way.

I'd known I wanted to talk to her about this for a while. The woman at the restaurant had simply opened the door.

We moved to the couch as soon as we came in. One cushion held the stack of sheets and blankets I was using for sleeping, so we sat close together on the other side. I pulled her legs across my thighs and settled my hands on her calves.

"Alright, Leo. I've been patient. What is this obviously significant thing you need to tell me? Are you dying or something?"

I took a deep breath, exhaling it loudly. She immediately sat straighter.

"Oh my god! Is that it? You don't want to get too close because you're sick?"

"No, no. Nothing like that." Patting her shin, I managed the semblance of a smile. After giving me a once-over as though to confirm there were no visible terminal illnesses, she relaxed back against the cushions.

"Then what?"

I rubbed her ankles absently, grounding myself. "Maybe I should start at the end, when we were at the restaurant earlier." She bobbed her head. "The reason I'm sometimes a bit touch-feely with you—sorry, I can't think of a better way to phrase it—and the reason I liked it when that woman thought I was your boyfriend, is because those aren't things I've really gotten to experience."

Her jaw flexed. "Leo, I know we haven't talked about this stuff much. Which is kind of weird when you think about it since we talk about everything else. But are you trying to say that you haven't had a lot of girlfriends?... Or boyfriends?"

"It would be girlfriends, if it were anything. At least I'm pretty sure." I dragged a hand over my face. "Being with you makes me feel like everyone else, like I get to have the same things most people take for granted."

She worried her lower lip. "I'm trying to understand here. I really am. And maybe I'm thick, but I'm not following. It's okay if you're not into me and want to just be friends. I meant it when I said I was fine with that."

"It's not that I *want* to be just friends with you, Panda. It's that I *can't* be anything other than just friends with you."

"Because of Marley and James?"

"No."

"Okay." Her expression pinched. "Are you in danger or something? About to enter witness protection?"

I released a gruff laugh. "Nothing that interesting."

"Then you're gonna need to help me out here. I'm running out of ideas and—"

"I'm ace—"

"Explana—... Wait. What?"

"Ace. Asexual." My slow-motion circles over her ankles continued. "I don't experience sexual attraction to women. To anyone."

She flinched but recovered quickly, placing her hand over mine to still my movements. "I know what asexual is."

"So you understand?"

Her head nodded subtly, and for a minute she appeared lost in her own thoughts.

Finally, she spoke. "Now that you say it, it makes perfect sense. Explains so much…" Bemusedly, she added, "I'm a little annoyed with myself that the thought hadn't occurred to me."

I chuffed. "Honestly, I do my best not to advertise it. But what I realized at the restaurant, and what I knew almost from the first moment we met, is that I feel different with you than I do with anyone else. It's not attraction per se, not in the way most people think of it, but from the beginning, I've experienced a level of comfort with you, an awareness that I haven't felt with anyone in a long time. When the woman at the restaurant called me your boyfriend, I liked leaning into that, even for a few moments." I inhaled another deep breath, and my chest tightened with purpose. "I couldn't go another day without telling you I've been letting myself have these moments, that I'm letting myself touch you and speak to you and be more intimate with you than I've been with anyone since my early twenties, when I figured out my asexuality. It felt wrong not to say it out loud, almost like I was using you. And now that you know, you can tell me to fuck off if you don't want me holding your hand or hugging you or whatever."

The fan kicked on, the rumbling noise punctuating my words. Miranda stared at me before her eyes drifted downward to land on the place where my palm held her ankle.

"It's hard to imagine a scenario where I'd ever tell you to fuck off," she said quietly. "And now that you've explained, I think I get it. Really, it's kind of an ego boost to know that I'm the person you're *comfortable* with... But can I be equally honest with you?"

"Of course."

"If you weren't ace and had been interested in pursuing something with me, I would have been open to it. Don't get me wrong. I'm not saying that because I think I can change your mind or anything. I'm clear on what asexual means, and obviously, I respect your identity. But I was feeling the same way you were, like it was past time to be honest about where my head was at. It felt gross being attracted to you without telling you, especially when you've been so clear that you only want to be friends."

I pulled her closer until her head rested against my chest. "We are a matched set, aren't we?"

She burrowed into me. "Where does this leave us?"

"You really don't care that I'm ace?"

"Why would I? If anything, I'm grateful for the context," she murmured. "As long as you don't care that when I see you without your shirt, it sometimes makes me want to lick you."

God, she really was my favorite person. "I take that as a compliment. Please ogle me all you want."

"Deal. As long as you touch me, hold my hand, and do whatever floats your boat to show affection."

"You wouldn't think of that as taking advantage?"

"No. You've been clear, and I trust your words, so there are no mixed signals. And I enjoy our closeness too."

I squeezed my eyes together, resting my chin on her head. "You have no idea how grateful I am for what you're offering, and for being able to communicate about everything."

"Did you really think I wouldn't be okay with this? That I would judge you?"

"Not really. But I've had a few unpleasant experiences."

"I'm sorry, Bear." She drew Xs over my heart with her pointer finger.

"S'okay. That's why I don't really talk about it. Easier to hide than risk blowing up people's expectations."

"Ah...I understand." She peeked up with a devilish glint. "People assume because you look like Thor that you must be interested in hammering?"

I laughed. "Jesus, Panda."

"Thunder between the sheets?"

This woman. My grip on her tightened.

"God of the bedroom?"

I kissed the top of her head. "I'm so thankful for you," I mumbled into her hair. "But in all seriousness, I decided a long time ago not to talk about it. Even James and my parents don't know."

I didn't go into detail. Maybe someday I'd tell Miranda about how I'd forced myself to try things when I was younger, thinking I just needed to find the right situation and get some experience under my belt. About how my college girlfriend broke up with me because of my lackluster performance in the bedroom. How I'd dated girl after girl in my early twenties, hoping to generate the spark everyone else seemed to feel. Eventually, I'd stopped trying because I felt so uncomfortable rebuffing their advances. Cringing,

I thought of the girls who'd angrily accused me of leading them on. I'd made women upset when they interpreted my lack of sexual interest as me thinking they were undesirable. I didn't know how to explain myself to them when I wasn't sure about things in my mind.

When I was twenty-three, I met Ilona, and she was the first person I had something of a genuine connection with. Feeling a seed of a romantic bond, I thought maybe I'd conquered whatever had been holding me back.

I got to know her, we went on some promising dates, and I began introducing her as my girlfriend. It elated me to feel so *normal*. But our bedroom problems started almost immediately. I couldn't get hard all the time, and I didn't want intimacy as often as she did. There was no way to hide how unenthusiastic I was about going down on her.

Ilona was the first person to propose to me that I might be asexual. Once she said it, I did some research, and everything clicked.

Asexuality was a huge spectrum, different for everyone, but the idea of not being sexually attracted to anyone resonated with me. And I had an aha moment when I connected the dots that my place on the ace continuum extended to having very few close friendships. I realized how difficult it was for me to connect with anyone in a truly emotional way. I was tight enough with my family, and I had some people I considered "good" friends, but even with them, it took a while to get there.

"It really is too bad," Ilona had said, walking out of my apartment for the last time. "You're so hot. What a waste."

Those final words, somehow both bitter and passive-aggressive, stuck with me. Echoed through the room and my brain. Stayed with me afterward. Was I a waste? I wrestled with that idea for a long time. Years. If I couldn't be someone's lover, was I less of a person?

Over time, I rejected the premise. I couldn't be a lover or an intimate friend. But I could be a good brother, a gym buddy, an excellent construction worker. I could have a fulfilling life.

Then Miranda laughed with me in her sister's carport and immediately guessed that people compared me to Thor. She liked the same things I did, called me Leo-Bear, and told me how she wasn't quite the person everyone thought she was. I recognized a kindred spirit, and for the first time in forever, I felt an immediate connection to someone. Comfortable enough to touch her. And be myself with her. It wasn't romance or sexual attraction, but it was love, in its way. And if she was willing, I planned to share it with her however she'd let me.

"I'm glad you told me," Miranda said, bringing me out of my thoughts. "It's brave of you to speak your truth. To own it. And I love you so much, Bear. You're even more my best friend now."

I ran my hand up and down her back. "Thank you."

She chuffed. "We certainly are good, both of us, at putting on faces for everyone."

"Nothing wrong with that. Keeping things copacetic. We can't help what comes naturally."

"True. But when it's just us, let's always be real."

"Deal." I kissed the top of her head again.

She sighed into my chest, and my dick twitched.

Wait...

My dick twitched?

What the fuck?

Chapter Nine

Miranda

NOW

I woke up the following morning with Leo's arm draped over my middle. The harsh late autumn sun sliced through the blinds, shining light on a brand-new morning.

And my new mindset.

I wanted him in my life. Full stop. But I also admitted to myself that things had changed since the summer, and therefore, we needed different boundaries.

Leo's deep breathing penetrated the still air, and I smiled. Lying next to him had helped me sleep, and thankfully, there was no repeat of the weirdness from the last time we shared a bed. In fact, his soft snores and even softer dick reminded me that I'd likely blown that incident way out of proportion. Just like I'd been confused for a beat when he kissed me at the arcade. I'd always been attracted to him. Not in a debilitating way, just in the sense that I would have been open to something if the possibility had been on the table. Even though I fully understood that it wasn't. I'd never lied to myself—or him—about that.

But I'd been lying to myself about what it had cost me.

My draw to Leo had kept me from sharing that closeness with another man. I'd never seen it as settling but rather *maximizing* what Leo was capable of. I wasn't secretly pining for my best friend, but now I saw that allowing him to have so much of me had prevented me from having it with someone else.

It was partly the reason I hadn't fallen harder for Stone. And why that hardly bothered me.

Yep, Leo and I needed new boundaries.

But not yet.

After the holidays.

Because I wasn't a masochist. I could not establish those lines with Leo in the middle of dealing with Stone's PR debacle. Last night, I'd slept better than I had in months. *And I'd needed that, dammit.* I wanted to sleep, to feel safe and cared for. No one did that better than Leo.

Leo nosed into the crown of my skull, tightening his hold from behind me. "Hello, girlfriend."

"Morning, Bear."

"Charlie texted that the sub is good for today. So I'm all yours." His gruff voice still sounded half asleep. "What should we do? More photo ops?"

I rolled over to share his pillow, tapping his nose with a finger. "I'm not sure we can top a day that ends with a giant sombrero ritual."

"We'll think of something. I believe in us." Smiling, he stretched his arms above his head. His shoulders cracked noisily.

"Oh no. Did I make you uncomfortable last night? Hog the mattress or something?"

His features softened. "Not at all, Panda. My shoulders pop because I work in construction. Plus, I'm old. You'll understand soon enough since you're starting your late twenties on Monday."

"Is twenty-seven *late* twenties? I figured it was still mid."

"Well, whatever. But don't worry about my decrepit bones. I slept more soundly than I have in months." Rising from the bed, he padded his way into the bathroom. A moment later, the shower flipped on.

After a beat of indecision, I grabbed my phone off its charger. I'd given myself yesterday as a reprieve, but I needed to know what was going on.

The answer came as soon as my texts popped up.

SHOSHANNA (STONE'S PA): The statement is getting traction. Comments look promising so far. Nice call on the photos. Probably good you left town too.

That text had come in around eight o'clock. Two hours later, she'd sent another.

SHOSHANNA (STONE'S PA): Watch this.

I clicked on the attached link. It was a video of an interview with Naomi, who was on set in Texas. She talked about how, as much as she appreciated the public looking out for her, she and Stone were doing great. She knew me through my friendship with Stone, and she also knew I was in a long-distance relationship with a man named Leo who lived outside Seattle. I gave Naomi credit. If I hadn't known it was bullshit firsthand, I would have believed her. She even spoke fluently about my @theadventurousmiranda account, saying she was glad Stone had friends who shared some of his more active hobbies.

Stone had posted a similar video to his YouTube channel, but Shoshanna and Lauren were clear that it was Naomi's voice that mattered most.

A few more texts had come through overnight. I wondered if Shoshanna ever slept. It would totally track if she turned out to be a vampire.

SHOSHANNA (STONE'S PA): These are some brilliant moves.

She'd sent a dozen links to videos and reels showing my date with Leo yesterday at the arcade and the restaurant. Someone had even posted the entire serenade I'd received from the restaurant staff. I appreciated being able to see Leo's amused reaction because I hadn't noticed it yesterday with the sombrero covering my eyes. It reminded me of how much I loved his laugh. Hopefully, he wouldn't mind all the comments along the lines of, *"OMG is this Miranda chick dating Thor?" "Seriously, this man is built like a God,"* and *"Um, yeah, so I'd pick this guy over prettyboy Stone Caseman any day of the week."*

Actually, Leo probably would like that last one.

Her last text came in during the early morning hours.

SHOSHANNA (STONE'S PA): Are you sure you want to stay in marketing? Because there is a future for you in crisis PR. Seriously, if I didn't know better, I would swear that you have been cheating on my boy Stone with this Leo person.

She'd attached pictures someone had taken of us at the arcade. Leo kissing my forehead and my cheek. My mouth. Both our eyes closed, his lips pressed into mine while he held my waist. His enormous hands looked like oven mitts clutching my small hips. The moment was intimate, even with dozens of people in the background and the glaring neon lights of the arcade games.

There was also a text from Naomi. We'd exchanged numbers a while ago for logistical purposes. Prior to today, I could scroll through all our communications with a few swipes, but this time, she'd sent me a book.

NAOMI BUTLER: Hello Miranda. I'm hoping you saw my interview. Please know that I don't blame you for any of this. (Just in case you were wondering and maybe you weren't because I'm reading this now and I see how I can seem like kind of an asshole just assuming you were worried about what I think at all). But anyway, just in case you were, I'm not mad. I know it was an honest mistake. This was always a huge risk, and we should have called it off a long time ago. There have been so many times over the past year when I've thought about texting you and really reaching out. At the time we started this stupid fake dating between me and Stone, I was so concerned with changing my image that I didn't really think about your part in all of this. And then when the movie took off—I guess I went a little crazy. I feel like I've spent the past ten years trying not to be controlled by other people, and then in a moment when I should have put my foot down, I failed the test. I feel like maybe I broke girl code or something by not trying to make this easier on you. Not checking in more. To be honest, I don't have a lot of friends. Not ones I can trust anyway. I've always envied Stone having someone in his life who kept him grounded and who he could trust. Seeing you called a home-wrecker and Stone a cheater made me sick to my stomach. Please know that

I appreciate everything you're doing and have done. You're not the only one who's trying to fix this. I know I owe you.

NAOMI BUTLER: Maybe after this is all over, we can be friends?

I wondered how long she debated sending the second text. It made me feel better that she'd taken the time to reach out. I honestly hadn't spared many thoughts for her since Thanksgiving. I texted back quickly.

ME: Thanks for sending this. No worries about any of it. We all made choices. I'm just glad we're on the same team. And of course we can be friends.

It was vague enough without being dismissive, and it would have to do for now. I followed it up with three heart-hand emojis, leaving the door open for us to touch base down the line, if either of us truly felt the urge.

There were other messages. I'd distanced myself from my college friend group since graduation, but a few of them had sent texts of the "WTF?" variety. It occurred to me that even if the public believed my story, many people in my life would have questions about my relationship with Stone. My friend Raven summed it up best.

RAVEN: Not cool, my dude. How the fuck did you manage not to tell us you were friends with Stone Caseman???????????? *frowny face emoji*

I hated upsetting people. My stomach roiled thinking that someone was mad at me. I hoped everyone would buy the argument that Stone and I had kept our friendship private at my request since I didn't want to be seen as a hanger-on or too much in the public eye.

I was most concerned that my sisters and Leo's family would be mad that we hadn't told them we were dating. It was trickier to explain away, but at least the story we'd devised sounded plausible.

As I scrolled, the good news was that our plan appeared to be working. No one could deny that Leo and I looked loved up, and there was significant blowback against commentators insisting that Stone must be cheating since I was a woman. When I'd proposed this idea to Shoshanna and Lauren, none of us anticipated the situation would reignite the age-old debate over whether *men and women can just be friends,* but that was exactly what happened. And it worked in our favor.

There also seemed to be a respect because I hadn't used my friendship with Stone to hype up @theadventurousmiranda. People found that to be evidence of my authenticity.

Still, even some of the supportive posts were oddly passive-aggressive.

They definitely look like a couple but I'm not a fan of blond-on-blond.

So Stone is a good boyfriend to Naomi and a good friend to @theadventurousmiranda? Yawn. If you're boring just say that.

That wannabe Thor guy is old, right? It's not just me. I think he's, like, ancient. Over 35 for sure.

"Ouch," Leo said, reading over my shoulder. I hadn't noticed that he'd finished his shower. I kept my gaze averted from his damp chest as he clutched a towel around his waist. His eyes scanned my phone as I scrolled through the comments. "It's like we can't win."

I chuckled. "Hey, at least they believe it."

Leo tossed his wet hair dramatically. "So that's the verdict? It's working?"

Humming, I looked up from the screen. "Seems to be. I haven't heard anything from Shoshanna this morning, and that's probably a good sign. She was happy yesterday."

"What did Stone say?"

I startled, realizing I hadn't gotten a message from him. "Strange. I haven't heard from him today." I shrugged. "He's probably busy on set. Or maybe Shoshanna told him not to use the burner too often."

"Seems like he'll be able to use his regular phone soon."

"I guess." Leo said nothing else, but I knew we were both thinking how odd it was that Stone hadn't messaged. Even Naomi had reached out. My stomach rumbled. "Brunch?" I suggested.

"Great idea. We can go out. Put some of that blond-on-blond action on display."

15 MONTHS AGO - SEPTEMBER

I sat on a blanket watching my friends play volleyball on the sand. It was our last day camping, and I was mildly grateful

I'd twisted my ankle. I'd be good to go when classes started next week, but for now, I enjoyed the rest. While my friends surfed and raced on the wet sand, I finished a book, journaled, and mentally prepped for my last year of grad school.

Raven came over to grab the ball pump, stopping to ask if I needed anything. I said thanks but waved her off. Within our group, she was the person I was closest to. As she ran back to the game, she fist-bumped another guy, Braden, who I'd also known for years. From their body language, it was obvious they were sleeping together. Our circle was incestuous in that way. New people came and went, but one thing that stayed constant was everyone's openness to casual sex and transient relationships that began and ended within months or weeks. Everyone except me, that was.

During my first few years in school, I'd participated in the round robin of partners. I'd tried to care, mostly to fit in, even feigning some elaborate emotional responses to breakups, as though eating cookies and watching cheesy romcoms would prove that the time spent together had meant something. But those rituals wore thin quickly. Eventually, I realized casual encounters weren't my jam, and I stopped engaging in one short-lived relationship after another for the sake of appearance. Then, after my mom died, I gave up even considering the possibility. Between grieving and schoolwork, I had enough on my mind without adding in romantic pressure.

A year ago, as the worst of my grief cloud lifted, I started dipping my toe back in the dating pool. Seeing my sister and James so loved up during the holidays made me reflect on how much I wanted something similar for myself.

I'd gone on a few first dates, mostly using apps. Some men recognized me from online and were keen to take out

@theadventurousmiranda. That was a no-go. I couldn't see introducing them to my honest self—hashtag-boring-and-tired Miranda. With others, the conversation was stilted and awkward. Or we had nothing to talk about at all. The number of men who could carry on funny, coherent conversations over messages but who were stone-faced and humorless in real life shocked me.

So far, there hadn't been any second dates. Making the effort was the win.

As I watched Raven smile at Braden as he squeezed her hip, the idea entered my mind that life would be so much easier if Leo weren't asexual. I sighed guiltily. That demonic little brainworm of a thought popped into my head way too often.

I needed to stop wishing things were different. Leo was perfect just as he was.

Glancing to my left, I saw two guys filming themselves, sitting on top of their surfboards.

I'd noticed them in the water earlier, wearing waterproof cameras strapped to their heads. I bet they'd gotten some great shots since both were clearly expert surfers.

One man looked older than the other. He'd unzipped the top of his wetsuit to reveal a smattering of gray hair on his chest.

The other guy, fit and tan, seemed closer to my age. His damp hair was curly and multihued, the kind of style people described as "beachy." When he laughed, it showed off his gleaming white teeth.

The younger man appeared to be interviewing the elder, both speaking to a camera mounted on a tripod in the sand. I couldn't hear their conversation, but it was enthusiastic, with lots of accompanying hand gestures. At one point, the older man demonstrated a paddling technique. After about ten minutes, they shook hands and turned off the camera.

The older man headed toward the parking lot. To my surprise, the younger guy walked my way.

"What'd you think?" he asked, coming to stand next to me, holding his hand above his brow. At this angle, he was merely a silhouette with the sun behind him. A toned, muscular, golden silhouette.

"I'm sorry?" I looked from side to side, just to make sure this beach Adonis was speaking to me.

"My interview. I saw you watching us. Can't believe I got to interview Jerry Scott for my channel."

A zip of recognition invaded my brain. Jerry Scott was a name I knew. A legendary surfer around these parts. This guy must have been a journalist or influencer then.

"I was watching," I said. "Sorry. It caught my attention. But I couldn't hear."

"No worries. Watching's the whole point, right?" Surprising me again, he plopped down in the sand, wrapping his arms around his knees. "I think it went okay, but I had to keep reminding myself to ask questions and stop, like, fanboying, ya know?"

I turned to him, the sun no longer blinding me. "You're Stone Caseman."

A flash of something—*disappointment?*—crossed his features before he wiped it. "You know me."

"Doesn't everyone? You have a million followers. My friend Raven practically wore out her laptop watching the video of you BASE jumping in Mexico."

He chuckled delicately, studying the horizon. "More like half a million, and yeah, that was a day."

Braden glanced over from the volleyball game. He must have noticed a random guy sitting next to me because he raised his brows, giving me a *you okay?* look. I nodded subtly. Braden obviously didn't recognize my companion, because all my friends would have raced over if they knew I was talking to Stone Caseman.

When Stone didn't say more but also didn't make a move to leave, I asked, "So the interview went well?"

"I think so. Everyone knows Jerry is a nice guy. He has that reputation. I was just trying to be respectful, so he'd think I was more than some stupid kid with a YouTube channel."

His candor was another surprise. "I get it," I said. "You don't want to be the *Which One of These Fruits Looks Most Like a Dick?* guy forever."

"Duuuuuuuuuude." Red-cheeked, he face-planted into his knees. "Of all the things to go viral."

I snickered teasingly. "Hey, every hero has their humble origin story, right? Besides, surfing with Jerry and interviewing him is a long way from that. I'm sure it will be great."

"I hope so." Stone scooted slightly closer, and I registered him giving me an appreciative up and down—not in a skeevy way, but in a normal checking someone out way. I straightened my shoulders and sucked in my stomach. "When I first started the channel, I had a lot of different types of content. But it was always the stunts and nonsense that took off and got the views. Now that I have a big enough following and can afford to lose a few, I'd like to transition away from that."

His voice changed as he went on. Like the leisurely drawl he used on his channel faded as his thoughts solidified into sentences.

Clearly, the Stone Caseman people saw on social media was only one version of him. Just like @theadventurousmiranda.

As we continued talking, I gave him my name and also shared my online identity with him. Turned out, he recognized the handle and already followed but hadn't recognized me. I took no offense, considering how small my numbers were compared to his. Plus, I didn't have a YouTube channel. Or even a TikTok. I'd chosen to stick to pictures and not videos a long time ago. That was a place where Stone and I diverged. He wanted to grow his following and make his living as the online version of Stone Caseman, whereas I wanted to wind down my page.

My friends began arguing, and I knew their game would be over soon.

"You should probably take off," I said to Stone. "I mean, you're welcome to stay for our bonfire if you want, but my friends will definitely recognize you, so you'll get stuck telling a bunch of stories and whatnot."

He stood, brushing the sand from his backside. "I should get home and start editing this interview anyway. My PA wants to look at it too. Make sure it hits. There's an indie movie I might get cast in, so I'm trying to keep focused."

"An indie movie sounds cool. Congrats. Probably fits in with your master plan to make a living at all this."

Stone gave me a pointed look. "Yeah, actually. It does." He pulled a pair of sunglasses from his pocket and slipped them on. "It was really nice talking to you, Miranda. Thanks."

"Same. And good luck."

With that, he walked away. When Raven asked me later about the hottie I'd been talking to, I told her I hadn't caught his name.

Two weeks later, Stone reached out via DM to ask me to coffee. I replied that I'd love to see him but suggested he come to my apartment (clarifying that this was not an invitation for anything other than coffee). My reasoning was simple. With his rising popularity, he was sure to be recognized in public. The last thing I wanted was for my online persona to be linked with his. I didn't need my follower numbers to go up solely because of a connection to Stone. I'd worked too hard to build up my brand on my own terms.

I supposed the easiest path would have been to turn him down, but his offer intrigued me, because he'd already been more "real" with me than he was with his audience.

Plus, he was gorgeous. Even though I'd sworn off casual encounters, I could imagine making an exception for someone with Stone's perfect body and smile. Remembering the way he'd looked at me made me shiver. He was interested. Maybe a relationship that needed to be kept behind closed doors was a good thing. We could explore the possibilities between us without external pressure.

If Stone was even interested in that. Perhaps he was only after a hookup.

I hoped he wasn't just looking for a friend. If that were the case, I wasn't the girl for him.

Because I already had a best friend who knew me in a way the rest of the world didn't. And I didn't want that with anyone else. Only my sweet, perfect Leo-Bear.

Chapter Ten

Leo

NOW

Miranda and I decided not to drive into Seattle. Instead, we opted to get pancakes at the little diner by my house, which we'd been to before.

When we walked in, a harried middle-aged server carrying a steaming coffee pot told us to sit "wherever." She paid us little mind, but the younger server on the other side of the restaurant looked up and did an immediate double take.

"I guess that's what we wanted," Miranda said under her breath. "To be recognized."

We sat down, shedding our coats, and I recalled the first time I'd brought Miranda here nearly two years ago. She'd exclaimed over the sticky plastic menus "with nary a QR code in sight."

The younger server motioned to the other woman that she'd take care of us. "Would you like some coffee while you're deciding?" she asked.

"Decaf for me," Miranda replied. "Cream and sugar, please."

"I'll take the hard stuff," I said.

The server's cheek stuck out, like she was pushing her tongue against the inside. Her hands fiddled with the short apron she wore, and I caught the outline of her phone in the pocket.

She left to grab the coffee, and when she returned, she lingered after taking our orders for pancakes and bacon. Rocking back on her heels, she gave the impression of wanting to say something else before abandoning the notion and walking away. Less than a minute later, I clocked her balancing a dish towel-covered phone on the counter.

"Not very subtle, is she?" Miranda guffawed.

"No. Maybe we should turn and smile and get it over with."

"Let her have it. We'll leave a big tip and maybe she'll post about that."

When the server brought our food ten minutes later, she'd reached the limit of her restraint. "I can't believe you're here," she said. "I just watched a video about you and Stone this morning."

Miranda smiled widely. "We were wondering if maybe you recognized us but didn't want to presume. Hopefully, whatever you watched was positive."

"Oh, it was. One of my favorite creators. It's stupid, you know, how so many people jump to conclusions. Of course men and women can be just friends. You and Stone, I mean."

I winked at Miranda. "Men and women can definitely be just friends."

"I'm Neveah, by the way," the server said.

"Nice to meet you," I replied. "Are you new? I don't think I've seen you before."

"This is my third week. Dorothy mentioned you're a regular," Neveah said, gesturing to the middle-aged server. "But she had no clue you two were internet famous. When I told her, she laughed and said you're friendly. She also said you'd be okay if I mentioned that I knew who you were."

I leaned out and tipped my mug at Dorothy, who gave a little wave in return. "Perfectly fine. But for the record, my girlfriend and I aren't famous, or maybe Miranda is a little. Stone and Naomi are the famous ones. We're just randos waiting for all this to die down."

"That's why I flew up from Los Angeles," Miranda interjected. "Leo and I usually do the long-distance thing, but I wasn't going to face all this while we were apart."

Neveah seemed to consider her words. "It must suck to have everyone talking about you when you're just trying to be a regular person."

"True," Miranda agreed. "I'll probably stop doing my Instagram account after this, too, since my identity has been exposed."

"Well, you're cool to eat your pancakes in peace," Neveah said. "If anyone asks, I'll tell them you're nice… Also, don't listen to the trolls. There's nothing wrong with two blonds dating each other."

With that, she turned her attention to another table.

"I'm getting a very real urge to dye my hair," I said dryly.

"Don't do it, Bear. Don't let the haters win." She shook her fist in the air like a gladiator.

"Are you really going to stop doing your Instagram?"

"You say that like it's a surprise when you know I've been looking for an out. It's no longer a brand experiment if people know it's me. If there's a silver lining to this situation, it's that it gives me the perfect excuse to sunset the account."

"She was fun while she lasted."

"She's still fun. Just slightly less adventurous."

Later that night, after going to the movies and walking the lake loop at a local park, Miranda opened up her feed to see a trending post. Neveah had put up the pictures she took of us eating—which turned out surprisingly well, considering the dish towel subterfuge—along with a caption talking about how friendly and "in love" we were.

"You really have executed the plan beautifully," I said, kissing her head. "Cluing Neveah into your thought process on flying up here so we could endure this terrible internet injustice together was a nice touch."

"Thank you. I'm glad she mentioned that part in her caption. Does our work for us."

I was in the kitchen boiling pasta when Miranda's phone rang. She stepped into the second bedroom to take the call.

Five minutes later, she emerged with a bewildered look on her face.

"Everything okay?" I asked, turning off the burner.

"That was Stone," she said. "He was just calling to check in. I guess Shoshanna told him everything was going well, which is true, but he just seemed...not stressed about it at all. It was almost bizarre how calm he was. I was worried when I hadn't heard from him earlier that something might be wrong, but it's obvious that he's just super chill about the whole thing. He didn't call because he straight up sees no urgency here."

I stepped to the side of the counter. Stone would always be a sticky topic, and I knew I needed to tread carefully. "Does it bother you?"

"I don't know if 'bother' is the right word. It's more like you and I have turned our whole lives upside down to fix this. Even Naomi is in on the game, giving that interview and reaching out to me. His people are buying burner phones and working on crisis management. Meanwhile, Stone is like, 'Man, the prop guns they have us using on this shoot have a real kick. I almost fell over today.'"

I knew she was annoyed because she did a *voice* imitating Stone, and it wasn't her usual MO to belittle him.

As much as I didn't want to defend Stone, I was fairly sure I knew what was happening.

I drew out my words. "Panda, from everything you've told me, it sounds like Stone has been happy to hand off the business side of all this to his PA and the other people who work for him. And it's basically their job to make him feel as little discomfort as possible. I'm guessing they've been underplaying the potential damage to his career, trying to fix it for him, because that's the dynamic that exists. The plan for triage with you and me—it's dictated by Stone's handlers, correct? Even if the solution was your idea. He's good at the videos and being charming, and it's clear he loves to act, but he's also in the habit of not worrying about this type of stuff."

Her nod filled me with relief. "You're right. Shoshanna pulls the strings. I'm sure she just gave him the burner phone and told him she'd take care of it and let him know if he needed to do anything."

"That would be my assumption."

Miranda sat down heavily on the couch, placing her elbow on her knee and leaning her chin into her fist. "I can't imagine letting someone have that much power over me." She put her arm down, leaning back. "But Stone is incredibly busy and dedicated to his career. There are so many places—this problem, our relationship, the possibility of standing up to Shoshanna—where what looks like a lack of effort is really just him not seeing that effort is needed."

He doesn't see you, I wanted to scream. *Not the way he should.* I gritted my teeth as Miranda excused Stone's behavior. Then again, she had been a willing accomplice in his lack of effort. Because, as bad as it was that Stone basically half-assed everything other than his career, she had noticed his lack of attention to their relationship and shrugged her shoulders at it.

She deserved so much more from him. And settled for so little. Why?

As if on cue, her phone buzzed. She stared down at it before holding it up for me to read.

SHOSHANNA (STONE'S PA): Thanks for your hard work. Pretty sure you're winning the internet. Please keep doing what you're doing.

SHOSHANNA (STONE'S PA): I'll tell Stone not to worry and that everything is handled.

13 MONTHS AGO - NOVEMBER

I arrived at Miranda's place in record time, even stopping to nap. The drive from my apartment in Tacoma to hers in Los Angeles was a long one. But the more I did it, the shorter the distance seemed.

We had decided that I would come down and spend a few days with her before we drove back to Coleman Creek together for Thanksgiving.

The holiday was early this year, and afterward, she had to fly back to LA for school, then back to Washington the first weekend in December for James and Marley's engagement party, then back to California to complete her classes for the quarter, and finally back to Washington to spend Christmas and New Year's in Coleman Creek. It was a dizzying schedule with lots of flying, so I figured driving this first time might be fun.

My initial guess was that I'd get into town around eleven in the morning, but when I rang Miranda's bell, it wasn't quite nine.

And it wasn't Miranda who answered.

The door swung open. A young, tanned surfer-type dude stood on the threshold. He was shirtless, with a smooth chest, and the band of his underwear stuck out above the top of his low-slung shorts. His skin practically glowed with energy.

He stepped back and opened the door wider. "'Sup, man. You must be Leo." I walked in, the heavy footfalls of my boots somehow a contrast to his tone. "Miranda's still in bed, I think."

Depositing my duffel near the entry, I eyeballed the couch. It didn't look like it had been slept on.

The guy wandered into Miranda's kitchen. No, it was more of a swagger. A saunter, even. He pulled a package of donuts off the top of the fridge, extending the box to me. "Want one?"

I put up my hand. "Um... No, thanks."

He pulled out a chocolate donut before putting the box back. "Cool. I just made some fresh coffee. Still in the pot. You're probably tired after your long drive."

"Uh-huh." Utilizing my knowledge of Miranda's kitchen, I pulled a mug from the cupboard and poured myself a cup.

"You take it black?" The guy smiled—his big white teeth sort of pissed me off—and gestured to my mug. "Hard-core."

"I take it however," I clarified. A few seconds passed. I sipped. He chewed noisily. Finally, I asked, "It sounds like you know my name, but what should I call you?"

"Huh? ... I'm Stone," he said, confusion evident. Like I should have known that.

"Oh." I waited for him to say more.

For the first time, his smile faltered. "Did Miranda not...tell you about me?"

Now I was confused. "No. Should she have?"

"Well, yeah. She mentioned you wouldn't recognize me since you're not online much, but I've heard so much about you, I just figured she'd tell you about me. Even though we're keeping this whole thing on the down-low."

"She's never mentioned a Stone."

"That's strange because—"

"Stone? Who are you talk—" Miranda stopped short in the bedroom doorway. "Oh."

Startled, she ran a hand through her unbrushed hair. The gesture drew my eyes to her, and I noticed she wore only a large T-shirt with a skate company logo on it, barely covering the tops of her thighs.

Stone eyed her hungrily, walking over to wrap an arm around her waist before kissing her forehead. To me, he said, "Nothing like when your girl wears your clothes, amiright?"

If I'd had any lingering doubt about who Stone was to Miranda, that cleared it up. As did the plus signs he drew on her hip with his palm.

Alright, dude. I get it.

"I see you two have met," she said, extricating herself from Stone's grip. "Gimme a sec."

She went into the bedroom and returned wearing sleep pants underneath the giant shirt.

"I thought you wouldn't get here for a few more hours." She gave me a hug, although not our usual lingering one.

"Made good time," I replied stiffly.

"That's great," she said, with a brightness that didn't reach her eyes. "And you met Stone."

I nodded. "I did. Except he seems a little surprised you haven't mentioned him to me."

"Yeah, babes," Stone piped in, still munching his donut. "I feel like 'Leo this' and 'Leo that' works its way into every conversation we have, but somehow you never mentioned me to him?" It didn't sound like an accusation, but there was an edge to his voice.

Miranda met his stare directly. "I haven't told anyone about us. That was our deal. But to be honest, I was planning to break that agreement and tell Leo." Swiveling her head to me, she explained, "I wanted to talk to you about Stone in person."

I understood immediately. As much as I didn't want to acknowledge the gravity of the situation, I couldn't deny it either.

In theory, if she was getting involved with someone—and I didn't know the level of involvement she had with this Stone character—she could shoot me a text or tell me on the phone. But that would mean denying what we'd been to each other these past eleven months. Our closeness. Would she need to save some of that closeness for this guy now? The thought made my lungs constrict.

"Right," Stone said to Miranda. "I know how much you like keeping our thing private. Especially now that I've got the movie." He shoved the last of the donut into his mouth. "Speaking of which—" Crumbs flew from his lips. "I'd better get moving. I need to meet Shoshanna at ten."

"Your PA?" Miranda asked.

"Yep. Signing contracts this morning. Naomi's gonna be there too. I'm excited to finally meet her."

He bounced into the bedroom, returning with a backpack slung over his shoulder.

A bolt of annoyance sped through me when he kissed Miranda and murmured, "I like you in my shirt," loud enough for me to hear.

I shoved the feeling aside. I had no right to be possessive. Miranda deserved to find her happiness.

And I couldn't give her everything she needed.

But I struggled to believe the surfer-bro shaking his ass as he walked out the door could either.

Chapter Eleven

Miranda

NOW

Waking up on Monday felt like I'd fallen into a parallel reality, one where my life hadn't completely jackknifed on Thanksgiving.

If someone had asked me a week ago, I would have guessed the day would go like this: I'd wake up to a happy birthday text from Stone, and perhaps a flower delivery. Then I'd go to work, and in the break room, there would be a store-bought cake, along with a card everyone in the office signed with only their names, maybe adding something like "Have a good one." In the afternoon, I'd treat myself to a Mocha Cookie Crumble Frappuccino and probably get more texts from friends I hadn't seen in a while. I'd made a half-hearted promise to have dinner with Raven, but it was more likely I'd order in and video chat with Stone. And the whole day, I would have felt awful about the fact that Leo and I weren't talking.

But instead of the California sun, I'd woken up to Puget Sound drizzle, and Leo's weighted blanket had replaced my light duvet. A Post-it Note on the bedside table informed me he had already procured my Frappuccino. It waited for me in the fridge. Also, he'd gone to his jobsite and would be home around five. Rather than smiling through a tepid office birthday, my work time would be spent on Leo's couch, staring at the giant painting of London's melting skyline. And instead of fretting about how Leo and I hadn't spoken in weeks, he'd be taking me to dinner.

I still got the birthday text from Stone, though.

STONE: Happy Birthday to My Favorite Girl! *cake emoji* *party hat emoji* *happy face blowing streamer emoji* *present emoji* *red balloon emoji* *red heart emoji* *pink heart emoji*

My apartment manager texted to let me know a massive bouquet had been delivered to my apartment and was sitting outside my door. I supposed Stone, or Shoshanna more likely, had forgotten to cancel it. I replied that he could have the flowers for himself. Or toss them.

Stone also left a voice message apologizing that he wouldn't be able to call later since he had a night shoot in a remote location.

I went into the kitchen to find my Frappuccino. The cup had another Post-it Note on it. *I hope you're able to get to this before it melts. I didn't want to put it in the freezer because I thought that might mess up the whipped cream. If it's too soupy, let me know and I'll have another delivered. Happy Birthday.* He'd put the cup in a bucket of ice, which had only melted halfway. The temperature was perfect.

Leo had certainly gone to a lot of trouble to get me my birthday treat of choice. Despite the success of the past few days, we were still a little nervous around one another. Still overcompensating. I figured it was because we hadn't truly worked through the fallout from our fight, other than both of us being apologetic. But that didn't change what we'd said.

I'd spent the last three nights in Leo's arms, knowing he was giving me everything he could, and realizing I could no longer square the circle between my relationship with him and my relationship with Stone.

My workday flew by in a barrage of Teams calls, emails, and virtual client meetings. I was grateful that my current notoriety hadn't penetrated those spaces. And when I snuck peeks at my phone during the day, it seemed like the world was moving away from the notion that Stone was a cheater.

Ironically, they seemed to have wholeheartedly embraced the idea that Stone and I were *goals* for what platonic friendship should look like between a man and a woman, and extended this praise to Naomi and Leo for being examples of how trusting partners should behave.

JFC. The internet couldn't decide if it was smart, dumb, a teacher, a judge, a toddler, or a demon. Luckily, a confluence of factors had benefited us. This happened on a holiday weekend, so people were in good moods and not paying attention to the news, which let us get ahead of the narrative. Not to mention there were other stories to provide distraction—bigger celebrities doing nastier things, or crazier things, or simply behaving in ways that demanded more attention than Stone did.

Shoshanna let me know that Naomi planned to fly out to Vancouver tomorrow and would stay with Stone for a few days so they could be photographed together. She also told me to keep up the good work with Leo. I almost replied that it wasn't work at all. I wasn't doing anything different, and neither was he.

Other than that kiss in the arcade. The one he'd done for show.

Even with work to engage me, spending the day alone with my thoughts and scrolling on my phone wasn't ideal. Pacing around the silent apartment in the late afternoon, I felt my mood spiraling. Things were falling in our favor, but despite that, there were *a lot* of comments. When I logged off work for the day, I was pretty much the definition of someone who needed to touch grass.

By the time I heard Leo's key slide into the exterior lock, I ached for the comfort and grounding only he could provide.

"Happy Birthday!" he shouted, grinning widely as the door swung open.

I attacked before he was all the way inside.

"Oof," he sputtered as I launched myself against his middle. One of his arms came around my torso, and the other pressed the back of my head, holding me to him. "Hey, hey, Panda... What's wrong?" His voice was a whisper as he kissed my hair.

I rested my cheek against his wide chest, soaking up the overwhelming sense of gravity that flooded me. I'd missed it all day. His solidness. Tears threatened, and I pushed them back. "It's okay, Bear. Just birthday blues."

How had I lived without Leo these past weeks since our fight? Duh. Because you were doing okay. You were always going to make up with him the minute you needed him.

I considered what I'd realized over the past few days. For both our sakes, we needed healthy boundaries. *But how would I ever survive without this?*

"Are you sure?" he asked, rubbing his hands up and down my back. I arched into his touch. "This seems like more than birthday blues."

Wiping my eyes, I forced myself to step back from him. "I think—"

"Hmm?"

I gulped down the emotions working their way up again. "After this Thursday, you're off until New Year's, correct?" I asked him.

His brows furrowed at my non sequitur. "Uh-huh. It might be Wednesday, actually. If we're finished by then."

I nodded. "Then, if you're not opposed, I'd like to go to Coleman Creek. I know my sisters won't be back until this weekend. But with everything going on, I just want to be someplace that feels like home."

He huffed. "My apartment not cutting it?"

I answered seriously. "Honestly, your apartment would be my number two. Even more than my place in LA. I hope you know that." Leo would always be home for me, but I didn't want to put that on him.

"Thank you," he said with equal sincerity.

"Will you come with me, Bear? Stay in Coleman Creek for the month? I know it might be asking a lot, but even so..."

He didn't hesitate. "It's not a thing. When your boss said to take a break from LA for December, I knew you wouldn't want to stay in Tacoma the whole time, and being with you is necessary to sell our relationship. Things are going our way now, but it's probably not a smart idea to take our foot off the gas."

"Very true."

"My parents and I were already planning to go to Coleman Creek for the holidays, so it's really just a few weeks early for me."

Relief flooded me at his quick agreement. "Great. So we'll leave Thursday." At that moment, our conversation reminded me of something else. "I just realized you never told me what your parents said when you called to tell them we were dating."

Leo smirked. "They were thrilled. Like, genuinely and enthusiastically over-the-top happy."

A knot formed in my gut. "As much as it helps that they buy our relationship, that sort of makes me feel icky. I hope they're not too disappointed when we split up. Or come clean."

He smiled sadly. "It's okay. When it comes to my love life, they're used to disappointments. At least it should be a nice Christmas."

My heart flipped at the thought of spending the season on Leo's arm. Marley was our family's designated holiday fanatic, but I still loved the lights and decorations and food. I was a good vibes girl, and nothing said cheer and joy like Christmas.

"I'm excited you're coming with me, Bear. We can do all the things. Drive around and see the window displays. Go to the official tree lighting. The Holiday Hoopla. You've already been to the high school talent show, but you might enjoy it more when James isn't embarrassing himself singing." I felt my spirits lifting as I imagined it.

He drew me into another hug, this one much less fraught. "Sounds like going to Coleman Creek is exactly what you need."

"With you, Leo. What I need is to be in Coleman Creek with you." At his questioning look, I hastily added, "Gotta remind the universe we're dating, right?"

His lips flattened. "Right."

13 MONTHS AGO - NOVEMBER

Driving north on I-5, Leo and I got stuck in traffic in Central California of all places. Usually, that was a dependably smooth part of the drive. But thanks to road construction, we lumbered behind a line of semi-trucks.

We'd spent a fun couple of days together, once Leo got over the initial shock of seeing Stone in my kitchen. Given a do-over, that would not have been my choice for introducing them. I meant what I'd said. I hadn't been hiding my relationship with Stone from Leo. It deserved an in-person conversation.

I explained to Leo how I'd met Stone on the beach and that we'd been dating under the radar for a few months. Because of what he'd seen when he showed up, I hadn't needed to clarify that Stone and I were sleeping together. But I did not clue him in to the fact that the sex was...ahem...pretty mediocre. Decent, if I were being charitable.

Once he had the basics, Leo offered an acknowledging grunt and didn't bring it up again. I knew he would, though. Just like when he told me about his asexuality. He had a process for working up to things before discussing them.

We'd spent his first day in Los Angeles touring the Science Center and Olivera Street, and the second day we went sideways of Disneyland to hit up California Adventure. The picture I grabbed of Leo having a discussion with Lightning McQueen in Cars Land was officially my new favorite.

Now, stuck behind the semis, Leo decided he'd stumbled upon the moment to speak his mind.

"Panda, I need to understand more about this Stone situation."

I smiled, pulling my knee up onto the seat to rest my fist on it. "Only took you two days to get curious, huh? What more do you want to hear about?"

"I know you said that you guys agreed not to date publicly, since he's a *celebrity*." Leo took his hands off the steering wheel long enough to curl his fingers into air quotes. "I guess I'm just confirming that keeping things under wraps is really what you want." He moved his head to look at me. "You deserve better than being someone's secret."

"I promise you I'm okay with it. I'm the one who insisted. Stone would have been public from the get-go, but he understands my reasoning. He's a good guy. I think you'd like him if you got to know him better."

Leo mumbled a noise that sounded a lot like "doubt it" under his breath.

I grinned. "That's okay, Bear. I realize you don't have much in common with a twenty-something bro. But it's like I said, we're not serious enough to justify the hassle of going public. Not at this stage. I have too much on my plate without adding being *Stone Caseman's girlfriend* to the mix."

"And if it gets more serious?"

I hummed thoughtfully. If Leo had asked me that a month ago, I would have assured him it wasn't an issue. I'd have said Stone and I got along great, but we were only having fun. Now I wasn't so sure. Every day, as I got to know the true Stone beneath his public facade, I liked him more. In private, he was funny and articulate. Nerdy even. Before he'd dropped out to pursue influencing full-time, he'd been in school for environmental science, and I admired his strong interest in conservation.

Still, I couldn't see myself ever wanting to be in the public eye. Not the way he was. Most of the time, that obstacle felt insurmountable to having a deeper relationship.

"Honestly, Leo, I don't know. We're not in that place now, and I can't predict the future. The only thing I'm sure of is that, at this moment, going public with Stone is more than I want to deal with. I've seen his DMs. You should see the amount of unsolicited boobs he gets sent—not to mention dick pics—and I don't want to be subjected to any extra scrutiny by his crazy fans. Not now that I'm finally past the worst of my grief. Plus, I'll be launching myself into the job market in less than a year."

"You've told him all this?"

"Some of it. I don't talk about my mom, or about the future. He's very much a *live in the moment* type of guy, so that's what we're doing. I think he likes our little cocoon when we're together because he's so busy with his career. He's got a new movie with Naomi Butler coming up—"

"The child actress?"

"That's the one. It's an indie film called *Panic in First Class*. It's mostly for Naomi to redefine herself. Stone is what you'd call 'stunt casting,' which he's okay with. But he's also nervous about getting it right. He knows this could catapult him into a real future in entertainment."

Leo let out a hissed breath, the sound vibrating through the cab. "It seems like you and Stone are in such different places," he finally said. "But I trust you. If you're telling me this works, then I respect it. But I want to be honest that the secrecy concerns me." He ran his thumb and forefinger over his chin. "It could fall apart in a bad way, and I can't help worrying."

"I know. And thank you. If this blows up, or I need someone to talk sense into me, you'll be the first one I call."

I reached for his hand, kissing his knuckles before pulling our twined fingers into my lap.

He kept his eyes on the road as I squeezed our palms together.

"We're still going to be us, Bear. We're still going to be...the way we are. That's not going to change. Your friendship is important to me. And I made it clear to Stone that it's a priority."

"As long as you made it clear to him that you're no one's afterthought," Leo said fiercely, disengaging his hand once we started moving again.

I rested my head against the window. Truly, I didn't mind if I wasn't Stone's priority all the time. When we were together, I enjoyed getting to know him. But when we weren't, I didn't pine for him or anything like that.

There was only one person whose thoughts and regard I truly cared about. Only one person I missed when he wasn't around.

Did it matter if Stone floated in and out of my life like the wind when I had Leo to be my rock?

Chapter Twelve

Leo

NOW

Tuesday morning, on my hands and knees, putting the finishing touches on the entryway staircase at the jobsite, I peered at the floor in front of me to see a pair of red Converse, the right foot tapping aggressively against the hardwood.

My eyes lifted as I sat back on my haunches. "Hey, Amala."

My coworker folded her arms and glared at me. With her blue one-piece utility suit and hair pinned under a red scarf, she gave off unmistakable Rosie the Riveter energy. Assuming Rosie was pissed as hell.

"Why didn't you tell me?"

I sighed. "About Miranda?"

She threw up her arms and made a face. "Yes, about Miranda. Obviously. You've been telling us for two years that you and she are just friends. Now we find out—from the fucking internet—that not only are you dating, but she's also friends with Stone Caseman.

Why didn't you say something when I was talking shit about him on Thanksgiving? I can't believe I didn't put it together that *adventure girl* Miranda was *your* Miranda, but whatever."

I rose. Since I was on the stair below her, we stood eye to eye. "I'm sorry. I guess when I heard you and Lisa talking, I panicked."

"But why bullshit us about being a fan or whatever? Why not just say then that you knew the story wasn't true because that's your girlfriend?"

Amala was hurt, and I understood. I'd known her for five years. I bit my lip, pausing before I explained. "That morning was the first I'd heard of it, honestly. And I didn't know what Miranda wanted me to say. She's known Stone for a while, and it's always been on the DL, you know. I was sort of...information gathering, I suppose. Just worried about my g-girlfriend." I barely stuttered over the word. "That was my thought process. Once you showed me what was happening online, I felt frantic to check on her."

That last part was certainly true.

"You could have told me," Amala grumbled. "Not just about her being friends with Stone, but also about dating her." She put her hand to her mouth like she'd just realized something terrible. "Or did you believe at the time it was true? That your girlfriend was cheating on you with Stone?"

Damn, this was convoluted. I shook my head decisively. "No. Miranda's not a cheater. It wasn't a surprise to me that there are pictures of her and Stone. They're, um, good friends."

"I feel like a jackass that I tried to introduce you to my sisters. Or pointed out women when we went out. You could have just told me you were with someone."

Again, I didn't want to lie. I struggled to come up with a half-truth that might make her feel better. "It's complicated between Miranda and me. I'm sure you remember that her sister is married to my brother. We kept it quiet because we didn't want to cause a big family drama in case it didn't work out."

Amala choked a laugh. Her anger seemed to have faded. "My man, I've seen you with that girl. And I've heard the way you talk about her. Not to mention those pics that got posted. I was an idiot to believe it when you said it was just a friend thing." She chortled again. "Trust me, it's gonna work out." She put her hands on her hips. "Charlie said he thinks you've been dating this whole time, since when you first introduced us to her."

"Charlie is...incorrect."

Amala snorted. "Well, I'm still not thrilled you didn't feel you could tell me right off. But I know one way you can make it up to me."

"How's that?"

"The next time Stone's in town, maybe you can have a party or something, and I can just swing by..."

I grinned in relief. I was sure she'd think of more questions later, but for now, I didn't have to worry about digging myself out from under a bigger pile of lies.

"Stone's actually fairly down-to-earth," I said. Grudgingly. "And he's more Miranda's friend than mine. But I know he loves his fans, and I'm sure he'd be happy to meet you." I planned to make sure of it. Stone could do me a solid after this.

"Cool. And if he ever does break up with Naomi, maybe you can put in a good word for my sisters."

Amala leaned down to look at the joints on the balustrade, and I reflected on how much Miranda and I were lying to our friends and families.

It was convenient that I'd bought myself some peace from having my coworkers wonder about my love life, but it was coming at a moment when I finally thought I'd be okay telling people about my asexuality. For years I'd felt like I needed a cover story, that I couldn't risk being upfront about why I didn't date. But that had changed. The shift had come so slowly, I hadn't registered it, but I didn't feel the same *otherness* I always had. The instinct to protect myself from being seen as "a waste" had dissipated.

Miranda and I had solved the immediate problem with Stone, but we hadn't talked much about our exit strategy from this deception. My parents were so happy to hear we were dating. Would Marley, James, and Maureen feel the same? Probably. And how long would we keep it up? Were we going to stage a breakup or eventually reveal the whole truth? Would it hurt them that we hadn't been honest in the first place?

There were so many X-factors we hadn't considered. Even if Stone kept his word and "broke up" with Naomi around Valentine's Day, how long would he have to wait before dating Miranda publicly? Would they ever be able to? No matter how long they waited, wouldn't it always look suspicious? I imagined if they waited a year, once me and Miranda and Stone and Naomi were all single again, they could do it. Sell it as a whole friends-to-lovers situation.

But that was a long time from now. More waiting for Miranda. I doubted she'd thought that far ahead.

The only person who'd probably thought that far ahead was Shoshanna, and she didn't care if Miranda had to lie to everyone she knew. Stone also didn't seem to have imbibed what this was costing his girlfriend.

Evidently, protecting Miranda's interests would be my job. As much as she'd let me. I could get her through this. Because no one cared about her the way I did.

I recalled that day almost two years ago, when she'd stood in my living room, dripping wet from her shower, and I'd been unmoved.

Not a whisper of a sexual thought. She was simply a beautiful woman who intrigued me, someone I wanted to know.

Now that same image had my cock at half-mast. In my mind's eye, I pictured her—face open, eyes soft and vulnerable. Bolstered by two years of knowing her, the memory hit different.

And thank god for that. Thank god Miranda had shown me what was possible. I could love someone.

I could love her. Even if she didn't know my feelings had changed.

Amala's voice broke my reverie. "Hey Leo?"

"Yeah?"

"Sorry I called your girlfriend a ho."

13 MONTHS AGO - NOVEMBER

Miranda and I spent Thanksgiving at Marley and James's house in Coleman Creek since my parents had gone on a cruise. Maureen had been laid off at the end of the summer and was living there, using the time to regroup. Miranda bunked with her while I took the third bedroom.

Thanksgiving morning, I stepped out for some fresh air and found Maureen on the front porch. She sat on the top step drinking coffee from a mug that read *On the Naughty List*.

"Escaping the kitchen madness?" I asked, sitting down next to her.

"I'll help in a minute. Just needed a breather before Marley goes full drill sergeant about peeling potatoes and trimming green beans."

My cheeks lifted. "She has been...rather intense."

"She's not usually this bad, so I'm guessing it's the stress of the holidays, plus the engagement party being in ten days." Maureen gripped her mug with both hands, staring at it. "Also...I think it's hitting her that she's getting married without our mom."

Maureen's face remained unreadable, as usual. The only whiff of strong emotion I ever saw from her was the aggressive frown she made whenever anyone mentioned James's friend Will.

I shifted my position, leaning against the stair rail opposite her. "You know," I said, "I was looking at some of the old holiday pictures Marley put up in the living room—"

"You mean the North Pole?" Maureen snort-laughed. "Barely December and Marley's already gone hard on the decorations."

"I kind of like it." I chuckled. "What I was going to say was that looking at all those family photos drove home what a special lady your mom was. I know Miranda misses her too. Especially this time of year."

"You certainly are close with my little sister."

I didn't bother downplaying it. "She's one of my favorite people in the world."

Maureen's reply was a keen perusal before she said, "On paper, it's weird, since you live in different states and you're older than her. But when both of you are in the same room, it's always obvious."

"What is?"

"That you guys are perfect together."

My spine went rigid. "You know we're just friends, right?"

She quirked an eyebrow. "My best friend Bren and I are perfect together too."

I relaxed my posture. "You're right."

Maureen hummed, taking another sip before placing the mug down beside her. "So here's an interesting story," she began, resting her elbows on her knees. "I used to have this real woo-woo coworker at one of the retail stores I worked at. Super into spirituality and all that shit. One of her big beliefs was that everyone had a twin soul. She thought the reason for being a good person and treating others well was so the universe would reward you by putting your other half in your path. Otherwise, you'd be condemned to walk the earth always missing a piece of yourself. Always feeling a little...lost."

I swallowed as my heart beat faster. "And do you believe all that?"

She smirked. "Leo, the only woo-woo shit I believe in is that a good outfit can change your day. As for the rest of it—who knows?"

We sat in silence, her words hanging in the air. Finally, she punched my shoulder before picking up her mug and going back inside the house.

I contemplated our conversation, not entirely sure what she'd been trying to tell me. Did she buy into the idea of twin souls or not? It amazed me that someone like Miranda could have a sister who was a bit of a misanthrope.

When I discovered Stone in Miranda's apartment, I'd felt something akin to jealousy, knowing he'd had her in a way I never would. At that moment, I'd seen the inevitable heartbreak ahead. For both of us. Even if Stone went away, eventually another man would come along who could meet Miranda's needs.

All her needs.

Could I truly be her other half if I couldn't give her everything?

For now, it was fine for her to have a casual physical relationship with Stone and an emotionally intimate one with me, but at some point, she'd want the total package. She deserved that. Not for the first time, I wished I could force myself to be *more* for Miranda. It was true I'd felt a twinge here and there, small slivers of awareness I didn't feel with anyone else. But was that enough to build on?

I knew some ace people had romantic lives and families, but many didn't. What I didn't know was exactly what was possible for me.

Once I reached my thirties with no signs of attraction to anyone, I'd resigned myself to a monastic life. And even if I somehow magically developed sexual feelings toward Miranda, there was no guarantee they'd ever grow to the degree that we'd be compatible that way. And I could never ask her to wait around while I figured it out. She was worth so much more than being my...experiment.

No, I knew where this was headed.

Eventually, I'd have to give her up. Or at least take a step back.

I stood, grasping the stair rail with both hands.

It had been a long time since I'd felt the otherness that came from acknowledging my authentic self. By hiding my truth, I'd insulated myself from the discomfort. But I felt it now. The flicker of shame. The modicum of anger. Bare rage that my dick didn't get hard the way everyone else's seemed to.

That I was a waste.

I felt the warm press of hands circling me from behind. Miranda pushed her chest against my back, forehead nestling between my shoulder blades.

"What are you doing out here, Bear?" she mumbled into my coat.

I patted her hands on my stomach before turning around to hug her. Resting my chin on her head, I reveled in the way she fit so well against me.

"Just thinking," I said. "You slept in late."

"I wasn't sleeping. I was talking to Stone on the phone." My shoulders tensed. She gripped me tighter, burrowing into my chest. "He can be such a goober sometimes about forgetting things. He left his lucky flip-flops at my place, and he has a key but apparently doesn't know what 'front closet' means. We spent five minutes on the phone while he tried to find them. I got so confused when he described everything he was seeing until I realized he was in my bedroom closet and not the hall one." Against my shirt, I felt her head shaking. "Should have just started out on video."

The way Miranda used "goober," as a term of endearment, accurately described Stone. He was essentially harmless, maybe even a good guy, but he was no match for Miranda. I gnashed my teeth, eager for the day she realized the fun-loving doofus was unworthy of her.

Just like I was unworthy of her.

Because I couldn't snap my fingers and make myself different.

But I also couldn't let her go.

I pulled out the sides of my coat to wrap her inside it, embracing her more fully.

With a burst of clarity, I knew the truth. She might belong to someone else someday, but no matter where our lives took us, there was a piece of me she would always carry.

My twin soul.

Chapter Thirteen

Miranda

NOW

Driving into Coleman Creek usually made my heart swell up a bit, but driving in with Leo after the eventful week we'd had felt more like coming home from a wartime deployment.

The holiday decorations wrapped around trees and sparkling in storefront windows made the warm embrace of the familiar even more appealing. I noticed the Hawaiian-shirted Santa outside the bowling alley had a friend this year, a six-foot tall sunglasses-wearing penguin with reindeer antlers. The official city holiday tree would not be lit until the ceremony this weekend, but we saw it as we passed, already decorated with an array of red, pink, blue, and silver bows. The high school tree lot was open, beckoning eager residents who felt confident in their ability to keep a fresh fir alive for a month. At the end of Main Street, my sister Maureen's consignment shop beckoned, with a piece of paper in the window that read "On Vacation. Back December 9."

I couldn't imagine a shop in Los Angeles sticking a sign on the door so the owner could spend a week in the woods. But Maureen was a one-woman show for now, and the locals didn't mind. That was one thing I loved about my hometown. As much as it sucked to have everyone in your business, it was good to know people had your back.

"Do you want to stop at the pub and grab something to eat?" Leo asked, humming along to the Dean Martin Christmas standards he'd queued up an hour ago.

"I'm not ready to face people just yet. Everyone in town probably knows about Stone by now, and I'd rather deal with it later."

"Understood."

We'd broken up the long drive grocery shopping near the highway, so I figured we could hide for a while before anyone realized I'd come to town. My sisters would be back in two days, but Leo and I had the house to ourselves until then.

We'd been quiet during the journey, content to listen to the music as the miles passed. I thought a lot about what this past week would have been like with Stone if I hadn't messed up and posted the pic. Video chats. Counting down the days until he staged his breakup with Naomi. Waiting for him to come home so we could have a real discussion about our relationship.

To the core of my being, I believed posting that picture had been an accident, but I couldn't stop the suspicion that—subconsciously—I'd been trying to bring things to a head. My entire relationship with Stone had been a waiting game I'd willingly participated in. A waiting game that began as commitment aversion, grew into bored complacency, evolved into paralyzed inertia, and eventually became avoiding the situation altogether. For the past few months, every interaction with Stone filled me with low-key dread because I couldn't lie to myself anymore. The whole time I'd been convincing myself we were in a relationship, we'd actually been waiting to start one.

And part of me knew that when I posted the picture.

Yesterday, when the photos of Stone and Naomi in Vancouver surfaced, I'd barely blinked. In them, he held her hand and pressed a kiss to her cheek in front of a little club in the Gaslamp district. My primary reaction was indifference. I wondered if Stone felt the same when he saw pictures of Leo kissing me at the arcade. Or maybe he hadn't bothered to look at them.

I thought I'd gained a sort of peace with Stone, an ease. But that was merely a story I'd told myself.

I owed it to him to clean up this mess, whether or not I'd caused it intentionally, and then it was time to set things right. No more waiting game.

Not with Stone.

Or Leo.

The past nights sleeping in Leo's arms had been both torturous and telling. I couldn't be with him the way I wanted to be. But I also couldn't keep pretending I didn't want what I did.

There was a word for what I felt toward Leo. I'd read it in a novel once. Limerence. Unrequited love. The concept wasn't a perfect match, since Leo loved me back in his way. Also, I wasn't obsessed to the point of paralysis. My limerence was gentler. I desired someone who didn't desire me back. And as much as I respected Leo's right not to want me, the intensity of my own feelings was becoming a pain I could no longer live with.

I'd used Stone to assuage the disappointment of not being able to be with Leo—I saw that now—but it hadn't worked, and it needed to stop.

After the holidays.

For the next four weeks, I planned to indulge myself like the Leo addict I was. It was probably unhealthy, torturing myself this way. I probably needed therapy, but I didn't care. If this was the closest I'd ever come to being his girlfriend, I was going to enjoy it. I was going to pretend that Leo wanted me in all the ways I wanted him. And I was going to do it in my favorite place in the world. At my favorite time of the year.

When we got to Marley and James's house, I was unsurprised to find they'd already put up a ton of exterior lights. Leo practically tripped off the front porch when he stepped on the themed welcome mat, which blasted "Rockin' Around the Christmas Tree."

I pulled the key from the fake rock near the door. Flipping on lights along the way, we walked to the kitchen and deposited our grocery bags on the counter.

"I can't believe they did all this before they left," Leo shouted from the living room as I put the fresh food in the fridge, and I knew he was taking in the decorations.

"Don't play like you haven't met Marley." I laughed. "She starts in early November, and everything is up by Thanksgiving. The only thing missing is a live tree, which I'm sure they'll get next weekend."

Leo popped his head into the kitchen. "There's already a tree."

I snorted. "Um, that's tree number one. I guarantee you tree number two is set up downstairs in the family room. Tree number three will be the live one."

"Wow. I thought it was over the top last year because of the engagement party."

"The themed onesie duos didn't clue you in that she's more than a little crazy about the season?"

His eyes crinkled as he smiled. "I forgot about that."

"By 'forgot,' you mean pushed the embarrassing memory into the darkest recesses of your mind?"

"Hundred Percent."

I threw bags of chips into the basket in the pantry. On the top shelf, I saw stacks of red decorative glitter and peppermint candy melts and realized my sister had already started assembling ingredients for Christmas cookies and treats. "Honestly, I'm glad she's like this. It's something she and our mom had in common. I don't think Maureen and I would have kept all the holiday traditions alive if we'd been left to our own devices. Marley's sort of been our anchor like that."

He went back into the living room to put on a record, commenting about how weird the house seemed without Bambi and Oscar, Marley and James's dogs. It was nice that mentioning my mom no longer felt like an arrow to the heart. I'd healed a lot in the two years since Leo and I first talked about my grief in the carport, drawing some of that strength from our friendship.

After a quick dinner of chicken and rice, we watched TV until I started yawning. The house had two guest bedrooms, and his face flashed when I suggested we share the bedroom by the kitchen.

"Your childhood bedroom?"

"You remembered," I said. "It wouldn't make sense to mess up both of them, since they'll be expecting us to sleep in the same room."

After we brushed our teeth, Leo put on his pajamas in the hall bathroom while I did the same in the bedroom. I turned my head when he stepped wordlessly through the doorway, a flat look on his face, before stumbling to his usual side of the bed. He stood by the mattress, punching the pillow to fluff it. I fanned my fingers in front of my chest, the air in the small room thick and heavy.

I wasn't sure why we were tiptoeing around each other. We'd been okay in his apartment.

"Why does this feel so awkward?" I forced a laugh.

He smiled, but it didn't reach his eyes. "Because it's different in Marley and James's house."

I waited for him to elaborate, but he didn't. We slid into bed, and he flicked off the lamp, shrouding the room in moonlight. A moment later, his arms wrapped around me.

"This okay?" he asked gruffly.

"It would have been stranger if you hadn't." I melted into his embrace. For the past week, we'd shared a bed. Once I'd gone to him the night of the sombrero serenade, we'd never stopped. Never talked about whether we should. But I understood why he was asking. In Coleman Creek, everything was magnified. Being together in this house, surrounded by my past, meant something.

"Do you have specific plans for when your sisters get back? Anything I should know?" He whispered into the darkness.

"What do you mean?"

His hold on me tightened. "I know we're going to tell them we're dating, that we made it official after the wedding, but is there anything else? Some piece of backstory you wanted to get straight?"

I bit my bottom lip, considering. "I don't think so. They've seen us together... just...make it seem real."

His warm breath caressed my neck as he splayed his hand across my belly. "That won't be hard."

I knew he meant it wouldn't be difficult since we'd shared a bed so many nights before, and we'd been doing a good job with this ruse for a week.

But oh, how I wished he meant it another way!

His soft shaft against my backside and his forearm over mine were nothing new. And it had all been fine a year ago. Manageable. This closeness. But now, things felt less benign. Dishonest somehow.

Since I'd decided to put distance between us after our fake dating was over, that expiration date made the moment bittersweet.

But I couldn't keep banging my head against the brick wall of knowing Leo didn't want me. After the night he'd pushed his erection against me and whispered my name—I continued to force that memory aside, knowing he hadn't meant it—and after the vehemence of our fight on Halloween, I'd accepted that we could never go back to the way things were before the summer.

We'd reached a tipping point. The past week had proven that.

So why did lying in his arms feel completely, utterly, indescribably right? My beautiful, painful limerence.

12 MONTHS AGO - DECEMBER

"You want to do what?"

"Fake date her."

I jumped off Stone's couch and began pacing in the open space between it and the dining table.

"Naomi Butler?" I asked again, as though having him repeat what he'd just said would change it.

"Yes. Since it's a quick shoot, this could help generate buzz until it comes out in the summer."

"You think people will talk about your movie because you and Naomi are dating?"

He shook his head with a smile, as though I'd asked a silly question. "C'mon. The public eats that shit up. And it wouldn't be real. Just for, like, the internet and stuff." He leaned back. "I know you get it. I saw you watching a reel about Zendaya and that Spider-Man guy."

"Pretty sure they're *actually* dating."

"But would anyone even care if they weren't?" Stone reasoned. "Shoshanna suggested it. She thinks it's a great idea—"

"Oh, well, if *Shoshanna* said it—"

"Babes, be so one hundred right now. You know how it is. Naomi's people were into the idea too."

"I don't know... It just seems a little...unhinged. And risky."

Stone stood behind me and put his hands on my shoulders. "Miranda, think about it. It's perfect. You and I are already completely undercover. No one in your life knows about us except your friend Leo, and you can tell him what's up. Then we can just keep doing exactly what we're doing. No cap. The only difference is that when I'm out in public, sometimes I'll be with Naomi. Shoshanna told me celebrities do this all the time."

"And Naomi's okay with it?"

"Yeah, she's on board."

"And does she know you're a twenty-seven-year-old man who still says, 'no cap'?" I shook my head with a grin, beginning to resign myself to this scheme.

He huffed good-naturedly before continuing. "Darlin', I hope you don't mind, but I had to tell Shoshanna and Naomi about you. About us. They won't tell anyone, but I had to explain that I was already in a real relationship. So they'd understand my limits."

"Limits?"

He hummed, looking guilty. "Shoshanna was pushing for a lot more physical stuff. Frenching on the sidewalk or whatever, so paps would be sure to get the shot. She said it would just be more acting, like with the movie, but I said no. When she—and Naomi, for that matter—pressed me on it, I had to tell them about you so they'd stop pushing. But don't worry, they won't say anything."

I snorted. "Obviously, unless they want to sabotage their own plan."

"Exactly. I told them that if they really believe it will help with the movie, I could be fine with fake dating, as long as we fake a breakup after the release. I also said that I didn't want to do physical stuff. Maybe a quick kiss on the lips or holding hands, really whatever you're comfortable with, but I draw the line there."

"And if I don't agree?"

"Then I don't do it. Full stop. I told Shoshanna and Naomi too. That this wasn't a done deal until you and I talked."

"You'd be willing to give up this supposedly amazing PR opportunity for me?"

"Don't give me too much credit. I'm only halfway on board with it myself. But if you say no, then the whole idea dies... But, babes, I really hope you can see your way to agreeing. This would be stellar for my career."

I sighed. I was already twisted up enough since I'd come home from Coleman Creek. Every time I was with Leo, it reminded me of what was missing from my relationship with Stone. It occurred to me that Stone wanting to start a fake romance with Naomi might be the perfect excuse for me to simply call it on our relationship, to walk away before it got messier or I became more invested.

But then I took an objective look at the way Stone was handling this request. The fact that he was asking for permission, that he was considering my boundaries and was willing to walk away. He cared about me. Maybe I didn't have the same connection to him I had with Leo, but I didn't want to sell him short. Or give up on our potential too soon.

As to the question of his publicity stunt with Naomi, with the level of indecision and ambivalence I felt toward our relationship, it wasn't fair to hold him back from something that might be a great career move.

"I'm okay with it, as long as we're clear about those ground rules. If Shoshanna wants you to stage a choreographed fuckfest with Naomi in some Vegas hotel, I'm out."

His shoulders shook with laughter. "Nah. That's the image of me I'm trying to get away from. The idiot bad boy. If I'm gonna be somebody's fake boyfriend, I'm gonna treat her like a lady."

I couldn't stop my smile. Despite everything—staying casual, keeping our relationship a secret, all our various external pressures—Stone had treated me with nothing but respect over the past three months. He would have gone public already if I'd allowed it. Instead, he'd waited for me. On some level, it felt nice to do this for him.

At least in theory. I was going to hate it the first time I saw a picture of him holding hands with Naomi online. Pushing the thought aside, I relaxed my expression. I could give him this.

My arms rested around his neck. "It won't require much acting on your part to convince people you're a great boyfriend."

He kissed the tip of my nose. "Good to know."

Chapter Fourteen

Leo

NOW

The first night in Marley and James's house, I didn't sleep much. I held Miranda in my arms and let my thoughts run wild.

Nosing her hair, feeling the rhythmic rise and fall of her stomach beneath my palm, I drank in the absolute miracle that was sexual attraction.

I'd given up on the idea of finding someone. I'd let Ilona's words condemn me to being alone instead of taking them for what they were—an indicator that she and I were a bad match. Her hurtful insult had landed like a bomb in my life, landing squarely on my insecure and questioning mid-twenties self.

I understood only now how much power I'd given Ilona's *disgust,* that once I'd gotten into the habit of hiding my asexuality, I'd stopped trying to understand myself.

Telling Miranda was the first step in a new direction. And I'd finally opened up to my brother after his wedding in July. Our talk helped me be receptive to other ways of defining myself, options beyond being like everyone else or being alone.

There were loads of articles about ace people who found companionship with other ace people, or with non-ace people who found ways to make it work. Some couples even opted for non-monogamy. I couldn't see myself being okay with an open relationship, but I could be amenable to talking about it, keeping an open mind. Ilona calling me "a waste" had come at the worst possible moment, at a time in my life when that sentiment did the most damage. And as much as I'd found fulfillment and a happy life without a romantic partner since then, I was ready to explore alternatives.

Even if Miranda could never be mine, if she and Stone made it work, she'd given me a tremendous gift in showing me that I deserved to be loved. And also that I could love someone else. There were a million ways to be asexual, and I was ready for something different from what I'd been doing.

But discovering my path forward was a goal for post-New Year's Leo. For now, I was going to enjoy every moment I could with Miranda. She'd asked me to make it look real, and that wouldn't be an issue.

I pressed my lips to the juncture between her neck and shoulder. It was real to me.

I must have fallen asleep because the next thing I knew, sunlight streamed into the room. I woke slowly, squinting, to find my leg slung over Miranda with the bedcovers bunched at the bottom of the mattress. She lay on her back, trapped beneath my bent knee, cupping her arms underneath mine. Our heads shared a pillow.

She peered at me. "Finally up? I've been waiting twenty minutes to pee."

I blinked my eyes open. "You could have rolled me away from you."

She smirked. "I tried. Believe me. But every time I'd push an inch of you off me, you snapped right back." Her lips twitched. "I don't mind. You're a very cuddly blanket."

As I awakened further, I realized with horror that my cock was rock hard. More urgently, it was poking into Miranda's hip. My cheeks went hot as I shuffled back with a grunt of alarm.

"Don't sweat it, Bear. I know it's just a biology thing. Morning wood."

She seemed entirely nonplussed. Still, my face burned. "Uh, yeah."

Escaping to the bathroom, I gave myself a mirror pep talk as I willed my dick to de-chub. I certainly wasn't going to rub one out in my little brother's house with Miranda feet away.

I conjured mental erection deflators. Sitting on a bench with fresh bird poo. The old spaghetti jar full of bacon grease my mom kept in the fridge. Cleaning a hair clog from a shower drain. Using a bench at the gym right after the sweaty guy who didn't wipe it down.

There. Done. Shaft wilted. I glanced down at my pajama pants to confirm. Just the normal soft bulge with no tent in sight.

Splashing water on my face, I shook my head at Miranda's reaction to getting a hip massage from my penis. Totally unfazed. But of course she was. She was completely convinced of my asexuality and would assume nothing different. Damn. Would I ever tell her? Or would that be selfish since she was with Stone?

Another problem for post-New Year's Leo.

MIRANDA HAD TO WORK, SO I KEPT MYSELF busy doing yard maintenance for James. I knew he hated it, especially during the colder months, so I figured it could be an early Christmas gift. At least it hadn't snowed yet this year.

For dinner, we chose to make our first public appearance in Coleman Creek by eating at The Landslide, the town's popular pub. Icicle lights covered the exterior, and a blow-up Rudolph greeted guests in the parking lot, which was close to full at six p.m. on a Friday. I'd been here enough times on other visits to know that the bar's small dance floor and pool tables were Coleman Creek's major claim to *nightlife*.

When we arrived, I immediately spotted Katy, a friend of Marley and James's I'd met before. I knew Katy had worked at The Landslide since high school and was in the process of buying the business from the owners.

"Oh my goodness, Miranda!" Katy exclaimed, hugging her. "I didn't know you were in town. I saw all the gossip online, and I've been thinking about you." She pulled back, stretching her arms to hold Miranda by the shoulders. "I can't believe you know Stone Caseman!"

Katy led us to a corner booth, bringing water glasses.

"Mm-hmm," Miranda said. "We met on the beach in Los Angeles, but all this social media stuff is the reason I never made a big deal about it. This past week has been precisely what I tried to avoid."

"Did you not even tell your sisters? Marley never said anything."

"No. I never told them any of it." Miranda gestured to me. "When they get back into town, they're going to have a bunch of surprises waiting for them."

Katy bobbed her head. "I'll say." She volleyed her gaze between us. "I can't believe you guys are dating. Actually, scratch that. I'm not surprised. What I don't get is why you kept it a secret."

"It's complicated," Miranda said.

I grasped her hand, lacing our fingers. "Our relationship has some weird implications for our families. We were keeping it private while we figured things out, but of course everything with Stone forced our hand."

"That tracks," Katy mused. "It sucks having to live out your life when you feel like everyone is watching." She squared her shoulders. "Leo, you drink Guinness, right? And Miranda, I have that local hard cider you liked last time if you're interested? Or if you're in the mood for something sweet, we've got candy cane shakes for the season."

Miranda wrinkled her nose.

"She hates minty flavors," I told Katy. "Don't let her get started on her lack of toothpaste options."

Katie chuckled. "Noted. I'll remember for next time."

"The cider sounds great," Miranda said. "And I don't need to bother with a menu. I've been looking forward to getting a patty melt and fries here since the last time I was in town."

"Yes on the Guinness, thanks," I said. "With the French dip and fries."

"You got it."

Katy went back into the kitchen as the music switched and "I'll Be Home for Christmas" came on the vintage jukebox. From another table, several folks waved at Miranda. She returned the greetings, but no one bothered us. Hopefully, Stone's handlers wouldn't be too upset that the townsfolk in Coleman Creek had better things to do than try to grab under-the-table shots of us for the internet.

"I danced with Katy at the wedding. Seeing her reminds me that she spent the entire time we were dancing telling me how great you were." I chuckled. "Not even slightly subtle."

Miranda waved her wrist in a circle. "For sure. Everyone we know has been shipping us for years. They'll be thrilled about this development."

She was right, of course, but I noticed she stopped short of taking the thought to its logical conclusion—that our family and friends would be very disappointed when we told them we were breaking up. Or that we'd been faking the whole time. I still wasn't sure what our exit plan was.

For the millionth time, I wished Stone wasn't in the picture. Then I could tell Miranda how I felt, how things had changed for me over the past few months. But even asexuals knew the rules. You didn't declare yourself to other people's partners.

Instead, I switched the subject. "Katy sounded like she had something in mind when she mentioned how tough it is to have your life play out in front of people."

"You know she's a single mom, right?"

"Sure. I've met her kids a few times." I laughed heartily as a memory surfaced. "Wasn't it her kid who had a meltdown and tripped you, and you ended up spilling all the champagne at James and Marley's engagement party?"

Miranda covered her face with her hands. "Too soon! I'm still traumatized. I know Braxton didn't mean it, but that is one of the most embarrassing experiences of my life." She shuddered, but her words were light. It was good that she could see some humor in the situation now, a year later. She'd been so on edge that night, partly because she knew I wasn't thrilled about her relationship with Stone.

"Alright," I said. "Point taken. But what does her being a single mom have to do with her airing her shit out in front of people?"

"I don't want to speak out of turn," Miranda said. "But there're parts everyone in town knows. She had a pretty shitty divorce. Long story short, her husband turned out to be a cheating bastard. Besides having to raise tiny children mostly on her own, she also has to deal with some of our less-awesome neighbors giving her smug *I told you so* faces because Mike was not well-liked, to put it mildly."

"Say no more." I put up my hands. "I've talked to Katy enough to know she's awesome, so whoever this Mike is, he's the loser in this situation."

"Huge understatement." Miranda grinned, and my heart skipped at how radiant and lit from within she appeared.

Fifteen minutes later, Katy dropped off our food. The Landslide's basic menu obviously hadn't changed in decades, but the fare was delicious in the way only small-town bar food could be. Like the recipes had been perfected over generations. The walls of the place reflected the same hometown aesthetic, covered in photos of Coleman Creek citizens over the years.

After finishing our dinners, we played pool, and I caught Miranda staring at a faded color photo tacked up near the restrooms. In it, a couple sat at a booth near the bar, smiling widely, brown beer bottles in hand. Based on the clothes and hair, I guessed the picture was taken in the mid-to-late 80s. The man had silvery-blond hair and deep wrinkles next to his eyes. The woman appeared significantly younger.

And familiar.

"Your mom?" I asked. I'd never seen photos of Alice Davis at this age.

"And my dad." Miranda's response caused me to do a double take. "He was twenty-five years older than her." She tsked. "It was quite the scandal back in the day, but they didn't care. They made it work for fifteen years."

I knew Miranda's father died when she was a baby, but I didn't know he'd been that much older than her mom. The only picture of him at the house was a faded wedding photo.

Staring at the image, there was no doubt in my mind that Miranda's parents had been deeply in love. "Fifteen years doesn't seem like a long time," I said. "Then again, some people go their whole lives without ever finding love for even a day."

She must have caught the hitch in my voice because she coiled her arm around my elbow. "I know it's been a while since we talked about...about..." She whooshed out a breath. "It's been a minute since we did any kind of deep dive into your being asexual. And I know you're living a perfectly complete and full-throated existence without a romantic partner. But I hope you never forget how much love you have in your life. You're my best friend in the world. It might not be the same as what my parents had, or what people imagine when they think of a relationship, but I do love you, Leo-Bear."

I leaned over to kiss the top of her head. "I love you too, Panda. And trust me when I say our relationship has fulfilled me in ways I didn't even know were possible." She had no idea how much.

Her expression was serious as she gazed up at me. "No matter what happens, after all of this. With Stone or...whatever. Never forget that I love you. Even when we were fighting and not talking, I never stopped."

I couldn't decipher her words. Or figure out why she sounded so forlorn. My guess was that she wanted to make a real go of things with Stone and was trying to put me on notice that she might need to spend time working on that.

She reached out with a finger to touch the image of her father. "He died when I was fourteen months old. Maureen has some memories of him, but it's sketchier for Marley, and I don't remember a thing. Our mom told us some stories, but mostly, he's an enigma. Except the one thing everyone who's known our family seems to agree on is that, of the three of us, I'm the most like him personality-wise. Mom used to say I got his cheerful temperament and wicked sense of humor. When I started traveling in college, she talked to me about how he'd done the same thing in his early years, before they met. His employees at the plant loved him because he was a good boss. The kind who let you off early if your kid had a baseball game and never had a harsh word for anyone. It makes me feel good to know we're alike, that I have something of his legacy even if he didn't get to raise me. I don't miss him the way I miss my mom, of course, but I wish I could have met him." She paused before concluding, "I feel his absence. Not like grief. More like a missed opportunity."

I pulled her to my side and glanced at the picture again. At her father's wide-open smile, so like hers. "I'm sure he'd be proud of you."

"I hope so."

"*Miranda?*"

We turned to see a man with curly brown hair lumbering toward us. I knew I'd met him before, but I couldn't place him.

"Kase! Hey." Miranda clapped her hands together, looking down at the two preschoolers giggling and clutching his legs. "I see you've developed a parasitic condition." I recognized the small boy and girl as Katy's kids.

The man chortled. "Alright, you hooligans," he said, peeling them off his jeans. "Go find Mommy."

As the kids scampered to where Katy waited by the counter, he walked over to us with a tentative smile. Miranda had no such hesitancy, pulling him into a hug.

"It's so good to see you!" she enthused. Turning to me, she asked, "Leo, have you met Kasen yet? He's a...friend of Marley's, and all of us, really." To Kasen, she said, "This is Leo, James's brother."

Kasen shook my hand. "Hey, man. I think we met at the wedding reception, right?"

I snapped my fingers. "That's it. I was trying to place you. How's it going?" I recalled hearing that Kasen and Marley used to date before she met James, and he'd known Miranda since she was young.

"Can't complain."

Miranda looked at where Katy was setting up her kids in a booth with a tablet and two headsets. "Babysitting?"

Kasen crooked an elbow to grab the back of his neck. "Yeah. Rosie, Braxton, and I are good friends. Since I mostly work from home and we're neighbors, I help out when I can."

"That's so sweet of you," Miranda said.

"Really, it's no big deal. They're great kids." Suddenly, Kasen's features changed like he'd turned on a mental lightbulb. "Oh, shit! I just remembered I read about you two online. Everyone's talking about it. My parents even mentioned it." He grinned at Miranda. "Your sisters are going to flip when they find out."

She rolled her eyes. "About Stone? They don't care who I'm friends with. They'll understand why I kept it quiet."

"Not that. They're gonna be pissed that you two have been dating in secret this whole time."

I curled a protective arm around Miranda's shoulders. "We had our reasons. They'll get over it."

Kasen lifted his hands. "Hey, man, no judgment here. I think it's great. Miranda's like a little sister to me, and if she's happy, then I am too."

Katy's younger child, the little boy who'd tripped Miranda at the party, shouted across the room, "Sen, come watch with us!"

Kasen smiled. "Duty calls." He slapped my shoulder and nudged Miranda into another quick hug. "See you soon, I hope."

We watched as he sat down with the kids and Katy brought over plates of mac 'n' cheese for them.

"I'm glad he seems good," Miranda said. "He was a little weird when Marley and James first got together."

"Yeah, James mentioned that. I guess enough time has passed."

"Sure. Time heals heartbreak and all that." She looked at the picture of her parents again. "Then again, Mom never dated again after losing Dad. One great love was enough for her."

A shrill ringing invaded the air. Katy went behind the bar and picked up the handset of a heavy, old-fashioned phone.

"I can't remember the last time I saw a landline," I said as Miranda and I slid back into our booth.

"If that gets you going, you should check out the pay phone at the bowling alley."

"Seriously? I'm totally doing that."

"Such a city boy," Miranda chided.

"And you're not a city girl?"

She shook her head. "As much as I love Los Angeles and even Seattle, I'll always be more comfortable here. It's hard to explain, but I've been all over the world, and no place makes sense to me the way Coleman Creek does. It's like it's magical. I know that sounds corny, but it's true."

I took in the pictures of Coleman Creek citizens plastered to every inch of wall space. While The Landslide's interior was clean, no one would describe it as "modern." But there was something cozy about the mismatched chairs and weathered booths, like the unfussiness welcomed everyone. A Christmas tree in the corner glittered with baubles and homemade ornaments. It listed to the side under the weight of a beer can star. Strands of twinkle lights looped around light fixtures with no rhyme or reason. It was the opposite of picture-perfect.

Just like the town. I could see why she loved it.

Miranda jumped in her seat when Katy slammed the handset onto the receiver, groaning.

"What's the matter?" Kasen asked with concern.

"That was the mayor. George and Kenny Waldman got into a minor fender bender tonight. They're okay, but they both need to stay off their feet for a week, plus George has a fractured elbow."

Miranda edged out of the booth and sat at the bar. "That's too bad, but...why did he call you about it?"

"Because The Landslide is a sponsor of the town's holiday events. We've got the tree all set up for the lighting this weekend, but the Holiday Hoopla doesn't start getting assembled until mid-week. George and Kenny own a construction company and always volunteer to help. The mayor wanted to see if I had any ideas about how we could replace them."

"I can help," Kasen offered. "My work hours are flexible, and both my elbows are unfractured."

At his deadpan delivery, I eyed him. I could be friends with this guy.

"We'll probably take you up on that," Katy said. "But no offense to your white collar, this isn't really your lane. As much as we need folks with strong backs to set up the booths, some prep tasks require professionals. It's not as simple as people think to make sure the lighting gets installed, that there's access to water, portable restrooms, and all the AV equipment and stuff for the stages. I don't want to take the risk that something gets assembled pell-mell and a booth comes tumbling down or a stage collapses." She sighed deeply. "I guess I should start making phone calls. It sucks we're probably going to have to pay someone, but—"

"I can do it," I piped up.

"I was just about to shove my elbow into your ribs," Miranda whispered.

"No need for violence." I poked her shoulder and turned to Katy. "I'm happy to tap in. Just put me to work."

"You're in construction?"

I tipped an imaginary hat. "Licensed and bonded contractor. At your service."

"I'm so grateful." Katy looked on the verge of crying.

We exchanged numbers, and she told me she'd text on Monday, once she confirmed the plan with the mayor.

Kasen spoke to me as Miranda grabbed our coats. "I'm down to help anytime, too. Just think of me as your unskilled labor force." He lowered his voice. "Katy's been stressing ever since she took this on, but she didn't think she could say no, ya know? She's been trying to get the owners to sell to her since they're mostly retired and she runs the operation anyway, but it's like she needs to keep proving to them that she understands the legacy of this place."

"Glad I can help," I said honestly. "I'll be in touch."

Kasen plugged his number into my phone, and I walked out with Miranda. "Check you out," she joked. "You came in for a sandwich and left with a new buddy."

She teased, but only to a degree. I'd had fun tonight. And it hadn't once felt like I was holding myself apart from people. Plus, we hadn't mentioned Stone in hours.

Maybe Coleman Creek was the magical place Miranda said it was.

12 MONTHS AGO - DECEMBER

Is this the hottest celebrity pairing in history?

OMG! Stone and Naomi are heating up Hollywood

Little girl all grown up? Naomi Butler falls for internet bad boy

I STARED AT THE HEADLINES IN FRONT of me. I wasn't a big celebrity gossip guy. More of a politics junkie. But the news about Stone and Miranda flashed across even the "serious" news sites. They'd captured the public's imagination. The laid-back surfer dude who'd never met a dare he wouldn't accept had fallen for the former child actress who was synonymous with uptight elegance.

He softened her edges. She polished his. A match made in tabloid heaven.

The headlines and accompanying articles also included photographs. So. Many. Photographs. Stone giving Naomi a surf lesson at Newport Beach. Naomi and Stone kissing on their movie set. Stone sneaking into Naomi's bungalow in the Hills.

A tornado of rage boiled in my core. Miranda would have told me if she and Stone broke up. Obviously, the bastard was cheating on her with his co-star. The story, confirmed by both their publicists, said it had been going on for over a month, that they fell in love while filming.

I stalked around my apartment, fingers flying over my phone, grateful it was Saturday and I didn't have a jobsite to get to.

ME: I'll kill him. Seriously, just tell me where he lives and I will come down there and seriously fuck him up.

ME: Also—are you okay? Do you need me? Should I fly down?

ME: I know you're coming up here in a few days, but if you need to get out of town sooner I'll make it happen.

MIRANDA: Down boy. Gimme a sec to get to a quiet place. I'll FaceTime you.

Ten minutes later—enough time for me to determine that I could be at SeaTac and in the air to Los Angeles within two hours—my phone rattled with the *dut-da-duh-da-dut-dut* of an incoming video call.

I hit the green button, and Miranda appeared. I'd expected her to look exhausted. Heartbroken. But the woman on screen was clear-eyed and stunning as always. Her expression sparkled with...*contrition*? And was that...*humor*?

"Leo, I am so, so sorry. I didn't get a chance to give you the heads-up before everything happened. I was trying to figure out the best approach, especially since you still seemed so salty about me dating Stone when I saw you at the engagement party. The PR teams were supposed to wait until after Christmas, especially with all the good press Stone just got promoting Maureen's video."

Taking a breath, I recalled that Maureen had recently re-launched her YouTube channel, *Fashion Vibes with Francesa*, and Stone had helped promote it to his followers.

"You knew Stone was with Naomi? Why didn't you tell me?" At her continued look of self-reproach, my confusion heightened.

A door opened off Miranda's side. To my bewilderment, Stone walked into the room, leaning down behind her.

"Yo, Leo, my dude, this mix-up is totally my fault. I've been, like, keeping Miranda locked down while we figured this whole thing out. Then there was a little snafu with me missing a text from my people about the timing of the info drop. Lolz. My bad, man. Bygones."

What the fuck? Was this guy for real?

Miranda swatted Stone on the shoulder. "Stop doing peak Stone right now. You can just be normal with Leo."

"No. Not bygones. No fucking way," I snarled. "I don't know what you think you're doing there with Miranda right now, but you don't get to cheat on my friend and—"

"Whoa—" Stone flinched.

"Let me—" Miranda put a placating palm on Stone's elbow. To the camera, she said, "It's not like that. No one's cheating on anyone. It's all for publicity."

"Publicity?"

"Yeah, man—" Stone started, but Miranda stopped him again.

"Their publicists cooked up this scheme to get publicity for the movie," Miranda spoke rapidly. "The photos are staged. They're not together."

I sat down, catching my breath as my arms fell to my sides. "What?"

"Bear, put the phone back up so I can see your face."

"Sorry." I flipped the kickstand on the case and set it on the coffee table.

"From this angle, you really do look like a big ol' Viking," Stone offered, grinning.

I narrowed my eyes at his ridiculous, massive white teeth.

"I'm so sorry I didn't call you before this got out because I knew you'd worry," Miranda said, and I saw her twisting her hands together. "But I'm telling you now. Stone asked my permission before they did anything, and I told him I'm okay with it. We're not known as a couple, so it's not like he's embarrassing me or anything. And if it helps his career, I'm all for it."

"But there were pictures. He was kissing her."

"You of all people should know that not all physical affection is as it seems." She raised her eyebrows meaningfully.

Stone decided it was okay for him to talk again. "Dude, how I am with Naomi is like how you are with Miranda. Just really good pals. She understands how hard it is to play the celebrity game. Naomi's trying to change her image, same as me, and she's been helping me learn the ropes."

I attempted to look directly at Stone. "Just because you don't have an issue with my friendship with Miranda—rightfully so—doesn't mean Miranda owes you this. This would be a huge ask under any circumstances, and it's even more so when your relationship is being plastered all over the internet."

Miranda sighed. "I'm okay with it. Promise." The picture distorted for thirty seconds, and I heard her mumble something to Stone. A moment later, her face reappeared, except this time, she was in an unfamiliar bathroom. "Okay, Leo-Bear. Stone can't hear us. So say whatever you need to."

I wasted no time. "I'm just struggling to believe you're really okay with this."

"Look, to be honest, when Stone initially asked me, I was hesitant but on board with it. Now that it's out in the world, I'll admit it makes me a little nauseous. Seeing them like that. All the fans gushing in the comments. I don't know if there's any way I could have prepared myself for it. But *I agreed*, so there's not much I can do now. Other than be okay with it."

"Have you said this to Stone? That it's bothering you?"

She shook her head. "There's no point. We can't put the genie back in the bottle. At least he's doing everything he can to show me I'm the one he actually cares about. I've also texted with Naomi, and she's made it clear I have nothing to worry about on her end."

"I still think—"

"Leo, you have to be alright with this. Because I mostly am. But in order to get all the way there, I need to know you have my back."

Vomit threatened. Stone was lucky enough to have her, and this was what he did? Put her in this position? It sucked that she had to settle for this bullshit. I didn't want her to settle. Not for anyone. Ever.

"Panda, you know I'll always have your back." My voice pitched higher. "I just want you to be treated like the treasure you are."

For the millionth time since I'd met her, I cursed the universe that I wasn't something else. That I didn't have more to offer. Why couldn't I give her everything she needed?

"Oh, Leo," she hushed. "I'm okay. I promise."

She was perfect. Vulnerable and joyful. With a huge heart.

Stone had that all in his grasp, and he was going to...date Naomi.

I hung my head. "Okay isn't good enough for you," I said in a broken-down rasp. "You deserve more."

She sucked in a breath, and the phone went black for a moment before her face sprang up again. "What do you think I deserve?" she whispered.

"You deserve..." *Someone who loves you as much as I do.* "I don't know," I finished lamely. "More than this."

Her face turned away. She scraped her hand through her hair, and I registered the rise and fall of her shoulders as she inhaled raggedly. The silence stretched, thick and uneasy in a way it rarely was between us. Finally, she gazed determinedly at the screen.

"You don't need to worry. I get more from Stone than you know." Her attempt at both gravitas and clever innuendo rang hollow.

My insides clenched. "You're honestly okay with this?"

She nodded wordlessly. Unconvincingly.

"Well, then, as your friend, I think you should tell Stone how you're feeling. At least be honest with him that you're having mixed emotions. It might help him make better decisions."

Her features wilted. She knew I'd never give her my full endorsement of this plan.

I could love her and be there for her, but I couldn't lie and say I thought Stone treating her this way was acceptable.

"I already told you, Leo. Putting that on Stone isn't an option. I gave my word."

"Panda—"

"I can't talk about this anymore. I hope you can support me. See you at Christmas."

She hung up.

I DIDN'T SEE MIRANDA AGAIN UNTIL I showed up at Marley and James's house on Christmas Day. Miranda had rented a car and driven to Coleman Creek from the airport since I'd had to stay in Tacoma for work until December 24.

My parents and I drove together and checked into the Hampton Inn near the highway. When we arrived, the hotel had boxes waiting for us. Marley insisted we show up on Christmas Day wearing footie pajamas.

Mom and Dad looked at this development with amusement, commenting that there was nothing they wouldn't do for their "delightful future daughter-in-law."

"At least yours are dignified," I grumped, envious of their blue snowflake onesies. "I look demented."

Heaving my massive frame into the gingerbread men-patterned zip-up bodysuit was a challenge, and my reward was having my parents pull out their phones to snap pics and laugh at me.

My dad called out my sour face. "Since when do you act like Scrooge before he met the ghosts?" he asked.

I shrugged. It was the best I could do.

When we arrived, I saw that Marley and James were wearing candy cane onesies. Maureen had recently fallen hard for James's friend Will, and the two of them were in a holly leaf pattern.

"Hey," came from the living room, and my spine went rigid. I hadn't heard Miranda's voice since she'd ended our call less than a week ago. "Cool," she said. "Ours are the same."

She also wore a gingerbread men onesie. "I think Marley wanted even pairs," I replied, not knowing what else to say.

As she stepped next to me, I saw the pleading on her face. She wanted things to be good between us. It was rare for me to get close enough to people that I could get hurt. But that was exactly how I'd felt when she hung up on me.

"That's right," Marley said, unaware of the undercurrent. "There were only four patterns and you guys are good friends, right? Good friends can be a pair."

"Of course!" Miranda said brightly. I grunted.

After Marley took at least a hundred pictures of the eight of us in our matching outfits, I excused myself to get some air. James found me slumped in a patio chair.

"You alright, man?" he asked, handing me a mug of hot chocolate.

"Mm-hmm. Just thinking."

"Are you thinking or brooding?"

I choked out a laugh. "*Brooding*? Am I a poet wandering the gray mists of the moors?"

"More like one of the sulky teenagers in my classroom."

My jaw ticked. "Not brooding."

He sat down in the chair next to mine. "Seriously. It's not your style to be so out of sorts."

"Probably just the holidays getting to me."

His face scrunched up. "That's not like you either."

I took a sip of hot chocolate. Too sweet for my taste. "Leave it, little brother. Thanks for checking in, but I'm fine."

Holding his drink with both hands, James sat quietly for a few beats before speaking again. "Just because I moved to Coleman Creek doesn't mean we can't still talk."

Had he always been this relentless? I blamed Marley for bolstering his confidence. "I don't need to talk. If something is bothering me—and I'm not saying there is—I'll get over it."

"Does it have to do with Marley's sister?"

"Maureen?"

"Don't play dumb."

"Fine." I scowled. "Miranda and I are having a difference of opinion at the moment. But don't ask me for specifics because I can't say."

He nodded. "Okay."

Although he didn't press for more, most of the fight left me.

"You know she and I are really good friends?"

James chuckled wryly. "I'd say that's a bit of an understatement. I've never seen you light up the way you do around Miranda." There was a question in his words, but he didn't ask it directly.

My asexuality was something I'd never discussed with my family. Over the years, they'd gotten the memo not to question me about my love life or inquire whether I was dating anyone. I'd turned the conversation away from the topic enough times for them to understand it wasn't something I would willingly discuss. I figured by now they might have guessed, but I had no way of knowing for sure.

"We're friends," I stated firmly. "Friends fight."

"Alright," he said, rising to his feet. "Then maybe count to ten and get your shit together. You know how much Christmas means to Marley. If you do anything to upset her, I'll have to kill you."

Smiling, I brought the mug to my lips again. "I hear you."

I didn't want to ruin Christmas for Marley. And I didn't want to stay mad at Miranda. Like I said to James, we were friends.

The thing I hadn't told him was that she and I were more than that. If we weren't, I wouldn't be so bothered right now.

A year ago, when I met Miranda, I noticed she was stunning and personable, but I hadn't been attracted to her in a sexual or romantic way.

But over the past few months, there had been flashes when I'd felt something. A spark under my skin where we touched. Butterflies in my belly when she grinned. An occasional stray thought that was more than platonic. I'd chalked it up to proximity, but perhaps it was something else?

It had been over a decade since I'd broken up with Ilona, long enough for me to have given up on the idea of ever developing feelings for another woman.

A big part of my mood stemmed from the fact that I needed to process these confusing new signs.

My lingering anger toward Miranda evaporated. She didn't know my head was spinning. And even though I still thought Stone was a dipshit who didn't deserve her, I wasn't in a place to make her an alternate offer. At least not yet. Maybe never, if it turned out Stone made her happy.

The only thing I could be sure of for now was that I needed her in my life.

Which meant I had to grit my teeth and hold her hand while Stone and Naomi made nice for the cameras.

Chapter Fifteen

Miranda

NOW

I woke up Saturday morning and saw I'd missed two texts from Stone.

STONE: I'm sorry I haven't been able to check in more these past few days. This entire production schedule has turned into all-day shoots and it feels like the only time I'm free is during the middle of the night. Thank god for texting. But I hear from Shoshanna that everything's going well. She said the internet thinks you and I are goals for men and women being friends. That was not on my bingo card but I'll take it. *thumbs-up emoji* *winky emoji* *Canadian flag emoji* (a finger slip, I assumed)

STONE: I miss you, kid. We'll talk soon.

We were on such different planes right now. There was nothing to show he understood how insane this situation was, how even though the plan was working, it had still thrown my life upside down. Also, if he really wanted to make a conversation happen, he could.

Did he realize how unattractive it was that he was just living his life while other people solved his problems? Clearly, Shoshanna was keeping him blissfully ignorant, but he was a grown-ass man, so that wasn't an excuse. The most Stone had had to do was get photographed with Naomi last week. And even then, Naomi had flown to him. She'd made the effort. Stone had merely done what he was told.

I shook my head. I didn't want to resent him. Especially when I'd caused the problem that required solving. But seriously, at what point had I atoned enough?

These flippant little text messages were unacceptable. How did he not see? I couldn't keep pretending that his behavior was acceptable. Even if Stone did eventually make it a priority to call me, I doubted it would be a good idea for me to take the call. After my terrible fight with Leo, I'd learned a valuable lesson. Some conversations needed to happen in person.

I exited my texts without replying.

Leo's surprisingly melodic shower rendition of "Good King Wenceslas" drifting down the hallway soothed some of my irritation, bringing a smile to my lips.

A smile that quickly faded when I heard cars pulling into the driveway.

I banged on the bathroom door. "Shower karaoke's over, Bear. Finish up, because our reckoning has arrived."

Besides Stone's messages, there had been a dozen from my sisters letting me know they'd seen all the gossip about me. Those texts had come in a few hours ago, I assumed as soon as they had service.

I hadn't responded, just like Leo hadn't replied to the ones he'd gotten from James. We preferred to wait so that we could talk to our siblings in the same room. They'd be surprised to find us in Coleman Creek.

Although Leo's truck parked outside the house probably clued them in.

"Miranda?! Leo?!" Marley's voice echoed as soon as the front door swung open. "Are you here?"

I stood next to the couch. "We're here. No need to shout."

"Oh, thank goodness. When you weren't responding to any of our texts, I got worried."

Marley enveloped me in a tight embrace. James, Maureen, and Will filed in behind her, carrying luggage and tote bags that they plopped down in the entryway. The appearance of my oldest sister and her boyfriend was unexpected. I hadn't anticipated facing the entire cavalry.

"You didn't go back to your house?" I asked Maureen.

"Some of the gear that needs to be stored in the garage is in our car. We figured we'd drop it here on our way." She gave me a hug, more reserved than Marley's but no less filled with love. "And now I'm glad I did."

"Hey, guys!" Leo piped up from the hall, towel wrapped around his waist, still dripping wet from his shower.

I walked over and whispered so only he could hear. "Really, coming out in a towel?"

He leaned in and gave me a kiss on the cheek, then rasped in my ear. "Just trying to sell it, Panda."

Pulling back, he winked at me, and I slapped him on the butt. "Go put some clothes on," I said.

"Yes, big brother, please get dressed," James added dryly.

Leo disappeared into the bedroom.

Will brushed his hands across his thighs. Even though my sisters and James looked a little rough after their long trip, Will looked ready to step out of a catalog for high-end business casual. "This seems like it might be a family-only discussion," he said. "I can go put the stuff in the garage."

Marley and James frowned as Maureen hissed, "Don't you dare. If you leave, plan on getting overly acquainted with the couch tonight."

Will grinned. "Good. Because I kind of want to hear this." He turned to me. "Guess we've solved the mystery of why Stone recommended Maureen's video."

"For the record," I said carefully, "Maureen's channel would be a success with or without the *Stone Caseman bounce*. But yes, let's just say Stone owed me a favor."

"True," Will agreed, kissing Maureen's cheek as she pretended to be annoyed with him.

"Why are we even talking about that right now?" Marley interjected, hands flailing. "I don't give a flying fig about Stone Caseman and all his...shenanigans. What I care about is the fact that you and Leo have been dating and didn't tell us." Her voice shook, but I knew it was hurt and not anger that drove her.

"I'm sorry, Marls. I promise it wasn't malicious. We just wanted to keep it private for a while."

Marley's expression dimmed, but before I could try to explain further, Leo re-emerged from the bedroom.

He wrapped his arms around me as we all stood in an awkward circle near the Christmas tree. "Obviously, it's a complicated situation. With our families so closely connected."

Leo and James exchanged an indecipherable look of silent communication, and I got the feeling the brothers would be having a private discussion soon.

Maureen put a placating hand on Marley's arm. "Miranda may be our baby sister, but she's a grown woman. We won't agree with every choice she makes." Turning to me, she said, "I think a more important question is how you're doing with all this. I haven't been off the grid since they invented the internet, so of course something like this happens the first time I unplug."

"Not gonna lie, I missed being able to go to you guys," I said. "But it's good to know I could handle it on my own. I think it's good for you guys to know that too."

"Miranda—" Marley raised her brows. "We know you can handle things on your own. You've been all over the world and have been living away from us for years. But you're still our little sister, and we want to protect you, and...know about you. I don't want to find out important things about you by going online."

"Exactly," Maureen chorused. "And it seems like things are improving now, but I still want to tear everyone on the internet a new asshole for referring to you as a 'ho' and a 'home-wrecker' and a 'slut,' and so many other vile things. Seeing comments on my little sister's Instagram littered with the c-word, I've never felt such pure rage. But there's no one to get mad at. Everyone is nameless. Faceless. Occasionally, I get weird comments on my channel, but nothing like that. I hate that you had to go through it on your own."

"I absolutely did not go through it on my own," I huffed. "Leo's been with me. I flew up the night the story broke, and he's been by my side the entire time."

James eyed where his brother's arms still locked around my torso. "You guys have always had a special relationship. Thank goodness you had each other." He gave Leo another odd look.

"Yes. You two being together surprises no one," Maureen said. "And I realize you had Leo to support you. I'm just sorry I couldn't be here." She folded her arms. "It's the whole situation that seems a little strange. Not telling us. You being besties with Stone Caseman—"

"Clearly, we're still missing pieces," Marley agreed sagely. "Starting with why you're in Coleman Creek. I'm happy to see you, but you've been saying for months that you couldn't get away until Christmas."

I sighed. "My bosses are pretty stodgy. They were worried about all this causing a circus, so I'm working remotely through the holidays."

"You're here for the entire month?" Marley, upset mere moments ago, now slapped her hands together in giddiness. I smiled inwardly. She was seriously made of tinsel, holly, and Hallmark movies. I loved it, feeling the gentle echo of our mom.

"Until after New Year's," I clarified.

"Me too," Leo added.

"That's amazing! You haven't been in town for that long during the season since you left for school." Marley squished my cheeks between her hands. "We can do all the things! Decorating, the Hoopla, the talent show, baking. Oh my gosh! I just realized the city tree lighting is tonight. Yay!"

James smiled indulgently at his wife. "We're not going anywhere until we get everything back in the garage. Plus, I need a proper shower." He glared at Will.

"What?" Will protested. "It's a million-dollar cabin. How was I supposed to know the highest level of water pressure was *sad, slow drip?*"

The news of my extended visit to town seemed to have softened Marley. Maureen—not so much.

"To be sure—" Maureen said to me and Leo, "when Marley says we can 'do all the things,' that includes figuring out whatever it is you're still hiding from us."

"I'm not hiding anything," I insisted, staring her down. "Like we said, it just made more sense to keep things quiet."

Maureen hmphed. "Obviously, you have the right to your secrets. We only care that you're okay." She squeezed my biceps.

I leaned back against Leo. "I'm good."

9 MONTHS AGO - MARCH

OUR LITTLE CABIN BY THE BEACH had everything. Cozy, lived-in furniture and a kitchen with a fancy espresso maker. An outdoor shower with foliage blooming above. Water views clear enough to see turtles swimming. But the only thing that seemed to interest Stone was the excellent Wi-Fi.

I knew he'd sensed my reservations about his public relationship with Naomi even though I hadn't brought them up. He'd convinced me to spend my spring break in Maui with him—his way of atoning—promising a romantic getaway.

Shoshanna had made the arrangements, choosing someplace far enough off the beaten path that we could be together, free from scrutinizing eyes or paparazzi lenses. Still, there was a fair amount of subterfuge involved in getting there. We took different flights and cars. I posted on Instagram about taking a solo trip to Hawaii. Shoshanna staged a photograph of Naomi hugging Stone goodbye at the airport. Finally, we both made our way to the little bungalow on the sand, blissfully alone together in paradise. But Stone didn't try to romance me.

Nope. He immediately opened his laptop.

I'd spent most of the past week by myself, taking short hikes through the nearby nature preserve and even shorter runs on the beach. I'd body surfed and napped in the sun. @theadventurousmiranda would certainly have some great new content once I had the chance to edit the photos.

Stone came out to join me intermittently, full of promises that he had just "one more phone call" to make, or "one last time-sensitive email" to respond to. We managed a few quick dinners together, some ocean swims in the morning, and one longer stroll along the shore, but mostly, he'd dipped in and out of our vacation like a boat dropping anchor for brief land excursions.

Gazing out at the orangey-red horizon, I thought back to my conversation with Leo three months ago. His disappointment. Why hadn't I gotten out of this when Stone first proposed his plan for fake dating Naomi? Why had I agreed?

A big part of the reason was that I liked Stone. He was attractive and funny, and once I dug past the shallow online persona he'd cultivated, I enjoyed spending time with him. And while I didn't think I was a person who needed a ton of sex, it was nice to be with someone in the bedroom again.

It also might have been simpler to walk away from Stone if I were someone who fell into relationships easily. But I wasn't. I hadn't been drawn to anyone other than Stone in years.

Other than Leo.

I shook my head. Nope. I needed to train my brain to stop going there. He was my best friend and soulmate. My Bear. But he would never be my lover.

I wasn't stupid. I knew my attachment to Leo was a big part of why I wasn't as invested in my relationship with Stone as I might have been and why I gave him so much grace with this Naomi nonsense. But I still didn't see enough of a potential future with Stone to risk diminishing my connection to Leo. When we'd had that stalemate before Christmas over his objections to Stone and Naomi, I got a taste of what it felt like not having him in my life.

It was unbearable.

Even though I could see the argument that my bond with Leo might prevent me from forming a stronger attachment to Stone, I certainly wasn't going to pull back from my best friend while my boyfriend pretended to date another woman.

Leo and I had settled into a comfortable new normal where we didn't discuss Stone. I could live with that. What I couldn't live with was the silence that had stretched between us for those days after I'd foolishly hung up on him.

I leaned back on my elbows, feeling the sun on my neck. This beach was supposedly private, but in the distance, I saw folks running away from the evening tide. I'd also noticed a few other couples during our stay, but so far, no one had ventured close enough to chat. I chuckled. *Hope they don't have a long-range camera lens and are big Stone and Naomi fans.*

Peering at our cabin, I watched Stone pace back and forth in the front room window, phone glued to his ear.

I pushed down my annoyance and attempted to give him the benefit of the doubt. At least he tried. He was here, with me, and he'd turned Shoshanna down when she'd suggested flying Naomi out for a few hours to get a shot with Stone on the beach.

Within the confines of our behind-the-curtain relationship, Stone usually treated me well. By necessity, we spent most of our limited time together at my apartment. He listened when I talked about my classes, asking specifics about tests and online lectures. We cooked together and took long drives, finding lonely stopovers where we could get out and gaze at the stars. I told him stories about growing up in Coleman Creek, about Marley's students and Maureen's online styling clients. He rubbed my shoulders when I looked stressed, and he never failed to tell me how beautiful and amazing I was.

For sure, knowing there was an end date to his charade with Naomi helped me manage the secrecy. I just needed to hang on until the movie came out in July. But there was another issue in our relationship that wouldn't be as easily solved. Watching Stone on his laptop and phone this week, spending every hour of the day near him, it really sank in how busy he was chasing his dreams.

If I were to eventually become Stone's real, public-facing girlfriend, I would also need to accept that he would be gone a lot. Like, a lot a lot. Unlike the situation with Naomi, his travel schedule wouldn't be changing anytime soon.

Stone had been away from Los Angeles for at least half the time we'd known each other. Besides his movie shoot, he traveled constantly to film clips for his channel, flying regularly to other states to appear on podcasts or the occasional local morning show. He felt like he needed to say yes to every opportunity since, as he liked to remind me, his star could grow cold as quickly as it had grown hot. He rarely let his *I don't care* facade slip, but underneath, I saw how nervous he was about not being able to make his fame stick.

Mostly, the distance worked for me. Stone didn't make demands. He wasn't around much, but when he was, it was like getting a recharge on feeling attractive and desired.

It had taken me a while to decode what it was about Stone's fakery with Naomi that still nagged at me—the unease I'd admitted to Leo during our tense video call. At first, I assumed it was as Leo suspected, that I didn't like this plan because Stone was treating me more cavalierly than he should.

But that wasn't the truth.

What I truly disliked about Stone's arrangement with Naomi was that it forced me to put more thought and energy into our relationship than I wanted to. There was a reason I hadn't gone public with Stone. I'd liked having an excuse to put in so little effort.

Wandering around one of Maui's most beautiful beaches solo had driven home the point of just how little investment I'd made. Those first few months, I'd enjoyed spending time with Stone, the man, but what I'd really fallen for was the convenience of Stone, the boyfriend I didn't have to think too hard about.

Now I had to coordinate our schedules to avoid being seen together. I had Shoshanna hassling me to sign an NDA. The tactical maneuvering involved in making this vacation happen was worthy of a spy novel.

I recalled Leo's crinkled-up face and broken voice when he worried I wasn't getting what I deserved.

But it was more like I was getting much more than I'd bargained for.

I heard the snapping sound of someone walking in flip-flops. Stone came up behind me as the sun set. He rolled out a towel on the sand and pulled me into his arms.

"You look stunning out here in the evening light," he said, kissing my freckled shoulder. "I'm sorry I've been such a dick. Being on the phone and stuff."

"It's okay," I said. "It's given me a chance to think." I snuggled against his chest.

"Oh yeah? Watchya thinking about?"

"I was thinking that I can't wait until your movie comes out this summer. So you can end the thing with Naomi."

He pulled me away from him, fixing his eyes on mine. "I thought you were cool with it?"

"I am," I responded slowly. "But I don't love it. It's been...harder than I thought it would be." *There you go, Leo. This is me laying it on the line with Stone, just like you wanted me to.* "I don't like that it's put us in a stasis. I want to try being an actual couple, seeing what that feels like."

He sighed. "I want that too."

Nodding, I leaned back into him. "I graduate in June, so lots of things will change. When we first met, I know it was my choice to keep things casual and under wraps. It made sense to be on the down-low until we could be sure we were going somewhere. But what I realized is, we can't figure that out if we're hiding all the time. When we're together but also not. Like I said, stasis. I need a reason to put more energy into our relationship, not our deception."

He wrapped his arms around me. "That makes sense."

That settled it in my mind. Once Stone and I made our relationship official, I could decide if I wanted to invest more into it. We'd already put in six months. Maybe with more time, and hopefully a little less distance, I could form the sort of connection with Stone that I'd forged with Leo.

Chapter Sixteen

Leo

NOW

We went to the official Coleman Creek tree lighting celebration after Marley and James unpacked their car. To my pleasant surprise, I recognized many of the faces. Katy and Kasen were there, along with lots of people I remembered from James and Marley's wedding, including some of their students and fellow teachers. I also scoped out the six city blocks designated for next weekend's Holiday Hoopla, three on either side of the enormous tree. Several people who'd heard about my offer to help set up for the event sought me out to offer their thanks.

"It's crazy how so many people already know about that," I said to James after receiving a handshake of gratitude from the mayor.

He grinned and shrugged. "Small towns."

James still had classes to teach, but Will offered to assist me when he wasn't with Maureen at her store. In theory, Will was a property developer in Seattle, splitting his time between there and

Coleman Creek, but he'd mostly been on hiatus from that while he'd helped Maureen get her businesses up and running. After consulting with Katy and the mayor, I agreed to start construction on Wednesday morning, hoping that everything would be ready by Friday afternoon for the Hoopla on Saturday. It was a tight timeline, but since they always set up the event the same way, I could work with last year's plans.

Just after the mayor's speech, I glanced over and saw Miranda's phone light up with a FaceTime request from Stone. She ignored it and stuck the device in her pocket.

She did the same thing the following morning during breakfast, and again that afternoon while we were helping Marley and James put up more outdoor decorations.

I asked her about it as we were getting into bed Sunday night and she demurred, saying she'd been too busy in the moment to pick up. I wanted to press her on why she hadn't tried to call him back—and I knew she hadn't since we'd been together the whole evening—but I didn't want to spoil the ending of what had been a near-perfect weekend.

Instead, I pulled her into my chest and threw my leg over her. She giggled as the mattress protested with a loud squeak.

"Is that another way you're trying to sell the story, Bear?" she asked playfully before wiggling her midsection, causing even more noise from the mattress, not to mention a groan from the old bedframe. "Trying to fire James and Marley's imaginations?"

"Such a troublemaker," I admonished with a grin.

I wrapped my arms around her, calming her movements, but as she lay peacefully against me, I spared a thought for what my brother must be thinking.

Especially after our conversation this summer.

I could tell James wanted to ask more questions. About everything. I'd caught him staring at Miranda and me a few times, his features assessing and puzzled. But so far, he hadn't asked me directly. I owed him an explanation, but I couldn't talk to him about how things had changed with me without spilling the beans on the whole story.

On Monday, Miranda logged off an hour early and informed me that we were going on an adventure.

"I thought @theadventurousmiranda was hanging up her hat?"

She booped me on the nose. "This is a Coleman Creek brand adventure. No aesthetic edit required."

Ten minutes after leaving the house, we pulled up in front of the bowling alley. I laughed. "You could have just said bowling."

"We're not bowling. I already told you why we're here."

I thought about it. "Seriously?"

"Seriously."

We went inside, and Miranda waved to an elderly gentleman behind the desk before leading me to a far corner of the building, next to a bank of lockers. "There it is," she announced.

In front of us was a gleaming steel pole with a large black phone box attached. A paper phone book with "1995-1996" printed on its spine sat on top of it.

"Pick up the handset and pretend to make a call," Miranda instructed, holding up her phone. "And I'll take your picture. Very meta."

"I'll do you one better." I picked it up and produced a few coins from my pocket. After slotting the quarters into the massive box, I punched the buttons. A second later, Miranda's phone buzzed in her hand.

"You have my number memorized? That's hard-core, Bear."

I rolled my eyes as she took my picture. "You do realize I grew up in a world where there were lots of these," I said.

"Sure. But that was *your* childhood. Totally different. I envy it."

Without her needing to explain, I understood. The nine years I had on her meant she hadn't had quite the analog childhood I had. But we both had an attachment to simple things.

"Maureen once told me she left Coleman Creek because it felt like the land that time forgot," Miranda said wistfully. "And also that she came back for the same reason."

I nodded. "Not gonna lie. It's nice. The pace of things not being so quick to change. Like on Friday, when we were at The Landslide and I played a song on the jukebox. There was a diner in Seattle that had one when I was a kid, but I hadn't seen another until I came here."

"It's the little things," Miranda agreed. "The one-screen movie theater where you can't choose your seat or buy tickets online. Stan at the hardware store, whose version of store credit is a spiral notebook reminding him who to bill at the end of the month. There's a hobby shop in town that doesn't accept credit cards at all, and there's not a single parking lot or street in town where you need to pay to park. I don't mind the city, obviously. I love living in Los Angeles. But if I had to choose, I'd say this is more my speed."

Suddenly, her phone lit up with another FaceTime request from Stone. She frowned and declined it as I looked away. I'd noticed that he'd texted a few times since she got off work, and she hadn't responded to any of those either. Same as last night, I was curious but didn't want to push her or make it weird.

"Will you ever move back here?" I asked, returning us to our conversation.

"I'm not sure," she answered thoughtfully. "Both my sisters did, and knowing they're here is a huge incentive. But I also feel like I've just begun a real life in Los Angeles. Having my job and shedding my *Outdoor Barbie* skin—I finally have some momentum there, like waking up from hibernation."

I nodded, recognizing the sentiment. My wake-up moment came when I met Miranda two years ago. Her friendship added layers to my existence I hadn't even known to want. Now, I couldn't imagine living without them.

"Where to next?" I asked.

"We're on the clock since I promised Marley we'd be back for dinner, and I offered to stop by The Landslide to pick up some of that cider." She tapped her lips. "But I suppose we have enough time to ask Bert behind the desk if we can have the keys to his Honda, so you can remember the joys of hand-cranking a window."

I laughed as her phone buzzed in her pocket.

She ignored it.

6 MONTHS AGO - JUNE

MIRANDA FLOPPED DOWN ON HER BED and hooked an elbow dramatically over her face. "I was so close," she lamented, her slurred words evidence of the many drinks we'd imbibed. "One more hand and I woulda had 'em."

"Easy there, Panda. One more hand and the dealer would have been forced to give you a prize for being the world's worst poker player."

I sat down on my bed. Our room was on a higher floor, and we had a great view of the Strip. I had learned something new about Miranda today—she stunk at cards—but we'd had a ton of fun playing and exploring the city.

She turned her head toward me and opened one eye, pinching her thumb and index finger, leaving half an inch of space between them. "Soooooooo close."

I grabbed her a bottle of water from the room's mini-fridge. Our families had come to California to watch her graduate from her MBA program, but everyone else flew back immediately after the ceremony because Marley and James's wedding was next week. Miranda was the maid of honor, but Marley gave me permission to take her to Vegas for a few days to celebrate her accomplishment properly.

Miranda's friends from school were going to Chile on a hiking trip, and she'd turned down that invite. She told me she considered our Sin City adventure to also be a celebration of ending that chapter of her life. She planned to stay friendly with some in her group, but @theadventurousmiranda was winding down.

Unless, of course, her himbo of a boyfriend decided it would be good for his image for her to maintain it. I had a feeling she'd keep posting if he asked. I dreaded the next few months because Stone's movie was coming out and that meant he'd be ending his ruse with Naomi. Miranda told me they'd wait a few months and then bring her own relationship with Stone into the light.

Would I lose her then?

So far, it hadn't been as much of an issue as I'd feared. Stone was gone so often I could almost pretend he didn't exist.

And she never brought him up. He seemed to be a non-factor in her decision-making. When I'd suggested Vegas, Miranda had jumped into my arms and agreed with no hesitation.

I handed her the water. She chugged down half of it and forced herself to sit up, looking green.

"I know myself," she mumbled, as if her tongue were glued to the roof of her mouth. "If I lie down in this bed, I'm gonna wake up with a killer hangover. I need to take a shower and move around a bit." She reached out to tug my pants. "Wanna walk around the Strip?"

"It's two in the morning."

"Perfect." She drank some more water. "This is the only time of day the heat won't melt our faces off."

Rising, she began taking off her clothes. By the time she got to the bathroom, she was down to a bra and panties.

She must have been more inebriated than I thought. Since I'd told her about my asexuality, she always behaved modestly around me, treating me as though I was someone who could get aroused by her body. I appreciated that courtesy, one of many ways Miranda found not to "other" me.

Somewhat guiltily, I let my eyes roam over her backside as she attempted to open the bathroom door.

The sight of her rounded ass didn't exactly excite me, but combined with her cute little huffs of annoyance—reminding me that said ass was attached to my Miranda—something sparked beneath my skin.

My fingertips prickled. I wanted to touch her butt.

Shoving down the sensation, I stood behind her and slid the door to the side. "Apparently, you had enough rum punches to forget how a barn-style door operates."

She pffted. "It's confusing."

Walking into the brightly lit bathroom, she neglected to shut the door behind her, so I did it. A moment later, the water turned on.

I let my mind consider the moment, registering my reaction like I were taking an exam. Miranda was naked, the water sloughing over her shoulders and back. Her ass. I kept myself from attempting to picture it, but I wondered abstractly what her breasts looked like. Not in a pervy way. More like a clinician. The last pair I'd seen were Ilona's, over a decade ago. They had been teardrop-shaped, her nipples small and brown. Were Miranda's the same?

I had a vague recollection of wanting to touch Ilona's breasts. For the first six months of our dating, I *did things* with her because I thought I was supposed to. Eventually, I realized I was touching her out of obligation and not lust.

But that was what I felt now with Miranda. Lust. Desire.

It was a revelation.

An incredibly inconvenient revelation.

"Leo!" Miranda's shout rang out.

"What?" I called through the door. "Are you okay?"

"I forgot my shampoo. Can you get it from my bag? It should be right near the top."

"Sure." I found the bottle. Clearing my throat, I said loudly, "I'm coming in."

I slid the door open, averting my eyes from the glass shower enclosure.

"Thanks, Bear. You can just put it down by the edge."

Complying, I kept my gaze away from her, but in the mirror, I saw she was crouched down, using a washcloth to cover herself. With all the steam blanketing the small space, I couldn't see much, but my heart gave a thump at her blurred shape, knowing there was nothing but bare skin beneath the tiny towel.

She noticed my obvious efforts not to look at her. "Such a considerate gentleman."

Knowing the steam covered everything, I swiveled my head, looking only in the general direction of her face as I winked. "Such a beautiful lady."

I hurried out as her mouth dropped into an O shape.

Twenty minutes later, we'd bunched our hair into blond buns and were strolling along the Strip. Even at three in the morning, there were plenty of people out. To Miranda's point, the air felt mercifully comfortable for the first time during our trip.

Miranda ducked her head under my arm. We walked that way, with my arm slung over her shoulder, and I let myself imagine I was just a regular guy on vacation with my beautiful girlfriend. A girlfriend I'd wanted to touch earlier.

Without thinking, my hand moved. I felt each notch of her spine as I trailed it downward, ultimately resting on the soft hollow of her lower back.

She made a *mmm* noise and pressed herself into my side, wrapping her arm around my waist to grip my hip.

My hand remained on her back as we passed by one glittering casino after another. I even sneaked my thumb under her shirt, brushing it back and forth over the soft skin there.

With everything in me, I wanted to move my palm lower, to cup the curve of her backside like I'd thought about doing in our hotel room.

But I didn't do it. Because if I ever touched her with more-than-friendly intent, it wasn't going to be while she was dating someone else. Or while I was still so unsure of myself. It felt dangerous to even nurture a seed of hope that there might be a different future for Miranda and me than the one I'd resigned myself to.

No matter what happened, I knew that if I ever had the chance to love her, I'd only go there if I could do so fully and openly.

She might be Stone's hidden secret.

But she would never be mine.

I'd love her with no reservations. Or not at all.

I WOKE UP IN THE REST AREA TO FIND Miranda assaulting me with her phone. More specifically, her phone camera.

"What are you doing?" I asked.

I'd crawled into the back seat to nap for a few hours to break up our long drive from Las Vegas to Coleman Creek, and she'd attempted to sleep on the front passenger side.

Her seat was still in the full recline position, but she'd slid nearly all the way out of it to put her head in my lap. I'd come awake to find her snapping selfies of us.

"You just looked too cute, Leo-Bear," she replied. "You were even snoring a little. The moment needed to be captured."

I snatched the phone from her hand. "I look like a monster," I complained. "My chin looks like it's melting. Also, what the hell kind of a face are you making?"

She cackled. "Don't belittle my attempt at duckface. I dunno. I think I'm loopy going from the lights of Vegas to this drive through the desolation and despair part of Nevada."

"Central Nevada certainly gives new meaning to wide-open spaces," I agreed. "Now please delete those shots from your phone."

"Never! These might come in handy someday."

"For what? Blackmail material?"

"I was thinking LinkedIn profile pic, but blackmail works too."

"Delete them."

"We'll see."

Chapter Seventeen

Miranda

NOW

On Wednesday, two minutes after closing out of my work portal, I received an unwelcome message on my phone.

SHOSHANNA (STONE'S PA): Stone asked me to check in with you. He said you're not picking up your calls or answering texts.

Ugh. I liked Shoshanna, and I knew she was just doing her job, but dammit, this was weird. And invasive. I didn't owe her any more than what I was already doing. I'd gotten into a groove in Coleman Creek and was enjoying the breather. There were large chunks of time when I forgot the circumstances that brought me back to town. Because I could just exist here. And be happy.

With Leo.

I knew I should pick up Stone's calls, or at least reply to his texts, but a larger part of me wanted to...not do that. To allow myself to behave as if we were truly apart, to try that feeling on for size.

I couldn't get away from the situation entirely. Even though I wasn't providing more statements about Stone on @theadventurousmiranda, I did post pictures of me and Leo. In front of the Christmas tree. Outside playing with Bambi and Oscar. At the bowling alley. It was so much easier to process and commit to the playacting in Coleman Creek. There was nowhere I was more comfortable.

And Stone needed to let me handle it my way. He could try using Shoshanna as his errand person, but I didn't need to go along with it.

I closed the text app and shoved my phone in my pocket.

A moment later, Leo walked into the room.

"How'd it go?" I asked. He'd spent the day working with Kasen, setting up for the Holiday Hoopla.

"Good, I think. We're ahead of schedule because Will swung by for a few hours. And he may not be a professional, but Kasen is a huge help."

"I'm not surprised. He's always been a hard worker." I rubbed my temples.

"You alright?"

"Tired. I hate being on Zoom while the rest of the team is in the office. They don't seem pissed or anything, but it's hard."

"Still no work besties?"

I shook my head. "Hasn't been enough time, plus, you know—"

He didn't need me to say Stone's name. We both knew. When I'd made the comment at the bowling alley about starting my *real life*, it struck me how much my relationship with Stone had kept me treading water for the past year. Not just in the romantic sense, but in all aspects of my existence. Turning down Stone's FaceTime requests and not replying to his texts was petty, sure, but it was also liberating. Now that I'd separated myself from Los Angeles, I recognized how much of a hole I'd been in.

To be fair, I already knew. I'd already decided what I needed to say to him. But the past few days in Coleman Creek had strengthened my resolve.

I'd tried to start my *real life* once, the first time I'd planned to move on from my friends. Then my mom got sick, and I stayed in place rather than risk disappointing her. After she died, my grief paralyzed me again. Meeting Leo, being with him, I'd begun to heal. But then came the letdown of not being able to be with him the way I wished I could be. That chance meeting with Stone on the beach, so innocuous at the time, created another excuse for my inertia.

Leo was my safe place to be myself, to live as authentically as possible. That was why I'd lost my shit with him on Halloween. Because I knew nothing I could say or do would make him walk away from me for good.

That was also why I knew he'd understand once I told him I needed some distance. At least for a little while. I'd tell him how much I loved him, but that our love wasn't serving me at the moment. I had to resolve things with Stone and decide what came next. And I knew Leo would support me. It wouldn't break us.

"You look like your brain is melting, Panda."

I brushed away my thoughts. If this holiday season was the last chunk of time I got with Leo before putting space between us, I was making the most of it.

"I really am tired. The past few weeks of being on edge are catching up with me."

He stepped behind where I sat at the dining table and began massaging my shoulders. "Are Marley and James home?"

"They have a PTA meeting at the school, and then they're doing date night at The Landslide." As his fingers worked the tension from my sore muscles, I barely suppressed a moan. "I was going to make spaghetti for us, if that's okay?"

He pressed his thumb into my deltoids. "Spaghetti works. But you're clearly beat, so I'll be doing the cooking."

"Thanks. I'll make the salad, though."

I breathed deeply as he continued the massage, thinking about my day.

Prior to all this, I hadn't been in tune with my coworkers—still exuding *new-kid stink* around the office. Based on the reception I'd received in our online meetings over the past few days, working remotely hadn't helped matters, except for the few folks who hinted they'd love it if I brought Stone around.

Leo's magic hands helped ease some of the stress. My muscles turned to jelly as he worked his fingers down the center of my spine between my shoulder blades, the heat of his palms penetrating the thin material of my T-shirt.

His touch soothed my nerves. I'd missed him while he'd been out working with Kasen. I was used to Leo always having my metaphorical back. It was even better being in the same room with his hands on my literal back.

"I can't believe how tight you are," he murmured, close enough that the hairs on my neck stood at attention.

His index finger found a knot, and I couldn't stop my soft groan of satisfaction as he worked it out.

"Good?" he asked with a smile in his voice.

"Mm-hmm," I drawled. "The only way it could feel better is if you were doing my whole body."

His hands stilled for a moment before moving lower. I tilted forward in the chair to give him better access to the middle of my back.

"Is that something you want? ... Or need?" he asked. "Would it help you if I did this...everywhere?"

He sounded so unsure, and I had no idea how to read it.

Why would he be hesitant when physical touch didn't affect him? He was acting as if I'd suggested something *untoward*.

I pushed back my chair, and he stumbled. "Leo, it just slipped out." I forced a small laugh. "Because you totally turned my stiff shoulders into a puddle of goo. There's no day spa in Coleman Creek, so it's not like I'm used to getting massages here. Don't worry about it."

He grabbed my shoulders. "You don't need to take it back. It just surprised me, is all. But I'm happy to give you a...*more comprehensive* massage if you think it will help. I played football in high school. I lived for the trainer rubdowns after tough games."

"Oh yeah?"

"Yes, Panda. I've never given anyone a full massage before, but I'm sure I can do it. And if it makes you feel better, I'm happy to."

His words were soft, but his gaze was sharp. With any other man, I'd call the glint in his eyes *heat*, but with him—

Leo didn't desire me.

And yet—

He was also the same man I'd shared a bed with after Marley and James's wedding. The night I'd been trying to forget for five months.

A shiver rolled down my spine.

I wasn't going to overthink it. I wanted his hands on me. That was all I needed to know.

"I'd love a massage."

5 MONTHS AGO - JULY

"Explain it to me again." Sitting on Marley's couch, my voice was calm, but underneath I seethed. If Stone looked carefully enough at the tablet screen, I was certain he'd see smoke coming out of my ears.

"Wow, you're like, really mad." He sounded genuinely baffled. "I don't know if I've ever seen you this pissed."

"Can you blame me?"

He scratched his temple like a gorilla. "I dunno, babes. I honestly thought you'd be cool with it. Like you've been cool with everything so far."

Sometimes I thought Stone didn't understand me at all. Other times—like now—I *knew* he didn't.

"Just because I haven't been constantly getting upset with you or re-litigating this decision doesn't mean I'm just meh or whatever about the whole thing. Constantly raking you over the coals seemed counterproductive, especially since I agreed to this. But I also believe I was clear with you that my patience has a ticking clock. You know full well I've been waiting for you and Naomi to break up."

Maybe I should have expected this, since Stone was correct that I hadn't pushed back on anything so far. But I meant what I'd just said. Being sulky would have been hypocritical. But now he was breaking our agreement. And he was finding out that I had a lot more bite than he'd realized.

"Stone, I'm not just going to accept this like some docile little animatron. Naomi's the one who's your fake girlfriend, remember? I'm your *actual* girlfriend—supposedly—and I'm the one who should have a say in our relationship. I can't believe you talked to Shoshanna about this and agreed without even discussing it with me!"

"Babes, I'm sorry." He bit his lip, and I knew his regret was genuine. "I feel like a total ass now because it honestly didn't occur to me that you wouldn't be fine with it. I know you said so on the beach, but I guess... I guess you've just been so chill with everything so far, I didn't...think." He leaned closer to his camera, so his face took up almost my entire screen. "I'm just really stuck here. The public loves Naomi and me together, even more than Shoshanna thought they would. The movie is getting good buzz. If we break up right after it releases, it'll kill the vibe."

Panic in First Class hadn't even come out yet, and I was already over it. It was getting great reviews and even some awards chatter, so interest in Stone and Naomi had magnified.

I shifted on the cushions. Part of me couldn't believe Stone chose to tell me now, a few days before Marley's wedding. Then again, it shouldn't have surprised me. Stone had a unique sort of tunnel vision when it came to his career, especially when we were apart. He didn't mean to be thoughtless. He just couldn't seem to help himself.

Leo and I had driven straight to Coleman Creek from Las Vegas, and I intended to spend the next few months here, away from all of Stone's movie premiere craziness. I'd volunteered to watch the dogs while Marley and James went on their honeymoon, and I wanted to help Maureen with her new business before I headed back to Los Angeles. I'd accepted a junior marketing manager position that started in September.

The plan had always been for Stone to break up with Naomi in August, when their film's theatrical run would wind down.

"Why didn't you wait to tell me until after the wedding? If you've already decided, why complicate this for me?"

He had the good grace to look even more uncomfortable. "I guess I didn't think of it that way. More like, I'm about to get extra busy doing press and traveling and stuff, and I wanted to tell you as soon as I found out." He patted his hand against his chest. *Again with the gorilla motions.* "My bad with the timing. That was a dick move."

"No, Stone," I hissed, waving my hand at my screen. "The timing is just you being oblivious. The dick move is not sticking to the original plan." I stared directly at the camera. "I don't know if I can accept this. If I can keep existing in this...holding pattern."

He reared back from the screen. "Darlin', you're not gonna, like, end it with me, are you? After everything?"

His expression of sheer panic mollified my ego and dulled my anger. A little.

I sighed, calming down and trying to gauge my emotions. I was pissed at Stone for going back on his word, but I also recognized that I hadn't made this relationship my priority either. My anger didn't stem from having to face more months of seeing pictures of Stone and Naomi pop up online. It came from not being able to move past this phase. Of our relationship. And my life.

As I saw it, my choices were to stay stuck or break up with him.

It would have been so much easier to walk away if Stone was cheating, lying, or yelling at me. But he wasn't. He was trying. Constantly reassuring me of his devotion. While it might be less than what I could ultimately settle for, he was trying.

He'd tried to make our arrangement as meaningful as possible—figuring out clandestine travel plans, creating dummy accounts to order food and rideshares, and prioritizing spending time with me whenever he was in town. When he traveled, he sent flowers or gifts that let me know he was thinking about me. He'd bought expensive champagne for Marley's engagement party and re-posted that video boosting Maureen's channel. He never got jealous of Leo and trusted me fully even though he didn't know about Leo's asexuality.

While I was sure Shoshanna coordinated many of those specifics, she worked under Stone's direction. And on balance, his efforts far eclipsed mine.

My major contribution to our relationship over the past six months had been putting up with his shit with Naomi.

But that didn't mean I had to let him take me for granted.

Biting my lip, I gritted out, "I honestly don't know, Stone. I'm not sure how much longer I can do this." At his crestfallen face, I hurried to add, "But I don't want to make any decisions yet. I'm about to get busy with the wedding and its aftermath, and you've got the movie. Let's just take this time until we're both back in LA to breathe and think things over."

He looked sheepish. "Darlin', I'm really sorry. I know this is hard on you, and I promise I wouldn't do it if Shoshanna hadn't insisted that it's the exact right thing." His gaze deepened, and the Stone I thought I could maybe love someday appeared on the other side of the screen. "But just so you know, this is going to be your decision. There's nothing to think about on my end. I want to be with you. Full stop. I get that dating me feels like it comes with a lot of conditions, including hiding away like thieves. And maybe I'm wrong asking you to put up with all of it. But that's what I'm doing. Even if it makes me a selfish bastard. Because this thing with

Naomi won't be forever. How about I tell Shoshanna that I'm done by the end of the year? No matter what. Then you and I can be out in the open." When I didn't rush to either agree or stop him, he plowed ahead. "When we first got together, it was already a weird time for both of us, right? @theadventurousmiranda meets Stone, the internet dumbfuck. But a year from now, I want us to be Miranda Davis, marketing genius, and her movie actor boyfriend, Stone Caseman. We just have to ride through this rough stretch a little longer."

He made it sound so simple. And the words showed how much he cared. But in my heart, I knew I wasn't as all-in as he was.

He didn't realize that he'd fallen harder for me than I had for him. But I'd realized it. It was the reason I'd stayed in this as long as I had.

Because if I truly, truly cared for Stone, I'd never have allowed him to treat me this way.

I exhaled. "I promise to think about everything you've said. That's the best I can do. And I don't want this to ruin the amazing journey you're about to go on with your movie coming out. I want you to enjoy it, since I witnessed how hard you worked for it. Let's put this conversation on ice for now. We're cool to text or whatever until we're both back in LA, but nothing heavy."

He nodded. "Miranda, you are the only person in my life who couldn't give a shit about the Stone Caseman people see online. As long as we laughed and talked the way we do, I know you'd still be with me if I were in some boring-ass corporate job, or if I worked as a ticket taker at Dodger Stadium. Sometimes I think the universe put you on the beach that day because it knew I needed you in my life."

He was sweet to say it, and I believed he meant it. But being in his life and being his girlfriend weren't the same thing.

I glanced into the backyard to see Leo throwing a plastic stick to Oscar and Bambi.

Truthfully, it was hard to fault Stone for not putting me first. He'd never been my number one either.

Chapter Eighteen

Leo

NOW

I followed Miranda into our room. It was dark outside, so I flipped on the floor lamp. We stared at the bed for a second before she crawled onto it, lying down on her stomach.

This is normal. We've always been physically affectionate. She doesn't know what's changed. Just be cool. Don't make it weird.

Running through the mantras in my head, I reminded myself that this shouldn't be a big deal. But despite my affirmations, it felt like dangerous territory.

Or maybe it was just me. Projecting.

I sat down next to her on the edge of the mattress. She turned to face me, and I realized how awkward our positions were. I could understand why massage therapists had tables for their clients. It would be difficult to get a good hold of Miranda's shoulders from the side.

"Are you okay if I straddle you?" I asked. "I'll keep my weight on my knees, but it'll make it easier to do this." In for a penny, in for a pound. If it had to be dangerous, at least the massage could be good too.

"Whatever works." She seemed totally relaxed. Her eyes closed, and she melted into the bed.

I threw one of my legs over her thighs until my joggers-clad knees were on either side of hers. I rested back on my haunches, my thighs thick enough that I could still be comfortable without actually having to sit on her.

Leaning forward, I rubbed my thumbs across the juncture of her neck and shoulders. My fingers traced slow patterns down her spine and over the sinewy planes of her muscles, and I registered how enormous my hands were compared to the narrow expanse of her back.

Running my palms across her thin T-shirt, I rubbed circles along her sides as they tapered to her waist, working out any small knots I discovered along the way.

A groan escaped her. Guttural and deep. I squeezed my eyelids, drinking in the sound.

I'd done that. She'd made that noise because of me.

I reveled in the feel of her body beneath my hands. Contemplated my deliberate motions. Miranda might be unaware, but this was the most sensual thing I'd ever experienced. My cheeks heated as it hit me. We'd touched before. Cuddled and hugged. But this was different. This felt carnal, like I was *servicing* her.

I released a long breath, knowing I was on the edge of getting *excited*.

"Pressure okay?" I murmured, noticing how quiet the room was.

"It's perfect. I feel very decadent right now." She laughed lightly.

"Good. I never did get you a real birthday gift. We can consider this massage as me rectifying matters."

She twisted her neck slightly to peek at me. "Leo, you have been the most amazing friend. And you have given me so much. Not just since Thanksgiving, but always. That's the gift."

I smiled, and some of my more tumultuous thoughts eased. "I know, Panda. But I'm glad to do this too."

We stopped talking, and I moved my hands, kneading her lower back as she continued breathing deeply. My desire felt like a furnace inside me.

My fingers worked their way toward Miranda's ass, stroking along its upper curve. I dug my thumbs into the area just above the waistband of her leggings, the twin dimples there beckoning me like sirens. I longed to press my mouth to them.

But I resisted.

I ran my palms from her shoulders down the length of her arms, gripping her triceps, her forearms, her wrists. As my fingers grazed the sensitive skin there, goose bumps popped up, and she hummed. "Tickles."

"Sorry." I dragged my hands back to her shoulders.

With Miranda so open and pliant beneath me, the desire to kiss her intensified. I imagined brushing my lips against the back of her neck. It would be in bounds. I'd given her pecks like that before.

Except I couldn't do that now. Knowing how I felt. Knowing she belonged to someone else.

I arrived at the same impasse I'd been at for days. With the same lack of good options.

One path was to tell Miranda how I felt and leave the ball in her court. But it wasn't fair to do that when she was dating Stone. Putting aside our long history, deep friendship, and my evolving asexuality, it was uncool to tell another person's partner that you were into them.

Which left me with only one option—keeping my mouth shut.

I knew I needed to tell her about my new understanding of my sexuality, because holding back something that huge from her simply wasn't who Miranda and I were as friends. It could wait until after the New Year—based on the stiffness of her shoulders, she clearly had enough on her plate to worry about without me adding in any new wrinkles—but I couldn't keep such a big revelation from my best friend indefinitely.

"Everything okay?" Miranda's voice broke into my thoughts, and I realized I'd stopped moving my hands. I was basically just resting on my knees above her.

"Sorry, daydreaming."

She rolled over underneath me and I ended up straddling her thighs.

I hadn't anticipated the move. It had her grazing my dick, which thickened to half-mast.

She smiled, appearing oblivious to my distress, and I looked down at her. In all our times sharing a bed, we'd never been in this position. We'd lain next to each other, back-to-back, and spoon-style, but I'd never straddled her like this. Never felt so...dominant.

My instinct was to jump off, but I tamped it down. If she was going to act like this was perfectly above board and innocent, then it was.

"That was amazing," she said, grinning up at me. "For someone who's never given a massage before, you sure are good at it." She placed her hands on my thighs. "Thank you."

Her touch had my cock taking notice again, and I knew better than to keep playing with matches. I slid off her until I stood next to the bed. "Just wait until you taste my spaghetti."

She chuckled. "Can't wait... And Leo?"

"Hmm?"

"I'm sure you're tense too, with everything, and doing all that work for the Hoopla. If you ever want a massage, I'm happy to return the favor."

Hahahahahahahahahahahahahahahaha. Like that wouldn't totally kill me.

"We'll see."

5 MONTHS AGO - JULY

Miranda knocked on my hotel room door at two in the morning. Luckily for her, I hadn't been able to drift off since getting back from the reception a few hours ago.

"Everything okay?" I asked, blinking at the fluorescent lighting in the hallway.

"Couldn't sleep." I shivered as she dragged her fingertips casually across my bare stomach as she slipped inside the room. "Figured I'd see if you were in the same boat."

I chuckled. "Sure am. When days are this nice, it's hard to put a period on them."

She sat down on my rumpled sheets. Turning on the table lamp next to the bed, I sank down into the chair across from her.

"It was a beautiful day," she agreed. "Everything went so well."

"You were a very capable maid of honor."

James and Marley had opted for a low-key ceremony in a quaint nondenominational chapel downtown. He'd worn a gray suit with no tie, and Marley's white linen dress was equally unfussy. They laughed when James landed a few jokes during his vows and again when their overexcited dogs couldn't handle the twenty feet required for ring-bearing duties and detoured down the wrong aisle.

They'd held the reception at the high school, in the room next to the auditorium where James had sung to Marley eighteen months ago. The space accommodated the sizable crowd who turned up to wish them well. I met several of my brother's students, current and former, and was happy for the reminder that he'd found his true calling as a teacher.

One young man, a recent graduate named Fel, approached my parents to tell them what an impact James had made on his life.

"Mr. Wymack has a way of talking to me that makes me realize when I'm being kind of a dick," Fel explained with a smirk. "I think he's trying to knock me down a peg or two before college, you know, for my own good." He grinned wryly.

My dad raised an eyebrow. "Maybe for his next trick, my son can teach you not to say 'dick' in front of your elders."

"Elders?" Fel looked from side to side. "I see no elders here." He reached for my mom's hand and dropped an air kiss over her knuckles. "I see only beautiful young ladies."

"Cut the crap," James said, approaching Fel. "I hope you got us a really good wedding present to make up for being a pain in the toosh the past two years."

The young man shrugged. "Nah, we all chipped in and got you a new beanie. Because Ms. Davis deserves better than to be around that stanky one you always wear." With that, he hurried away to his friends, calling back, "It's been real, Mr. Wymack. Congrats on convincing Ms. Davis to marry you."

Our mom and dad looked at James with pride. And I knew it wasn't only because of his impact on his students. It was because of the wedding, Marley, setting up a life for himself in Coleman Creek, all of it. They never made me feel *less than* for not being able to give them a day like this, but deep down, I wished I could.

For Marley and James's official first dance, a senior student named Daniel played an acoustic rendition of "Across the Universe" on guitar while his friend Nan, a former student home from college for the summer, sang vocals. Daniel looked at Nan with such naked longing in his eyes that even my ace heart—normally not attuned to those signals—could see it.

"You think he likes her?" Miranda asked, a lilt of laughter in her voice as she came up beside me.

"Maybe just a teeny bit."

Daniel put down his guitar, and the DJ took over.

"May I have this dance?" Miranda asked prettily.

I wrapped my arm around her back, pulling her into my chest as we swayed to "At Last" and "Never My Love." I admired that she was petite but also sturdy. Unbreakable in body and spirit. That's what had drawn me to her in the first place, that toughness beneath the sweet exterior.

She leaned into me, exhaling a happy sigh. Closing my eyes, I felt the press of her cheek on my torso and the warmth of her skin beneath my hand. I breathed in the familiar scent of her shampoo and smiled at the gentle hum of her mumbling along to the music.

It wasn't unusual for us to be close like this.

But the way I felt now was new. The way my body reacted was new. Noticing how she molded to me, registering her soft curves.

The soul-deep contentment of knowing the woman in my arms better than I knew myself was like nothing I'd ever experienced.

My pulse sped up.

I'd loved Miranda from the start. But I couldn't deny that something had shifted. All of the sudden, I was *feeling* things.

My heart thumped in my chest. Could it be...?

I darted my tongue out to lick my lips before nosing the top of Miranda's head.

Could it?

Yes.

Holy shit... Yes!

I wanted her.

I let the revelation sit in my mind until I knew, with zero doubt, that it was true.

For the rest of the reception, whether she was near or far, I felt her presence, the kernels of desire expanding and bursting in my stomach.

I wanted her. Now what?

The possibilities were thrilling, but by the time I arrived back at the hotel, the full reality of my attraction to Miranda had set in, tempering my initial elation. I was questioning everything I thought I knew about myself. Things I'd fought hard to come to terms with.

I wasn't an idiot. I knew these things could *evolve*, that sexuality was fluid. But part of me resented having such a straightforward explanation. Almost like I'd betrayed myself. Although there weren't many people in my life who knew about my asexuality, it was a label I'd worn proudly in my mind. I'd used it to guide my life choices and interactions with others.

As much as having a romantic pull to Miranda ignited my senses, it also made me feel like a fraud.

Those were the thoughts going through my head as she sat across from me in my dim hotel room, appearing perfectly at ease in my disheveled sheets.

Was I really asexual if her hand brushing across my stomach made me tremble? Had I been holding people at a distance for no reason? Had I ever been true to myself? And how the fuck at age thirty-five did I not know the answers to these questions?

Perhaps more importantly, wanting her wasn't the same as knowing I'd be able to love her the way she needed. The way she deserved.

Faced with those complicated anxieties, I could almost forget Stone's presence in her life.

But Miranda didn't know what was happening with me. And she hadn't forgotten Stone. I suspected it was their situation that kept her awake tonight. She'd looked upset during their video chat the day before. I'd seen her slam her laptop closed from the backyard. But after our argument about Stone and Naomi, we rarely discussed her boyfriend, so I hadn't asked her about the call.

All the same, I sensed she needed me.

Her next words confirmed it.

"I don't really know why I came to your room, Bear. I guess it just didn't seem right to end this amazing day alone when I could end it with my favorite person in the world."

"You know you can always come to me, Panda. Whatever you need."

She yawned and scooted under the covers to the other side of the bed, patting the spot where she'd been sitting. I smiled and crawled in next to her. It wasn't the first time we'd shared a bed. I'd woken up more than once in my apartment to find she'd snuck into my bedroom during the night, claiming my "creepy" painting was attempting to steal her soul. I'd also graduated from the couch to one-half of the bed whenever I stayed with her in LA.

It would be different now, after what I'd discovered today, but I'd never deny her this comfort.

"Everything okay?" she asked, throwing an arm over my chest and snuggling into my side.

"Mm-hmm. Just tired."

She'd had her nails done for the wedding, and she scratched them through my chest hair. I felt my dick perk up under the blanket and hoped she didn't notice.

"You know," her tone teased, "I'm pretty sure I see a few silver strands."

I tilted my head and pretended to bite her jaw. "Are you saying I'm old?"

"No... Uh... Stone waxes his chest." She rested her cheek on my sternum. "This is nice. I like the furry...and the silver."

I harrumphed. She'd barely mentioned Stone's name to me in months. I tightened my arm around her.

"Can I sleep here?" she asked.

"Course."

A few minutes later, I heard her soft snores.

Unsurprisingly, I found sleep elusive and eventually gave up trying. My brain continued to churn with all its earlier worries, even as I enjoyed holding the first woman I'd been attracted to in over a decade. After so many years of nursing the same patterns, my life had turned a corner.

I'd entered a new era where I no longer fully knew myself.

I was officially having an identity crisis.

Chapter Nineteen

Miranda

NOW

Leo had gotten hard while he'd massaged me.

I'd felt the tautness in him at the dining table when he first touched my shoulders, and again after I unintentionally asked for a more comprehensive massage. Without understanding exactly what was happening, I knew I wanted his hands on me.

And I sensed he wanted that too.

Tension simmered as I led him into our room. To the bed we shared.

When he asked to straddle me, heat pooled instantly in my core. Then his thighs squeezed mine as he worked me over, and I couldn't stop the low moans that escaped my throat.

There was power in his fingertips I felt him keeping in check. Something had shifted. A weighty silence electrified the air, and I dared to hope...

Still, I'd needed to test my theory. So I rolled over, surprising him before he could conceal the evidence of his desire. And while he wasn't granite, he wasn't soft.

I could keep making excuses, keep telling myself he wasn't into me. *Our level of physical affection was normal between friends. His daily morning wood was pesky biology. Kissing me at the arcade was all for show.*

Or I could assess the evidence in front of me and think critically about the past two weeks.

My suspicions weren't solely based on Leo's physical reaction to the massage. I'd heard the hitch in his voice. Seen his expression.

He wanted me.

I was done pretending otherwise.

And even though I was sure he had reasons for not owning up to it, I would not let him get away with that.

I had lied to myself so much with Stone. Rarely confronted him. But Leo and I weren't like that. What was the point of being best friends if we didn't communicate? We'd been down that road before. Being too careful around one another and not talking had caused our blowup on Halloween, when everything beneath the surface exploded.

Leo and I were real with each other. It was kind of our thing. I might have gaslit myself into believing Stone's cavalier attitude toward me was acceptable, but I wasn't talking myself out of noticing Leo's response to touching me.

I'd put up with less than I deserved from Stone, but with Leo, I never would.

As he retreated into the kitchen to start the spaghetti, I released a shadow of a laugh. He truly thought he'd gotten away clean.

Silly Bear.

5 MONTHS AGO - JULY

I WOKE UP IN THE MIDDLE OF THE NIGHT to find Leo pressed against my back. Pulling his arm tighter over my waist, I snuggled against his chest.

This was why I'd come to his room. I knew he would settle me.

Watching Marley marry James had been one of the most joyful experiences of my life. The ceremony was beautiful, the reception loose and fun. Perfect for the happy couple. I was thankful my frustrating conversation with Stone hadn't tainted the day for me. I'd been able to put him out of my mind. It wasn't until I came back to my quiet hotel room—after deciding not to stay in my sister's guest room on her wedding night—that the doubt and irritation crept back in.

From the moment I knocked on Leo's door, I'd felt at ease again. Decisions about whether to cut ties with Stone or give him until the end of the year to stage a breakup with Naomi faded into the background.

Ever since a year and a half ago, when Leo first comforted me in the carport of my childhood home, he'd been my safe place. As I'd scratched my nails through his chest hair tonight, mentally contrasting the rough planes of his body with Stone's smoothly sculpted pecs, I felt so grateful for Leo's incredible friendship.

I'd fallen asleep thinking about how both Leo and Stone were physically absent from my life most of the time, but unlike Stone, Leo still felt like a solid, constant presence in it.

Only Leo felt necessary to my existence.

I'd miss him when he drove back to Tacoma tomorrow.

Before Stone dropped his bomb, I'd been looking forward to spending this time in my hometown. I'd had it all planned out—a summer in Coleman Creek away from the inevitable public interest surrounding Stone and Naomi's breakup, and by the time I was back in LA to start my new job, Stone and I could date openly.

Instead, our holding pattern would extend into the fall. Unless I ended things.

That was why I told Stone I needed time to think.

I linked my fingers with Leo's on top of my stomach. I wished I could ask for his advice. Maybe I would eventually, but since he was leaving town in less than twenty-four hours, it wasn't the right time. He had to get back to the city for work, and I didn't want him to feel obligated to stay, something I knew he'd do if he suspected I wasn't okay.

For tonight, it was enough to soak up his warmth and positive energy.

He grunted and pressed himself closer, shoving a knee between my thighs.

I froze as my butt made contact with an unmistakable object. An unmistakable *hard* object.

What the hell?

Leo's cock was pushing against my ass. I felt it clear as day, even through our pajamas. In all the times we'd shared a bed, he'd often held me close, but as far as I could recall, he'd never gotten an erection.

It had to be biological, right? Surely, even asexual guys sprouted wood sometimes. Maybe it was friction from the sheets. Yeah, that had to be it. The friction.

I stayed still, not wanting to wake him.

He rubbed it against me again.

Jesus, Leo, give a girl a break.

I could also tell it was...big. Not shocking since so was he. I wasn't a size queen or anything, so I didn't care, but for the first time, I imagined what Leo might look like fully naked. I'd caught him coming out of the shower enough times to have an idea, but I'd never seen the whole, um, package.

Pushing those wayward thoughts aside, I relaxed. It was fine to let my imagination take a ride, but I never got too far without remembering Leo was ace. I'd long since resigned myself to the fact that the attraction I felt to him was entirely one-sided. My old friend limerence.

I exhaled. Sometimes a hard dick was just a hard dick. It had nothing to do with the way Leo and I felt about one another.

Unbidden, a small voice in the back of my mind asked, *but what if it does?*

Chapter Twenty

Leo

NOW

Miranda and I prepared pasta, salad, and garlic bread together. She seemed more relaxed after the massage but not particularly talkative, so I put on records in the living room. Marley had an impressive collection of old Christmas albums.

Oscar and Bambi lay in front of the tree, snoring softly. They finally stirred when Miranda and I sat down at the table to eat, watching us with pleading eyes that would have given Oliver Twist a run for his money. I relented and grabbed Kongs from the freezer. I could have sworn Bambi bowed at me before taking his treat to the rug by the fireplace.

"The first thing I'm going to do when I buy a house is get a dog," I said, watching as Oscar rolled onto his back, wriggling like a worm with the bright red Kong sticking out of his mouth.

"You're close?" Miranda asked, and I realized it was the first time she'd spoken since we sat down.

"It depends. I could probably find something in South King County, but I'm not sure that's what I want. If I saved up to afford a place in Seattle, I could be closer to my parents, but sometimes I think I'd prefer something farther out, with more land."

"I could see that."

She brought a bite of pasta to her lips and chewed slowly before taking a sip of water. I hummed along to Sammy Davis Jr. on the vinyl player.

Miranda's phone rattled on the table, causing her to jump in her chair. She flipped it over and frowned. I caught Stone's name before she declined his FaceTime request. As before, I wanted to ask about it, but the storm on her face kept me quiet. Seconds later, a string of texts came through. She didn't even check them, calmly putting the device in the pocket of her leggings.

When the muffled *dings* of more messages sounded from underneath the table, I raised an eyebrow.

"It's nothing," she said, her tone clipped.

"You sure?"

Her fork clanked against her plate as it slipped through her fingers. "Actually...don't worry about the texts. But there is something else I want to talk about."

"Yeah. I can tell something's up. Did I massage you too hard? You can tell me if I suck at—"

"Stop." She put up her hand. "The massage was great. Very informative, in fact."

Informative? That was a strange word to—
Oh no.

She leaned back in her chair and threw her napkin on the table, then folded her arms across her chest. "You weren't touching me like a friend, Leo. You were touching me like a lover."

I froze, stunned, before sucking in a breath. She stared evenly at me.

"Miranda..." I struggled for what to say. Of course the person who knew me best would see right through me.

On some level, I knew she'd been talking herself out of the obvious for a while. During the massage. At the arcade. Probably longer. Because she respected that I'd told her I was ace. That I didn't want a romantic relationship.

But that delusion couldn't last forever.

"Be honest with me, Leo. Do you want me as more than a friend?"

Now it was my turn to drop my fork.

5 MONTHS AGO - JULY

By morning, I'd gained more clarity. I wanted Miranda. Full stop. Where did we go from here? That was still a wide-open question.

She wasn't in my room when I woke up. There was a note on my phone. She'd gone back to her room to shower before we needed to head to James and Marley's house. We were having breakfast with them before they left for their honeymoon.

Driving over in my truck, Miranda chatted about the wedding and her plans for spending the summer in Coleman Creek. Meanwhile, all I could think about was waking up in the middle of the night to find my fully hard cock pressed into her ass. I'd rolled away, and I didn't think she noticed, but it was still...fucking weird. Another new thing to get used to.

I halfway thought I'd need to rub one out, but it hadn't been an issue. Per usual, I deflated quickly. I'd read that some ace people still had high libidos—meaning many of them enjoyed masturbating—but I'd never run hot. For me, jerking off was a rare event.

After breakfast, Miranda helped her sister finish packing. Marley and James planned to spend a week in Greece, followed by a Mediterranean cruise.

James and I sat on his back porch, sipping coffee.

I flicked the bun on top of his head. "Hard to believe my little brother is a married man."

He laughed. "You remember I married Cindy six years ago? You didn't seem so surprised then."

"That was different." He didn't need me to elaborate. Before James met Marley, he'd had a disastrous three-year marriage to a woman who'd expected more from life than being married to a high school teacher. With Marley, he'd found his forever.

James relaxed back in his chair. "I feel like the luckiest guy in the world, you know? I turned thirty a week ago, and I have an amazing wife, a home, dogs, a job I love. Will and I are best friends again, and I'm about to go on an amazing honeymoon. Life is good, brother."

"I'm so proud of you," I said genuinely.

We sat in silence for a minute before he spoke again. "You know the only thing that could make it better?"

My mind immediately went to kids, but Marley and James had made a point of saying they planned to wait a few years.

"Winning lottery ticket?" I suggested. "New chalkboard for your classroom? A trainer who can actually get Oscar to shake when you ask him to, instead of just licking his butthole?"

James's cheek ticked. "I'd like to know that my big brother is just as happy as I am. But the butthole thing would be good too."

I eyed him. "I'm happy. Are you under the impression that I'm not?"

"That isn't it," he replied, sipping his coffee. "And I'm not making a judgment. You're such an amazing and supportive brother, I guess I just want to make sure I'm giving you that in return. This is me checking in to make sure you're okay. I know you have friends and a job you like, but I hope it's...enough. Maybe it's none of my business, but sometimes it seems like you're holding yourself back. And if you're doing that because something's wrong, I want to help you." He exhaled. "You can also tell me to shut up."

I let out my own thick breath. "James, I—" Tilting my head upward, I gazed up at the clear, cool sky. "I get how my life might look from the outside. I'm in my mid-thirties, and I haven't hit a lot of, let's say, typical adult milestones... And I know you and Mom and Dad wonder why I don't date. If it helps, I'm saving for a down payment on a house, so at least I'll tick that box eventually." I paused, patting him on the thigh. "But you're my brother. If something were wrong, it would definitely be your business. You shouldn't feel you can't ask me things. I might not answer, but you can always ask."

"Does that mean you're just—what? Taking things at your own pace?"

I raised a *don't bullshit me* eyebrow at him. "You want to know the reason for the not dating?"

"Obviously, I'm curious. I'd be an oblivious fool if I weren't. Especially since you're the *hot* brother."

A year ago, I would have worried his comment stemmed from the body image issues he'd battled since high school. But he'd come a long way since meeting Marley, so his teasing smile didn't surprise me.

"Are you trying to make me tell you that you're hot?"

"Duh." He chuckled. "But seriously, is it because you don't enjoy going out? I know the apps can be a minefield."

I gripped my mug. "It's complicated. Or simple, I guess, depending on which way you look at it."

Part of me wanted to blurt it out to him, but after keeping this piece of myself inside for so long, I was having trouble putting it out there.

When I didn't continue, James said, "I used to think maybe you just did everything on the down-low, like you're a secret player and wanted to keep it all private. But these past few years..." His expression pinched.

"What?"

James sat up straighter. "These past few years, I've seen how you are with Miranda. I know the two of you are just friends, but—brother—the way you light up when you're with her. How you play off one another. It's not something everyone gets." I stared hard at him. He must have mistaken my expression for annoyance because he added, "Sorry if I'm overstepping. Like I said, it's none of my business."

"No," I reassured him. "I understand. And you're not wrong. Truthfully, hearing you say it out loud makes it more real. Miranda and I completely click. I'm comfortable with her in a way I've never been before."

"That's major, Leo." He hesitated. "There's really nothing more than friendship there?"

I thought about how much James didn't know. I couldn't talk to him about Stone, about how Miranda was already in a relationship with an internet clown.

"It's okay," James said. "You don't have to tell me. Just know that I'm here for you."

I couldn't talk to my brother about Stone. But I could talk to him about me.

Adjusting myself in the chair, I twisted toward him. "Actually, I think it might be good to—... Things might be changing with me, so maybe it's time." I steepled my fingers together beneath my chin.

"Time for what?"

"You mentioned that it seems like I've been holding myself back? Well, there's a reason for that. Like, a specific reason."

"This is a thing that Miranda knows?"

"Mm-hmm." I ran a hand through my hair.

After a minute of silence, James laughed a little. "It's fine if you don't want to tell me, Leo."

"I'm working myself up to it."

"But you really don't have to. If it's going to cause you stress, we can wait until you're ready—"

"I'm asexual—"

"...to tell... Wait, what?"

"I don't experience sexual attraction to people."

James's head shook slightly. "I know what asexual means." His forehead furrowed, and I knew he was processing, reconciling what I'd said with everything he could remember. Finally, he asked, "Ilona?"

"That's how I knew, man. I liked her, maybe could have stayed with her, but in the end, I couldn't get it up enough to keep her happy, and she couldn't accept it."

"Damn." James sucked in his lips. "That's rough."

I nodded. "It was. And I recognize in hindsight that she was crueler than she needed to be about it. Especially at the end. She called me names. Made me feel like less of a man, I guess. And maybe it was my fault for letting her get to me, but you need to understand that I was in a much different headspace then. My experience with Ilona was enough for me to give myself the ace label, but I had a lot of mixed feelings—shame—around it."

James slid his patio chair closer to mine. "This seems like it might be a longer conversation."

"Probably not one to have right before your honeymoon. But you have the short version now."

He frowned. "You really thought you couldn't tell me? Did you think I would judge you?"

"Like I said, the breakup with Ilona was harsh. For a while, I had this feeling like maybe it was something to be embarrassed about. I've recovered from that. Mostly. I realize there's nothing wrong with being asexual. But even though not telling people started as self-preservation, it eventually became a habit."

"But you told Miranda?"

"I had to. You said it yourself. We have a crazy connection. There was no way for us to be how we are without her knowing. It would be too confusing otherwise. Blurred lines."

"Makes sense. Since you guys basically act like a couple."

"I know. But it works for us. I've never felt this close to anyone."

"Then I'm glad you have her."

"Me too." I took a swig of my now-lukewarm coffee. "But James?"

"Uh-huh?"

"There is something I can't tell Miranda. Not yet, anyway."

He stopped moving. "Alright. Do you want to tell me?" he asked.

I cleared my throat. "Um, yeah... Yeah... I think I need to tell somebody."

James studied my face, waiting. His forehead lifted in question.

After releasing a huge breath, I said, "The way I feel about her is...changing. Evolving."

He hummed. "Let me guess. Your feelings are no longer exactly asexual?"

"How did you know?" I frowned.

"Leo, you broke up with Ilona a decade ago. If Miranda is the first person to come along in all that time who you've connected with, especially considering"—he waved his hand in a circle in front of me—"how easily you attract people, then she must be pretty special."

"But it's hard. I achieved this baseline that worked for me, and now it's upended. All of a sudden, I'm not asexual."

James raised an eyebrow. "C'mon. You're not that old. You must know that sexuality is a spectrum."

"I know."

"Then you also know that you're still ace even if Miranda flipped your demi switch."

My brows shot up. "My what?"

He smiled. "I guess I'm sensitive to it since I teach high school, and this new generation is going to make sure no one gets stuck in a box. It sounds like you're making the jump from *asexual and I'm not attracted to anyone* to *asexual and I'm only attracted to someone once I've developed a deep emotional connection to them.* A.k.a. demisexual."

I pulled out my phone and did a quick search while my brother watched patiently. There was a reputable website for asexuals that had a lengthy list of sub-categories beneath it. And one of the more prevalent types of asexuality was apparently demisexuality.

"This says that demisexuals have to form a close bond with someone before any sort of attraction arises." I read out loud, but it was more for myself than for James. After finishing the brief paragraph, I looked up at him. "It's been so long since I went down the internet rabbit hole looking at this stuff. There's much more here than last time."

"You really didn't consider this?"

"That there was a word for it? No, I really don't care about that. Mostly, I just care about being sure that I feel something deeper than friendship with Miranda. And as of this morning, I'm one hundred percent certain that I do."

As I skimmed through the articles, I thought about my experiences with my college girlfriend and Ilona. In both instances, I'd gotten to know them first before we started dating. But now I wondered if we'd jumped to the sex part too fast.

With Miranda, there had been such a slow build from instant emotional connection to intense platonic friendship to an inkling of romantic feelings that it felt like that next step—sexual attraction—had actually had enough time to simmer.

"You don't need to have a name for it," James said. "There are no hard and fast rules. A lot of people meet someone and want to sleep with them right away. Some people don't form strong emotional connections but are attracted to everyone. You're wired the way you are. It's all good."

"Thanks. I've been telling myself that for years, and of course Miranda told me, but it's nice to hear it from you too."

"Are you going to tell her soon? That your feelings have *evolved*? Not gonna lie. Marley and I would be the first in line to congratulate you two if you made it happen."

I thought about it. Even if Miranda wanted to be with me in that way, I didn't see a scenario where I'd ever want to have a ton of sex all the time. Would that be a deal-breaker? It certainly had been for Ilona. Also, Stone was still in the picture.

"Honestly, James, there's more to it than just telling her. She has her own stuff going on—things that aren't my place to talk about—and it's waited this long. If we decide to hash this out, it needs to be under the right set of circumstances." I rested my elbows on my knees.

James clapped me on my shoulder. "You know Miranda better than anybody—I know Marley is grateful she has you—so I know you'll figure it out. In the meantime, I'm here if you need me."

I turned to pull him into an embrace. "Love you, little brother."

"Back atchya, big bro."

Miranda and I waved goodbye to James and Marley a few hours later. After they headed out, we went grocery shopping and hung out with Oscar and Bambi until mid-afternoon, when I hopped into my truck for the drive back to Tacoma.

Miranda looked sad as I slid into the cab, flanked by the dogs in the driveway.

"You'll be back at the end of August to pick me up?"

"Yep. We can spend a few days together before your flight to California." She still seemed down, so I added, "Panda, you know you can call me if you need me to come sooner, okay?"

Leaning in awkwardly through the window, she gripped me in another hug. "I know, Leo-Bear. I'm just going to miss you." There was a wobble in her voice.

"Sure you're okay?"

"Yes." She straightened, backing away from the truck. "Thanks for holding me last night. Drive safe, and I'll see you soon."

Before I could reply, she ran back into the house.

Chapter Twenty-One

Miranda

NOW

Leo's fork dropped onto his plate with the strength of a thousand hammers.

"W-What?"

Steeling my shoulders, I stared him down. "Are you interested in me as more than a friend?" I asked matter-of-factly.

"Miranda, I—"

"Answer carefully," I interrupted, wanting him to understand that I would only accept the truth. "Because I'm pretty sure I know. But I need to hear you to say it."

My mind was a hurricane of confused thoughts. I'd been too quick to dismiss things. Too quick to give him an out.

I thought back to July, to the night of the wedding, and also to the end of the summer in his apartment. And now the massage. I'd convinced myself that Leo consistently getting erections around me over the past six months—even though that never happened during the entire first year we knew each other, no matter how many times we shared a bed—was totally reasonable. Now I saw. Something had changed.

He opened his mouth a few times, but no sound came out.

I pressed him. "Are you going to deny it?"

A long, loud sigh escaped his throat. "No. I won't lie to you. I just—"

Pounding footsteps on the porch interrupted him. The front door swung open aggressively, rattling on its hinges.

James trudged in, panting with exertion, dragging an enormous Douglas fir behind him. The scent of pine overwhelmed the room immediately.

"What the—?" I burst out, rushing to hold the door open for him as he dropped the tree in the doorway, resting his hands on his knees. "I thought you were having a date night?"

"They opened the tree lot for special deals since there was a PTA meeting, so we figured we'd get the best pick." James huffed a laugh. "And by best pick, I mean the heaviest freaking tree in the lot. As far as date night goes, I'm sure you're aware that buying a Christmas tree is your sister's idea of the perfect romantic outing. We're still planning to head over to The Landslide. Just wanted to drop this bad boy off first."

Well, I supposed my conversation with Leo could wait a few more minutes. Lord knew I didn't want to have it while my sister and James were around.

Leo maneuvered himself to the bottom part of the tree and helped James carry it inside. They brought it to the far end of the living room, then knelt to remove the netting.

"Where's Marley?" I asked.

"Carport. I didn't want her to help me because she's wearing one of your mom's old sweaters." He glanced at Leo. "Nice that my lumberjack of a brother is staying with us. I'll have to think of more heavy things to move while you're here."

"Why is she in the carport?"

"She left the tree stand there when we pulled all the stuff out of the garage last month."

Marley needed to hurry because it was freezing outside. I was about to close the door against the temperature when my sister pushed against it, clutching the metal tree stand we'd used since I was a child.

"I found the tree stand," Marley said in an odd tone. "And, uh, while I was out there, I found something else."

Peering nervously behind herself, she pushed the door with her elbow, opening it wider.

"Hey, darlin'."

Stone smiled at me as he walked in.

4 MONTHS AGO - AUGUST

Leo offered to pick me up in Coleman Creek so we could spend time together at his place before my flight to Los Angeles. We'd been texting and video calling almost daily since the wedding, and although he hadn't been physically present in my life, he'd been a tremendous support to me—even if he didn't know I'd spent my summer going back and forth in my mind about Stone.

Except he seemed unusually quiet when he arrived. I wanted to ask him about it, but my sisters and their partners surrounded us. Leo declined Marley's offer to spend the night, preferring to make the long drive twice in one day rather than risk missing work tomorrow.

"I'm trying to get ahead on jobs and bank vacation time so I can be here for an extended period over the holidays," he explained.

"Maureen and I are taking a trip over Thanksgiving," Will said. "Buddy of mine has a cabin. It's big and modern but totally off the grid. We've almost got Marley and James convinced to go. You two should come too."

Since I'd spent the past seven weeks stressing over Stone, it hit me how the rest of the world saw Leo and me as a matched set. I tried to picture going on a couples' vacation with Stone and my family, but the mental image failed to manifest.

"I'll be back for Christmas," I said. "But Thanksgiving is a no-go since I'll be busy trying to make a good impression on my new team at work." I wagged a finger at Marley. "Of course you guys are doing something semi-outdoorsy when I can't go. My followers would probably love a cozy Thanksgiving in the woods."

Maureen guffawed. "Cut the shit. The internet may be fooled, but we all know the real @theadventurousmiranda is just as happy at a four-star hotel. Maybe happier."

"You mean like how the internet thinks your YouTube channel is full of good vibes when in reality it's run by a cynical malcontent?" I retorted.

"*Oooh. Cynical malcontent.* Sick burn," Maureen replied, winking at me.

"I'm putting that on a T-shirt," Will said.

Climbing into the passenger side of Leo's truck an hour later, I realized I looked forward to seeing my sisters again at Christmas. It had been a little touchy between us after my mom died, but we seemed to have found our way back to each other.

I didn't notice the tense set of Leo's shoulders until we were out of the town limits. It wasn't easy between us like it usually was. His left leg bounced as he drove. He fidgeted with his playlists, skipping every other song.

We were halfway to the freeway when I called him on it. "Bear, what is the matter with you? I haven't seen you in almost two months, and suddenly, you're wound as tight as a bow. It's not like you to be so nutso with the music."

His jaw flexed. "I want to tell you, but I don't want to risk pissing you off."

My forehead rose at that enigmatic statement. "Well, now you have to tell me."

He gripped the steering wheel. "Yeah, but...we don't really talk about...Stone."

I sighed. "I just figured you disapproved so much it was easier to avoid it."

He nodded. "But there shouldn't be a big thing in your life that's off-limits. Stone is important to you. What kind of friend am I if you feel like you can't talk about him with me?"

"Is that why you're acting so strange?"

"Not entirely. It's mostly because... Back in December, you said Stone was going to break up with Naomi after the movie came out. And I looked online the other day—" The pulse in his neck flickered. "I noticed that they don't seem to be broken up. I even saw one article hinting that they're secretly engaged."

My breath caught. I'd seen that article too.

I turned my face toward the window. "That was the plan," I said, hating the catch in my voice. Leo waited patiently as I gathered myself before continuing. "Do you remember when I was upset right before Marley and James's wedding?"

"Your video call with Stone?"

"Yep." I laced my fingers in my lap. "That as when he told me their PR teams wanted him and Naomi to extend their relationship past the movie premiere."

Leo gazed out thoughtfully on the lonely highway. "I thought it might be something like that. Truthfully, I worried for a minute it might be even worse—like he'd started dating Naomi for real and left you behind. I...I'm sorry I didn't ask back then. Sorry you had to go through it alone."

"You danced with me at the wedding. And held me when I couldn't sleep. That was what I needed."

"Still, you've been sitting with it on your own for weeks. Unless you've confided in someone else?"

I shook my head. "You don't need to worry. Honestly, the time in Coleman Creek was exactly what I needed. I asked Stone for time to think things through. We've still communicated, so it hasn't been a total break. Just surface-level, though. He messaged me about his press tour. I sent him pictures of the dogs. Stuff like that." Rubbing my palms against my thighs, I felt the relief of finally being able to talk about this. "Obviously, my first thought was just to end it. But I can't shake this feeling like I haven't given us a real chance. When we're together, it's good. But it's also a dreamworld that exists in its own reality. Being away this summer gave me a chance to get some perspective on that. Then again, it's incredibly rare for me to feel a connection with anyone. The past few years, it's only been him. And you, obviously."

Leo's eyes flashed, but he stayed quiet, an inscrutable look on his face. Finally, he asked, "So you're giving him more time?"

"I think I have to... You're sure we're okay to talk about this?"

"All good, Panda. I never should have shut the door on it."

"Let's never do that again," I said. "I want us to talk about everything."

"Agreed."

An enormous weight lifted off my shoulders at his response. As much as I'd proven to myself that I could live without his guidance regarding Stone, my time in Coleman Creek showed me that I didn't want to.

"Alright, then, as far as Stone goes, I decided not to end it before he and I have had a chance to make a real go of things. To be fair, I've been half-assing this relationship in the same way Stone's only been in it half-time. We've both been uncommitted in different ways."

"You want to wait until he actually ends the fake thing with Naomi and then decide?"

"Basically, yes."

"Is there a revised end date for that?"

"The holidays. I told Stone that even if I give him more time, I'm done if it doesn't happen by New Year's, and he promised and told his PA too."

"You believe him?"

"I do. When he broke the first agreement, I don't think he was being intentionally dishonest. He's just derpy sometimes, and he's pretty susceptible to being manipulated by his people."

Leo appeared skeptical but dipped his chin. "Okay."

"Bear, I realize that most women would break up with him. But like I said, I have to take into consideration that I haven't been interested in that many people. It's hard to give up on loving someone when you don't get that feeling very often."

Leo went still. "You love him?"

I crooked an elbow against the passenger door, resting the crown of my head on it. "No, but...I really care about him. I'm not in love with him, but maybe I could be."

"And you want that? To be in love with Stone?"

"I want to be in love with someone. Maybe it's Stone. Maybe not. But I want what Marley has with James. What Maureen has with Will. I want to feel like I belong with someone. Mind and body."

Leo's Adam's apple bobbed as he swallowed. "I want that for you too, Miranda."

THAT NIGHT, I KNOCKED ON LEO'S DOOR. For the past two months, I hadn't stopped remembering how good it felt to be held in his arms.

He lifted the covers sleepily and sighed as I crawled in next to him. There was no need to overthink it. I enjoyed being close to him, and this was one of the few ways I could be. Hopefully, he didn't feel like I was taking advantage, but I doubted it, since he seemed to like it too. The second my head hit the pillow, he emitted a little grunt and rolled over, pulling me back against his chest.

I'd missed the sense of security his firm grip provided.

On paper, it sounded insane. A bad melodrama. I was in a relationship with someone I barely saw, who was in a fake relationship with a coworker, while they were cheered on by an unsuspecting public, and the thing that made me feel better was finding solace in the arms of my asexual best friend.

In the morning, I woke up to the feeling of—

Oh. My. God.

Ohmygod!

It was just like after the wedding. That was Leo. *Again!*

I froze.

"Mmm," Leo mumbled, and the next thing I knew, he was pressing his lips to my neck. He was still sleeping, but *he was KISSING MY NECK!* Asexual Leo. Leo the asexual. My friend Leo, who had no sexual interest in me. In anyone. His lips skimmed the bare skin of my shoulder, next to my sleep tank. *Fuck! He smelled so good. And his lips were so soft.*

Maybe he was having a dream? Did he have sexy dreams?

"Miranda," his slumber-laced voice drawled.

Holy shit. Not only was he having some kind of sex dream but it was apparently quite specific.

Should I wake him up? He'd be embarrassed. But it didn't feel right to just let him—*Oh my god, he was full-on humping me now!*

I widened the space between my legs instinctively when I felt him shove his sweats-clad knee in between. I held in a moan as I clamped down on his thick quad.

Bad Miranda! Do not ride his thigh! He doesn't know what he's doing!

His arm held firm around my waist, pressing me to him. Oh man. If I didn't get a handle on this, he was going to *finish*. And how would we ever come back from that? And how the hell was this happening?

Mustering my resolve, I rolled over quickly and put half a foot of space between us.

His movements stilled. I bit my lip as his eyes blinked open slowly. The dawn light filtered in through the curtains, shadows falling across his face.

"Miranda?" he rasped. "What—"

I saw the brief dart of panic in his eyes as he registered his hardness. He lurched forward, half lying on his stomach, trying to hide it.

He was about as subtle as an elephant, but I pretended not to notice.

"You okay?" he asked. "It's early."

Okay? No, I'm fully fucking not okay. You were just moaning my name and rubbing your massive hard-on up against me, and I'm freaking out.

"I'm good. A little congested. I don't want to risk getting you sick, so I'm gonna head back into the guest room to catch a few more hours."

"Okay," he croaked, giving my arm a squeeze as I rose from the bed. "There's sinus medication in the bathroom if you need it."

I went into the bathroom and noisily opened the medicine cabinet, but all I brought with me to the guest room was a glass of water. I remained wide-awake, the nuclear sunrise painting mocking me, seeming a little too on the nose. Had I just blown up my entire friendship with Leo?

No. I could take this whole incident to my grave if I wanted to. Pretend it never happened. Just like last time. Both incidents could be my secret.

But now that this had happened twice, I had questions.

As with all things, the internet had answers.

Lots of conflicting ones, but I could confirm that it was normal for asexuals to experience moments of high libido, or even attraction. Everyone was different.

Leo having a fever sex dream about me didn't mean he wanted to ravish me in real life. If he wanted that, he would have told me, right? I'd been honest with him from the beginning that I would have been open to something more than friendship, if it were an option.

But I knew it wasn't.

As good as it felt to have Leo's arms around me, it wasn't a smart idea to wish it could be more than it was. Leo had stated plainly that he wasn't attracted to anyone, including me, and I owed it to him to respect that.

And as much as Leo was my best friend, I'd been dating Stone for the past year. And hadn't I just spent two months deciding that I wanted to attempt to salvage that relationship?

There was an intensity with Leo, but there was a simplicity with Stone. And despite all the current misgivings I had about our relationship, one thing I never questioned was his affection for me. I knew Stone wanted me. Not because of random erections we couldn't talk about, but because he told me so unequivocally.

Not to mention, I liked what Leo and I had as best friends. I didn't want to fuck it up. It was raw, and real, and worth protecting.

By the time I got on the plane to Los Angeles, after spending most of the two days alone in Leo's guest room with a supposed bug, I'd fully settled it in my mind.

Nothing had changed. My priority was settling things with Stone, hopefully before the end-of-the-year deadline I'd given him. The memories of Leo rubbing against my ass would stay just that—memories. Buried deep in my brain.

As if the universe wanted to give its stamp of approval, I arrived home to find Stone standing in my living room, flowers in one hand and a bag from our favorite burrito place in the other.

I literally leaped into his arms.

He kissed me soundly, doing his best to put the food and roses down on the table as I wrapped my legs around his middle.

Pulling one of my hands from his waist, he kissed my wrist. "I only have thirty-six hours," he said sheepishly. "But I wanted to be here when you got home."

"I'm glad." I tried to get down, but he held me firm.

"This is the best welcome I could have imagined, Miranda. After how mad you were, and the way our last few conversations have gone, I wasn't sure—"

"It's okay, Stone," I cut him off. "I'm taking a wait-and-see approach, but I'm not giving up on us. If you haven't broken up publicly with Naomi by New Year's, we're done. But until then, I don't want to fight with you."

He nodded. "Breaking up won't be a problem."

I leaned in to peck him on the lips again. He really was trying. I knew how busy he was with the movie still being in theaters.

"Miranda, you know I lo—"

I slapped my hand across his mouth. Nope. That was an extra complication I didn't need. "Stone, don't. Not yet."

He looked sad but nodded.

Stone couldn't love me. There was no way. We'd never had the chance to truly be together. Surely he realized that?

Or maybe I was the one who was wrong? Plenty of people in secret relationships genuinely loved each other. I mean, I assumed they did. I didn't know anyone else in this situation, but it seemed plausible. Couples in long-distance relationships certainly made it work.

But in my heart, I knew that the problem with Stone wasn't the distance. Or the secrecy. Or Naomi. It was about the fact that I was waiting to feel for him what I felt for Leo. That was my measure of what "in love" should feel like.

Stone went into my bedroom to "wash off the plane smell." I sat on my bed, watching him soap up his phenomenal body through the glass shower door. Willing myself to feel more than I did.

Chapter Twenty-Two

Miranda

NOW

At first, I couldn't process the sight in front of me. The fuzziness of my brain gave new meaning to the term cognitive dissonance. "Stone?"

"In the flesh, babes."

I looked him up and down, as though to confirm. "What...what are you doing here?"

"Figured I'd surprise you," he said. "Hope that's okay." His words were benign, but his face didn't match them. I'd been ignoring him for days.

He looked at Marley, who stood between us.

I recovered my equilibrium. "This is my sister, Marley."

"Nice to meet you," she said, clasping Stone's hand briefly. "I'm a fan. My kids—I teach high school—love you too. Our family was so shocked to find out you knew Miranda."

"I'm very glad to meet you too," Stone replied affably. "To finally put a face to the name. And as far as knowing Miranda, I'm just glad the secret's out."

"Can I have a minute with Stone?" I asked my sister.

"Wha—Oh, yes. Of course." Marley started toward the living room just as James and Leo appeared in the archway.

"Leo! My man," Stone exclaimed, stretching an arm out to clap Leo on the biceps. "Long time no see, bro."

Leo whipped his face to mine. All it took was a subtle shake of my head and a widening of my eyes to let him know I hadn't been expecting our visitor.

Stern-faced, Leo bobbed his head. "Stone." He stepped behind me and put a hand on my shoulder.

"Stone, this brown-haired version of Leo is his brother James, Marley's husband." I introduced the two men, and they shook hands.

Leo kept his possessive grip on my arm. Stone stared at it with consternation, but his expression turned knowing when he eyed Marley and James again, as though to say, *oh right. Leo's touching you because they think you're dating.*

"This is...a surprise," I said. A colossal understatement. Why was Stone here? I patted Leo's hand before removing it, turning to him, Marley, and James. "I'm going to chat with Stone on the porch."

It was cold outside, but I preferred to face the chilly air than to have this conversation where Leo or my sister could eavesdrop.

"Oh, of course," Marley said. "How nice of your...friend to visit." She turned her back to Stone and mouthed, "You sure you're okay on your own?" to me. I nodded.

"I'm filming in Vancouver right now." Stone grinned roguishly. "When I found out Miranda had come to Coleman Creek and was so close, I couldn't resist."

Marley seemed to buy it, and I breathed a sigh of relief. Evidently, she was not registering my lack of enthusiasm at the unannounced appearance of my *friend*.

"Need me?" Leo asked under his breath.

"No. I think it's better if Stone and I speak privately." He frowned. I leaned forward to whisper in his ear. "I don't know why he's here, Bear. It'll be easier if it's only me asking. Keep Marley busy so she doesn't try to listen in."

He grunted softly before turning to Marley and James. "Let's get this tree into the stand."

I heard Marley whisper, "His car pulled up when I was in the carport. Crazy. Stone Caseman in our house."

I grabbed my coat and exited onto the porch with Stone, closing the door behind me with a *snick*.

He reached for me, but I stepped back.

"So it's like that?"

I ignored his pouty tone. "I don't appreciate being ambushed. Why didn't you tell me you were coming?"

"You weren't picking up my calls, and you haven't returned a text in days. We wrapped early today, so I figured I'd drive here to find out why. Make sure you were okay."

From the way he phrased it, I gathered he would not have made the effort if they hadn't finished filming early. As far as grand gestures went, that made this one on-brand for him.

I took a deep breath. Gathered my coat at my chest.

"Stone, I wanted to be in person to have this conversation, and this wasn't the way I planned to do it, but you've kind of forced my hand here." My knuckles turned white as I gripped my lapels. "I think we're done."

He blinked. "Huh? ... Wait, what?"

"I'm going to see this latest PR scheme through, help you with all that, but you and I are over."

He slow-blinked again and put a hand on his hip, arching like I'd struck him in the gut. Sweeping his other hand through his hair, he scrunched his forehead.

"I don't understand, Miranda. What the fuck happened? *Over?* We were fine, like, five days ago when we talked."

"Keep your voice down. As far as my sister and her husband know, we're just friends, so try not to let on that we're breaking up out here." I kept my coat pinched around me as he began pacing. "And for the record, we weren't fine. We haven't been fine in a while."

"What's that supposed to mean? I'm so confused about what is even going on right now." He moved his hands to the sides of his head before fanning them out in the *mind blown* gesture.

Even in his anger, he was still pretty cute. I remained firm in my conviction that Stone was a good guy. He just wasn't the guy for me. "Stone, I wanted to wait until after all this was over, after the holidays. But since you're standing right in front of me, I don't think it can wait. I don't have it in me to pretend one more thing."

"How long have you been planning to break up with me?"

I sighed. "After the summer, I tried to let myself be open to not ending things, but I've known since Halloween."

"Halloween? That's more than a month ago. And you didn't say anything?"

"Like I said, by the time I'd firmed it up in my mind, you'd already left for Vancouver. And I really do care for you, so I wasn't going to just send you some lame breakup text or do it when I know you're trying to concentrate on work. I didn't see any harm in waiting. And then everything happened with me posting the picture, so again, I put it on the back burner."

"But *now* is your moment? When I just drove from fucking Canada to see you!"

"Shhh," I hissed.

"Sorry." He held up his hands, and I knew his contrition was genuine. "But, darlin', I'm reeling here. I thought we were good. Solid."

"If you think about it, I bet you'll see. We were solid—in our way. But we were fooling ourselves to imagine we could survive long-term. Relationships don't work just because two people are companionable, or because it's convenient. I need more for myself and—"

"Fine. If that's what you need, I can do more. Be in town more. I would have done that if I'd known things weren't okay with you."

He really was sweet. But not quite sweet enough.

"I believe you. And you're right that I was okay with it for a long time. And maybe that should have told you something." He started to speak, but I stopped him. "Hear me out. When you're ready to truly fall in love with someone, you're going to want it to be with a woman who gets a little more upset when you're gone so much. Or when you forget to call. Or when you cancel plans. Or when you fake date America's Sweetheart and get photographed with her while you ask your real girlfriend to hide away and keep quiet about everything. Trust me when I say that you'll want someone who would care way more than I did about being a part-time girlfriend. Or maybe you can find another person who wants to be a part-time girlfriend so you can stay focused on your career. But I'm not her anymore."

He dragged a hand over his face. "I can change."

"No. Even if I believed that, you shouldn't have to. Not for this. Not for me. What we have together, as sad as it is to say, isn't worth that."

I didn't bring it into the conversation, but I knew what was missing with Stone. How my thoughts and mind gravitated toward Leo. Leo was the one I wanted to talk to, the one whose opinion mattered. Even now, in the middle of breaking up with the man I'd supposedly been dating for over a year, part of my brain remained on the discussion with Leo that had gotten interrupted.

Stone slumped down onto the porch swing, and I sat next to him. "A part of me knew," he admitted. "When you weren't answering my texts or picking up my calls... That's why I got in the car. I couldn't not know anymore."

"Sorry for not replying. That was petty." Grasping his hand in my own, I laid my head on his shoulder. "But we've had a wonderful ride. I'm grateful I met you that day on the beach. Being with you taught me a lot about what I want from a relationship."

He chuffed. "You mean it taught you I'm not what you want."

I squeezed his hand. "No. We've had plenty of fun, and I don't have any regrets about being with you."

We sat in silence for a few minutes, and I mused on how fitting it was to have such a quiet end to our relationship. I wouldn't call our breakup dignified—it couldn't be when Stone wore a beanie with a *Your Mom Says Hi* patch on it—but it was soft. Unsurprisingly, the romance we'd never brought into the light floated away into the darkness, almost like it never existed at all.

"Was any of it real?" he asked quietly. "I really thought—I just...I really like the way you see me, the way we are with each other."

I gazed fondly at him. "Our bond is real, Stone. It's just not the love connection we've been pretending it is. And we don't have to lose that. If you're okay with it, I'd like to stay friends."

"Really?"

"Sure. The internet already thinks we're *goals* for men and women being friends. Maybe we can make one part of this farce real, after all."

"Just one part, huh?"

"What?"

"Nothing." He used his booted toe to rock the swing back and forth. "I can live with *friends*. As long as I don't have to miss you."

"I won't leave you on read again," I said. "If you call, I'll pick up."

"Same."

"Even if you become a big movie star?"

"Especially then."

I smiled. Stone could be a total potato, but sometimes he said the perfect thing.

He stretched his arms along the back of the swing, gazing out onto the street. Every house had lights and decorations.

"This really is one of the coolest small towns I've ever seen," he said. "I didn't pay much attention last year when I posted your sister's video, but this place is a total vibe."

"You haven't seen anything yet. Can you stay a few more days? We have the Hoopla on Saturday. That's peak holiday around here."

He grunted and shook his head. "I have to get back tomorrow. But I'm glad I came...even if it was to get my heart stomped on." His tone teased, but he couldn't totally disguise the regretful undercurrent. "Miranda?"

"Hmm?"

"I appreciate you waiting to break up in person. I think we deserved that. But now that it's official, can I tell you something...as your friend?"

"Of course."

"If I call you up to hang out in LA in, say, three months, and you tell me you're still dating Leo, I want you to know that I'm not gonna be mad about it."

I squirmed, feeling my cheeks heat. "What?"

"Ten minutes ago, you said I'd see that we fooled ourselves into believing we could be long-term. And I do see. Now. I see clearly for the first time since we met. And I think you do too." He brought my hand to his mouth and kissed my knuckles. "You said you wanted *more*... Darlin', I sincerely hope you get it."

6 WEEKS AGO - HALLOWEEN

It wasn't working.

I'd given it over two months, pushed myself to look past the distance and focus on the times Stone and I were together. Forced myself to enjoy his company, to appreciate his beauty and his snarky sense of humor.

But it wasn't enough.

I did not *love* Stone, and every time we talked, I fell increasingly out of *like* with him.

Plus, I'd stopped sharing his bed.

He'd flown into town twice more since August, and I'd begged off both times. Thank goodness he was thick enough not to question that I'd been on my period more than once in a four-week span.

In my heart, I knew it was memories of Leo that had me balking at intimacy with Stone. I was more excited by the recollection of Leo's unintended hard-on than by the prospect of actual sex with Stone. And that wasn't fair to either of us.

I needed to call it, but I also had to work up to that. Because I was great at keeping things static.

Change required a plan of attack.

Once I broke up with Stone, I'd be left with a job that still felt like being posted on an alien planet, an Instagram brand I was uninvested in, a group of friends who were now closer to casual acquaintances, sisters who lived twelve hundred miles away, and a relationship with my best friend that was a little choppy since I couldn't figure out if I should bring up the time (two times!) he'd jabbed me with his dick.

But first things first, I needed to come to a new understanding with Stone. An understanding of the *we should just be friends* variety.

I sank back on my couch and picked up the candy bowl from the coffee table. Considering I was in an apartment on the second floor, the concept of trick-or-treaters was aspirational at best, so I had to assume I'd subconsciously purchased the Costco-sized bag of Snickers, Three Musketeers, M&M's, and Milky Ways as my personal consolation prize for not being able to go out.

I wasn't a huge Halloween person, but my coworkers had invited me to a party in Pasadena that many of them were attending. I'd been down to go initially, even assembling a passable *Edward Scissorhands* costume for myself. But then Stone told me he'd be flying into town for the night.

Since his Vancouver shoot was scheduled to last months and I didn't know when we'd see each other again, I figured I should take the opportunity to end things with him before the holidays.

It was a bummer because it was the first time I'd been invited to something social with my coworkers that wasn't an official office function, and I worried they'd think I was blowing them off. I knew the *"Sorry. Not feeling well. Can't make it"* text I'd sent sounded flimsy. They didn't know me well enough to realize I'd never cancel plans without a good reason, and they also had no idea most people considered me fun to be around. So far, they'd only seen me nervous, triaging my way through assignments and navigating the new job learning curve.

I'd thought about finding a way to casually divulge my Instagram profile, but I really didn't want to be that girl anymore, even if having tens of thousands of followers might increase my credibility with fellow marketing professionals. Although I'd spent seven years building my online persona as a brand, and had mentioned it during the hiring process, I didn't want to make it a focal point. Or be tied to it.

I wanted them to like me, but I also appreciated that they thought I was boring.

I popped the last bite of a Snickers into my mouth and sighed. Stone should have arrived twenty minutes ago. Pretty sure that was candy number four.

Okay, fine, it was number seven.

STONE: Sorry, babes. Shoshanna found out Naomi is also in town. She wants us to be seen together at some party. Don't worry. I'll just show my face for a bit and then I'll be right over.

I hmphed. Darn it. I could have gone to the other party. *For a bit.*

Two hours later, I sat alone on the couch, two beers and a dozen more candies in, alternating between self-recrimination and anger at Stone.

He wasn't behaving in any way I hadn't condoned over the past year. It just hadn't bothered me before. And maybe that should have been my first clue. For months, I'd misinterpreted not being bothered as not needing to change it.

Rather than let my anger boil, I did the thing I knew would keep me sane and firm up my resolve. The thing that reminded me more than anything else of how shallow my connection to Stone truly was.

I called Leo.

Holding my breath, wondering if he'd pick up or if he had his own Halloween plans, I exhaled when the connection went through. His face filled my tablet, and I clocked the warmth of his expression. Only Leo ever looked at me like that.

"Panda!" he exclaimed. "Hey! ... Happy Halloween! Are you back from the party already?" He scratched his temple. "Or do I need to fly down and take care of some mean girl cubicle dweller for you?"

Right. The last time we spoke, I'd mentioned how nervous I was to finally be invited to a social thing with my coworkers. He knew I'd been walking on eggshells trying to make inroads with them.

Stone didn't know about my plans tonight, but Leo did.

"Actually. I, uh, had to cancel."

His eyebrows rose. "Is something wrong?"

"Yeah. I mean, no. I'm fine. It's just that... Stone came into town."

"Oh." The light behind his eyes dimmed. "He's there now?"

I bit my lip and tried to keep my irritation with Stone from my tone as I responded, "No. He's gotta make an appearance with Naomi. Then he'll be here."

Leo clearly had to choke down other words before muttering, "I see."

"What are you doing tonight?" I asked, switching topics. "I don't think you ever mentioned. No big spooky shindig?"

He held up a bag of the same candy mix I'd purchased and grinned. "Nope. My epic plan is to pick out and eat all the Three Musketeers from this bag. Also, I'm watching the original *Nightmare on Elm Street*. Did you know Johnny Depp is in it?"

I rolled my eyes, grateful to be back on even footing. "Yes, you philistine. Everyone knows that."

We were chatting about our favorite horror movies when I heard an alert on his laptop through my speakers. He clicked into something and frowned.

"What?" I asked.

"It's nothing." Maneuvering his laptop away from his face, he gave me a view of his profile.

"You sure?"

He ran a hand through his hair, the blond strands longer than usual. Finally, he said, "I have my computer set up to alert me when Stone gets mentioned online." I startled, and he defended himself. "Don't give me that look, Miranda. My best friend is in a secret relationship with a guy who is in a public relationship with someone else. And I'm the only one who knows. I just wanted to keep up in case you...needed me. Since I don't really do socials or anything."

The thing was, I believed him. I knew he was just looking out for me. Still, I recognized a knot of shame in my belly, thinking about how Leo had seen all the pictures of my boyfriend laughing, kissing, and going out with another woman.

It might have been irrational—probably the result of beer and candy on an empty stomach—but I resented the fact that Leo had seen those photos.

Despite already deciding to end things with Stone, I felt the need to justify myself.

"You know all that with Naomi is fake, right? It's just PR."

"I know." He gave me a soft look through the camera, facing it directly again. "I only want you to be okay."

Was that pity in his voice?

I pursed my lips before whooshing out a breath. "So what did your computer alert you to?"

His eyes darted to the right, like he was looking at something else on his screen. "A pic of Stone and Naomi at a Halloween party tonight. No big deal."

I opened my phone, and it popped up right away on my feed. Stone and Naomi at some producer's home in the Hollywood Hills. Dressed in a couple's costume as ketchup and mustard bottles.

I blinked hard when I saw it.

Forgetting that Leo could see me.

"What's wrong?" he asked.

"Nothing really," I hushed out, narrowing my gaze at the image. "It's just weird, you know. Ketchup and mustard. I could almost see it if he was dressed up as, like, a shirtless barbarian and Naomi was a sexy kitten or something." I released a humorless laugh. "This just seems so *wholesome*."

It wasn't real. The strain in Stone's eyes and the tightness of his jaw didn't escape me. I knew what it looked like when he didn't want to be somewhere. But it would look very real to anyone else.

"You're upset," Leo stated flatly.

I nodded. "I'll be okay. It just wears on me sometimes."

Seeing my boyfriend so committed to this act with Naomi reminded me again how I'd allowed myself to become a ghost in my relationship. Knowing I was going to end things with Stone, I found it easier to sit with my reaction to the picture. I'd be off this train soon.

But Leo didn't know that.

"Panda," he whispered. "Please. I hate this for you. Hate that he makes you feel this way. This isn't something you should have to live with."

It had been a long time since Leo voiced that sentiment out loud, even though his objections to Stone had never diminished. Part of me wanted to inform him that I'd decided to end my relationship, but Stone deserved to know first.

"It's fine, Bear. I'm fine. Promise."

His expression fell. He'd heard—and obviously misinterpreted—the resignation in my voice.

"I don't believe you," he said, gritting his teeth. "I see how this is getting to you, and now I have to wonder how many times it happens when I don't see it." The camera angle changed, and he placed his laptop on the coffee table. His disembodied torso filled my screen as he stood. "How many times have these pictures made you miserable?" he demanded, arms waving in front of him. "You're asking a lot of me to watch this and not be infuriated on your behalf."

"Who's asking you to do that? Certainly not me." As much as I understood that Leo was coming from a good place, this wasn't what I needed right now. My tone pitched higher. "I don't need you to lecture me about Stone."

"Are you sure?" he growled, flopping back down on the couch. "Because it feels like someone needs to. I thought staying quiet was the right thing to do. But maybe that makes me a terrible friend. Maybe I should have been pushing you on this all along."

I huffed. "I guarantee you I do not appreciate being pushed. Not then, and definitely not now. This"—I flicked my finger back and forth between my chest and the camera—"isn't helping. You've made your position clear. I know exactly where you stand on my relationship with Stone. No good can come from your reminding me. Now you're just making me angry."

"But what kind of friend am I to just…just…stand by while—"

"The kind of friend who respects my will! The kind of friend who truly knows me, and who knows my mind. Dammit, Leo! I don't need you to tell me I'm wrong. Or right. I'm a grown woman, and I get to make choices all on my own, even if you disagree with them. Even if they turn out to be wrong!"

"So I'm supposed to just watch you teeter on the edge of a cliff and say nothing?"

I tried to slow the beating of my heart. "Maybe not every cliff, but when it comes to Stone, you have to trust me to make my own decisions. Even if it means watching me fall."

"I don't know if I can do that anymore," he rasped. "Sometimes it feels like I'm enabling you."

Something about the way he said it—like I was a recalcitrant teenager he needed to steer away from *bad life choices*—rubbed a raw place in me. It scratched below the surface of the Miranda who made a point of never being *too much*. The happy, perky, undramatic, flat-dimensioned Barbie most of the world saw.

"The only thing you're enabling right now is my getting pissed at you—"

"Why?! You're only pissed because you know I'm right. And because you know I'm going to love you all the way through it. Besides, I'm not the one you're mad at—"

"Leo, you need to stand down—"

"If you need to make me the bad guy because you don't feel like you can yell at Stone, then do it! Get pissed at me. I can take it. But don't pretend you don't see this situation for what it is!"

"And what's that?" I folded my arms, feeling my blood race through my veins.

"Totally fucked up! It's time to call it! Get out. You don't have to put up with this shit. You have options—"

His words cut off abruptly as his chest rose and fell.

Options.

An unspoken understanding reared up between us. A heavy burden fueled by countless conversations and nights spent in each other's arms. But this time, the truth of it wasn't just in my mind. It was written across his face as well.

We would be together if he weren't asexual.

And even though it was irrational, I suddenly felt angry with Leo for not being able to give me what I wanted from him.

That was why I couldn't let him have the satisfaction of telling him I knew Stone was bad for me, that I'd already decided to end things.

Leo wasn't wrong. He was the only person I ever allowed myself to go off on, because I knew he would never walk away from me. But at that moment, that knowledge made me bitter.

I resented loving him almost as much as I loved him.

"Don't fucking tell me I have *options*! Not about Stone. Not about anyone. Since you can't give me what I need, you don't get a say in what comes next!"

He reared back as if I'd slapped him, and I felt the echo of my words like a physical force.

For nearly two years, I'd been so careful never to make him feel deficient for being who he was, to never push on his most sensitive nerve. And now, I'd gone and done exactly that.

"Leo—"

He shook his head aggressively. "I wish... I wish I could give you everything, Miranda. More than anything, I wish that."

I felt the heat under my skin drop from a boil to a simmer. "Okay. Let's take a step back. I'm sor—"

"No," he said softly. "No. Don't do that. You're so good at making things neat. And I'm telling you that it is okay to rage. You always put the pins back in the grenades. You don't need to make me comfortable. I can take it."

My shoulders trembled.

"What do you want me to do?" I asked dully. "Call you names? Curse you out?"

"No. I want you to know it's okay to be mad. If you get mad enough, maybe you'll demand more for yourself."

My molars clenched. "I'm going to do exactly what I think is right. I'm clear on your position, but I can take it from here."

"Shutting me down won't make this any better."

"Oh, and fighting with you will?"

"I prefer that to your accepting being treated like shit." He ran a hand through his hair. "I feel like I have to keep trying here. Even if you hate me for it."

"Well, I don't want to get to that point."

I'd said something awful, and Leo's reaction was to love me through it. He thought he was making me see the light about Stone, but all he'd really done was show me how much he cared.

I couldn't shut off wanting him.

And that was probably the only thing I could ever hate him for.

He blew out a careful breath. "You know I'm not judging you, Miranda. Or your choices. I'm just worried about you."

"Well, you don't have to be." He needed to stop being so understanding. "I don't know why I called. And I'm not really mad about the picture—"

"Are you trying to convince me or yourself?"

"You know what, Leo? I can't deal with this right now. And that's on me. Because I'm the one who called. I shouldn't have."

"I never said that."

"Just stop, okay? Let's just hang up and cool down and talk later."

He paused before finally nodding. "Alright. I'll call you tomorrow. Happy Halloween."

"Night, Leo."

We hung up, and I went to bed. Feeling like utter shit. Surprisingly, I fell asleep quickly. Then again, I'd never wanted to put a cap on a day more.

STONE CAME IN DURING THE NIGHT, bearing flowers and apologetic words. I huffed and rolled over.

In the morning, I slept late. He was eating breakfast when I came out of the bedroom. His duffel sat by the door.

"You're leaving?"

"In about an hour," he replied, munching a spoonful of cereal. "I wish we had more time, but I have to jump on a Zoom in five minutes." He padded over and gave me a kiss on the forehead.

I studied his big smile and his sweet, uncomplicated face. After my fight with Leo, I wasn't in the mental headspace to break up with him. It would need to wait until the next time he was in town. I supposed that was okay. It had kept this long.

"Sorry I got in so late last night, babes," he offered sheepishly. "There were a lot more VIPs at the party than I was expecting, and Naomi offered to make a few introductions."

I snorted. "It's fine. Since you're jumping on a call, I'm gonna grab a shower."

Stone was sitting at the kitchen island, sipping coffee, when I came out of the bedroom twenty minutes later.

"Meeting over?" I asked.

"Rescheduled." He shrugged. "Oh—Leo called while you were in the shower."

Memories of last night rolled over me. Acid churned in my throat, reminding me of words I desperately wished I could take back. Willing myself to act nonchalant, I asked, "You picked up?"

"Yeah. I know he's basically your family, and since he knows about me, I figured it was okay. In case it was an emergency, you know, since he was calling and not texting."

"I understand. But...what did he say?"

"Nothing. Said he'd text later."

Stone left for LAX after eleven. Hopefully, he'd get a few days off soon to come home so I could do what needed to be done.

But my impending breakup wasn't the main thing on my mind. For the rest of the day and into the night, I paced around my apartment, picking up my phone and putting it down. Alternately waiting for Leo's text and dreading it.

But he never texted.

Not that day.

Or the next.

Or the next.

No calls either.

And I was too scared to call him. Too scared that I might discover I'd lost the best thing in my life.

I went to work, trying to be friendly with my still-chilly coworkers. I went on a hike outside the city and posted the pictures to @theadventurousmiranda. That made me feel worse.

Weeks passed, and I felt hollower and hollower.

I was so good at faking, I didn't think anyone noticed. Marley and Maureen seemed hesitant about leaving me alone for Thanksgiving, but I assured them I was looking forward to it and too bogged down with work, anyway. My college friends invited me to a Friendsgiving, but putting on a cheerful face for them was an absolute nonstarter.

Stone never got away for a visit. I muddled through a few calls with him, but mostly I brooded and let the empty feeling take hold. The thought that I might have pushed Leo too far had me reeling.

The night before Thanksgiving, halfway through a vodka bottle and at the bottom of a french fry carton, I opened my Instagram app and began scrolling through my photos.

I might not be happy, but if there was one thing I was good at, it was pretending.

Chapter Twenty-Three

Leo

NOW

By some miracle, I managed to keep my mind focused on holding the tree upright. Marley and James knelt by the base, trying to secure the metal screws into the trunk. Oscar and Bambi observed from their rug in front of the fireplace, staring at their owners with *we can't believe you brought a tree into the house we're not allowed to pee on* energy.

It took several attempts to get the tree secured without an obvious tilt. I appreciated the distraction, since a not insignificant part of me wanted to bum-rush Miranda and Stone on the porch.

Maybe having him show up was the reminder I needed to keep my selfish desire for her under wraps. I'd had my chance, and it was nearly two years ago.

I wished I had figured out before then that I was the type of person whose feelings developed over time, that, in fact, time was the only way feelings could develop. If I had known that was a possibility, I could have given her the information and let her decide if she wanted to be patient, to see if more than friendship grew between us.

But I hadn't done that. I'd drawn a line in the sand that first weekend in my apartment, telling her I wanted friendship and only that. When I'd disclosed my asexuality a few months later, she'd bravely admitted she would have been open to something between us. But by the time she started dating Stone last fall, our moment had passed.

And yet...

She clearly wanted the truth from me. I'd been about to confess when Stone showed up.

After we got the tree set up, Marley sat on the couch to admire it. "Looks good. We can put the lights on tomorrow."

James gazed at it too. "Do you think if we stare at it hard enough, it'll decorate itself?"

"Decorating can wait a day or two." Marley laughed.

There were already two other trees in this house brimming with ornaments, lights, and garland. How much stuff did she have?

Marley smirked, reading my mind. "I have infinite capacity to Christmas-ify the house, Leo."

"I don't doubt it."

James picked at something on his shirt. "Shoot. I'm covered in sap."

"I guess that's a sign for us to take a rain check on date night," Marley said, patting him on the belly. "You need a shower, and I don't know if our unexpected guest is going to be staying." She eyeballed the front door.

"I admire your restraint," James said. "I know you want to listen."

"Do you blame me? I can't believe Stone Caseman is at our house. I'm not a superfan or anything, but I don't think we've ever had a celebrity in Coleman Creek."

"He's not that big of a celebrity," I muttered. "In Los Angeles, he's barely a blip."

"But you've known this whole time that they're friends?" James gave me a meaningful glance. He hadn't brought up the conversation we'd had after the wedding, but I knew he had questions about how I'd gone from not even realizing I was demi to dating Miranda.

"They've only been friends since last September," I answered. "Not the whole time I've known her."

James's cheek ticked up. "Thanks for the clarification."

I glared at him.

"Well, I can't believe neither of you ever mentioned anything," Marley said.

"More Miranda's call than mine. And I think you can answer your own question. All this attention she's getting now. She didn't want any of it."

"I understand." Marley nodded. "As outgoing as Miranda's always been, even with her Instagram, she's never been a fame-seeker."

"True," James added. "I'm just curious why Stone is here. I mean, Will's my best friend and I love him, but when he's in Seattle, I don't just make the five-hour trek to pop in unannounced to say howdy."

The front door opened and closed as James spoke.

"It's my fault," Miranda announced, coming into the living room. "I wasn't replying to Stone's texts and calls about everything going on, so he drove down to check on me. He's filming outside Vancouver, so it wasn't too crazy of a drive."

"Did he leave?" James asked, looking over her shoulder toward the door.

"He got a room at the Hampton since he needs to head back in the early morning."

"He drove all this way to have a twenty-minute conversation with you?"

"Uh-huh," Miranda answered Marley's question but kept her gaze on me.

"What about?"

Miranda frowned at her sister. "I just said. Everything going on. Friend stuff, Marls. *Private* stuff."

"Sorry. I wasn't trying to pry. It's just weird, but... You're okay?"

"Everything's fine. Like I said, it's on me that I didn't respond to him sooner. Obviously, he's concerned about what people are saying about us. As much as my accidentally posting the photo was the catalyst for all this, he blames himself for putting public scrutiny on me."

Countless times over the past few days, I'd seen her deny Stone's call requests and sigh over his texts without replying. I'd assumed she'd been talking to him when I wasn't around. Apparently not.

"Why weren't you responding to him?" Marley asked gently.

"Just being sulky," she said, lifting a shoulder. "Not my finest hour. I am a little teed off that all this happened, and especially how it affected my job. You think I'm all kittens and fresh-baked banana bread, but I can be as passive-aggressive as the next person if I'm pushed hard enough. I figured he'd be irritated. I didn't think he'd get in a car and drive here."

Everything Miranda said made perfect sense. Marley and James seemed to take her explanation at face value. But I could tell—it wasn't the truth. Or at least, not the whole truth.

"Did you make it right with him?" James asked.

"We're good," Miranda said. "Our *friendship* is back on solid ground." She emphasized the word in my direction. "But once we resolved things, he was wiped out from his drive, so I told him to go to the hotel." Her eyes softened as she told Marley and James, "Sometimes he has trouble being himself around new people, and I think he was just too tired to play the part of Stone Caseman tonight, if you know what I mean."

"Man, it sounds like being a celebrity sucks," James said. He twirled a strand that had fallen from his man-bun before grimacing. "Dang. Now I have sap in my hair."

"Stone seems okay with the attention most of the time," Miranda said with a smile. "But I gave him a pass tonight." To her sister, she added, "I'll plan it so Stone is in town for longer some other day."

A sick feeling swept over me. I'd hoped that Stone's hasty exit, combined with the fact that she hadn't been answering his messages, meant that she was waking up to their situation. But if she was planning on introducing him to her family, maybe I'd misread?

Marley pushed James down the hallway. "C'mon, big guy. Let's get you in the shower and take care of the sticky stuff."

Miranda coughed. "That...didn't sound right, Marls."

"Definitely dirty," I agreed.

James pumped his eyebrows at me as he followed his wife to their bedroom, Oscar and Bambi trailing behind. A moment later, the door closed with a *snick*.

Miranda turned to me. "Alone at last."

I snorted. "Understatement. That was quite the interruption."

She walked toward me. "But I haven't forgotten what we were talking about before Stone showed up."

"And I want to discuss that, Panda. Except first you need to tell me the real reason you haven't been responding to him these past few days."

She didn't hesitate. "I needed the distance… To know for sure."

Taking me by surprise, she wrapped her arms around my waist and pressed her body against mine.

My immediate reaction nearly knocked me off my feet. Electricity zipped down my spine.

"Know what for sure?" I murmured.

She lifted herself on her toes and nipped at my chin. I felt the softness of her lips as they traveled to my cheeks and jaw. Mouthed my neck. Finally, she lowered herself and mumbled into my shirt. "I needed to know which one of my boyfriends was the fake one."

I froze, still as a statue. Her words lingered in the air, teasing the edge of my mind. Giving me hope.

The buzzing in my ears amplified and there was no way Miranda could miss the rapid-fire rhythm of my heart beneath her nose. I swallowed, a golf ball of emotion clogging my throat, almost painful as it worked its way to my lungs.

"And did you figure it out?" I whispered.

Instead of answering, she tilted her head back.

Keeping her arms around my waist, as though to reassure me—or stop me from retreating—she asked, "After we had our fight on Halloween, you called the next day, but you never called back. Or texted. Why?"

I squeezed my eyes shut, wanting to give her the truth while still barely understanding it myself.

"When Stone picked up, it reminded me that he's your boyfriend. And I realized it wasn't fair of me to…insert myself. The way I'd pushed you during our call. I meant what I said—it has been hard to watch him keep you a secret. But when he answered,

I realized that I had other objections, different motives for trying to get you to see how unworthy he is. And I felt like I needed to get a handle on those before I tried to…patch things up between us."

"What motives, Bear?" she asked quietly.

My mouth opened, but no words came out.

I'd stuffed it down for so long. Denied myself even before I knew that's what I was doing.

She recognized my indecision. Gently, she prodded, "That night, when you said I had *options*, what did you mean exactly?"

This question was easier. "That you didn't have to be with Stone. You could be with someone else."

"Who?" The word fluttered from her lips, barely audible.

Again, I got stuck. I'd lived so long not letting myself imagine the possibility, let alone voice it.

"Who, Leo?" She leaned into my chest and tightened her arms around me, drifting a finger into my back belt loop.

"Miranda—"

I groaned as her mouth trailed up my Adam's apple, leaving a path of heated skin as she planted tender kisses along my neck.

"You never gave me an answer before," she said, moving one hand forward to squeeze my waist. "Are we just friends? … Or something else?"

"Mir—"

Suddenly, her hand stopped moving.

She pulled away.

It happened quickly, as though someone had thrown a bucket of water on us.

I stared down at her. One second, she'd been like a siren, and I'd never felt so *seduced*. But now, her expression was more *disoriented*.

She worried her bottom lip with her teeth.

"Panda?"

Her forehead tipped onto my chest.

"I'm sorry, Leo." She sighed. "I don't know what I'm doing, and I'm so out of my element. I was trying to be…sexy, I guess. Because I'm pretty sure I'm not wrong about what's happening here." Almost guiltily, she continued, "But I just realized the playbook with you might be different. Something is changing between us, but I shouldn't assume that means you want me to…touch you. I don't want to do anything that doesn't feel good to you."

I gazed at her. She didn't want to risk hurting me.

She wanted to know how to be with me.

And that understanding helped me be honest.

"For the record, I loved everything you were doing just now." I stepped back and put my hands on her shoulders, meeting her gaze. "When I said you had options, I meant that I am an option. Me." Breath whooshed from my lungs. "Over the summer, I figured out that I'm not as ace as I thought I was. At least not when it comes to you. It feels selfish to say it because I don't know exactly what I'm capable of. But I know I want you. As a man. As…a lover. Watching you with Stone made me crazy—not just because he didn't deserve you, but also because I was jealous. I didn't call back after Halloween because I was confused about how honest I should be. I'm not anymore. Cards on the table, Panda. I want you. And I know you well enough to know you wouldn't be kissing my throat and pushing me like this if you hadn't just broken up with Stone on your sister's front porch—" I paused, and she nodded. "I guess that's where we stand now."

"You want to be with me? Be my boyfriend for real?"

"I've always been yours, Miranda. Boyfriend is just a new title. You are the person I've been waiting for all my life. And that's true whether we're friends or something more. You're everything."

Her face lit up, and she placed her palms on my chest. "And your asexuality?"

"Still feels true. Evolving, maybe. There's another label, demisexual, that might be more fitting, but to be honest, I don't really care about having a specific word for it."

She hugged me again. "Then you don't have to. It's nobody's business anyway. Never has been."

The negative associations I'd internalized about my asexuality had kept me from deepening my relationships with friends and coworkers. Even my parents and James.

"I don't need a label," I declared. "All I need to know is that the thought of being with you brings me joy rather than anxiety, and you're the only woman I've ever felt that way about. I don't know if I'll ever have a huge sex drive, but if you still want to be with me, knowing that, then I'm the luckiest guy in the world."

"Leo, I meant what I told you a long time ago. I like sex. But it's not the most important thing. And not having lots of it wouldn't be a deal-breaker. You're safe with me to be honest about whatever you're feeling."

"I know, Panda." I kissed her on the nose. "And if I told you that I want to be with you, but I don't know exactly how I want to be touched, or how often, what would you say?"

"I'd say that you just need to tell me what you would enjoy and what you want. I'll do the same, and we'll see from there. It doesn't matter if we have to muddle through. Loving you and having you as my partner is more important than whatever we get up to in the bedroom."

"Muddling through sounds like fun." I laughed.

She grinned. "If there's anything my lukewarm relationship with Stone taught me, it's what it looks like when a couple burns hot. That's what you and I have—heat. It has nothing to do with sex."

"Well, then, hopefully you won't be too disappointed to learn that I'm actually pretty interested in the sex part of things. That seductress routine you were doing earlier—? Next time, you don't need to stop. Don't hold yourself back because you're worried about my reaction. As long as it's you, I want it all."

"You're sure? And you'll tell me if something changes?"

I took the lead, running my fingers up her arms before cupping her face with both hands. "I'll tell you. You have my word that I'll never hold anything back from you again. Even if it's awkward or uncomfortable. Because I know we can make it through anything."

"I know so, too."

"Good. Then let me start by saying something that makes me incredibly nervous."

She pressed a kiss into my palm. "I've got you, Bear. Shoot."

"I'm done pretending. I want to take my very real girlfriend to bed."

Chapter Twenty-Four

Miranda

NOW

There were so many things that might have made going to bed with Leo awkward. I'd just broken up with Stone. Marley and James were sleeping down the hall. And he hadn't had sex in over a decade.

But in the end, it wasn't uncomfortable at all.

Leo had admitted he wanted me in the living room, but from the moment I took his hand and began walking us to our bedroom, his innate shyness and lack of experience came to the surface. He'd clearly surrendered himself to my expertise, such as it was, and that felt like an honor rather than a burden. We were so close and had been through so much together. We knew how to communicate.

All we had to do was find ways to explore each other's bodies that were pleasurable for both of us. And that task didn't seem daunting. More like a fun project.

In our room, I flipped the switch on the mini-Christmas tree on the dresser, casting twinkles of light across the room.

Leo watched hungrily as I undressed. Then he did the same. We stood by the side of the bed, and I allowed myself to look my fill, encouraging him to do the same.

His body was magnificent. I'd already known, had seen and felt it many times over the years, but this was the first time I'd seen everything altogether all at once. His broad chest and the line of hair leading down his belly drew my gaze. His soft cock, pink and thick, swung in a messy bush of dark blond curls. Evidently, Leo did not indulge in manscaping. I loved it.

I dragged a pointer down the center of his chest before trailing it back up to circle his nipples through his chest hair. The silvery strands shone in the moonlight pouring in through the gauzy curtains.

Leo's eyes blazed as he kept them on me.

Making a path through the hair at his groin, I ran my fingertip along the base of his cock, up past his circumcision scar, and over the head, where a dollop of pre-cum leaked. He held steady through my ministrations, but when I gathered the pearly liquid and circled the sensitive tip, his shaft twitched. Gently, I rubbed back and forth across the underside. He bit his lip and grunted, pumping his hips reflexively toward me.

Good to know, Bear.

I moved my finger farther down his shaft, feeling the pulsing vein along the underside. When I reached the base again, the rest of my hand got involved, my fist gripping his length. I stroked a few times and was rewarded by a louder grunt and more pushing into my palm.

My mind conjured so many ideas for what could come next. In a parallel universe, I was dropping to my knees and taking him into my mouth. Or lying down on the bed and pulling him on top of me. But in this world, I felt him shaking with… I wasn't sure. Emotion? Trepidation? Amazement? A combo of everything?

I dropped my hand. "Touch me," I murmured.

He nodded. Unlike me, he was not inclined to be delicate. He raised two eager hands to cup my breasts, palming them roughly, if reverently, squeezing them together as he gazed down like they were his new favorite toy.

Without preamble, his head dipped, and he tongued my nipples, first one, then the other, pressing them together to more easily flit between the two. He took my right nipple into his mouth and sucked firmly, tweaking the peak of my left breast between his thumb and middle finger.

His aggressiveness was unexpected. Unexpected but very welcome. My desire felt like a dam breaking. As much as I wanted to go slow and make sure Leo was comfortable, his raw lust lit me up like an inferno.

He pulled off my nipples and tilted his forehead into my chest, his heated pants causing goose bumps across my collarbone. A noise that sounded a lot like a laugh came from his throat. "Sorry," he said. "I wasn't expecting it to be so intense. Finally being in this moment with you has me going a little insane."

I smiled. "That's a good thing." Looking down, I saw him stroking his erection. He was fully hard now, red tip dripping with pre-cum. Still, he handled it like a foreign object. "How about we get on the bed?" I suggested.

"Alright," he said, nerves seeming to reappear.

Lying down, we continued to touch and caress as we faced one another. He ran a hand along my side before propping himself up to reach behind my thigh. Boldly, he tugged my leg over his hip, crooking my knee and bringing us close enough that his erection dragged across my center, sending a bolt of electricity through me.

"I'm not sure what you want to happen tonight," I said. "Just know that I'm not in any rush. We don't have to do anything you don't want to do. Ever."

"I know. And I'll be honest that I'm a little scared. Even though it was a long time ago, I have memories of...disappointing my partners." He exhaled slowly through his nose.

Placing my hand on his cheek, I reassured him. "It's not like that with you and me, Leo. I promise. You could never disappoint me because you're exactly right for me."

"And only you," he vowed, brushing his lips across mine. I held him there as we experienced our first real kiss. I kept my lips pliant, taking part but not leading, so he could show me what he wanted.

A flare of lust sparked when his tongue danced along the seam of my lips until finally, tentatively, he invaded my mouth. We kissed and kissed, tangling our tongues and laughing as we occasionally came up for air.

I was kissing Leo!

And it was as magical as I'd always known it would be.

After ten minutes, he pulled his head back. I could tell he wanted to say something but was having trouble getting it out.

"What is it?" I asked. "You can tell me."

He nodded, inhaling raggedly. "I know there are other things we can do. With our hands and...our mouths." His cheeks flushed adorably. "But I really want to make love to you. Like, be inside you. I'm still learning how to listen to my body, but I feel certain I'd like to do that."

"I want that too," I said quickly, so he'd know I had no hesitation. "But I don't have condoms."

His forehead raised. "Do we need them?"

"I have an IUD. And I haven't been with Stone in months. I got tested when I had my last physical, which was after that, when I started my job. So as long as it's okay with you, we can go without."

"I don't mean to sound like a caveman, but I'd really like that."

I guffawed. "Something primal in you, Bear? Feeling the need to mark me?"

Even as I grinned, his face remained unsmiling. "Is that so bad? All of a sudden, my world is different. I was happy before, and I made it work for myself. But now I can have a whole different future. And the best part of it is that you're with me. I don't want to freak you out, but I hope you know how much I love you." With intention, he rolled me onto my back and brought himself to a hands-and-knees position above me. "I adore you. And I'm so humbled and honored that you've changed my life. That I get to be with you."

Everything he said ignited my senses. Who didn't want to be loved so completely? But it was important to me that he understood we were on equal footing.

"I'm the lucky one, Leo. And you should know how much I love you too." I reached my arms up and touched his cheeks. "A week ago, I thought I needed to put distance between us because being near you reminded me of all the things I wanted from a relationship but couldn't have. Now I don't have to worry about finding the next best thing. Being with you is my dream. You're everything and exactly enough. And I'm going to make sure you never doubt that."

"Thank you," he whispered, tapping our foreheads. A moment later, he pushed my right knee to my chest and lined up the head of his cock with my entrance. Inch by inch, he pressed in, until he was fully seated. "I'm inside you," he rasped.

"You're inside me."

He kissed me again and began moving, rocking his hips slowly back and forth. Trying to find his rhythm in a dance that was new to him.

And because it was with Leo, it felt new to me too.

He gazed at me as he thrusted, smiling at his own brand of clumsiness, and I grinned back. I'd had sex before. I'd participated in sex before. But this was the first time it felt like I was *sharing* sex with someone.

A tear slipped out of my eye, and he caught it with his thumb, smearing the wetness across my cheek.

"It's a happy one, right?" he asked softly.

"So happy."

He hitched my other leg up, practically folding me in half, and I knew he was getting close. "I want you to come too," he said. "How do I make that happen?"

I smirked. "Another day, remind me to give you my lecture about how sex education needs to include giving boys the memo that making a girl come in missionary position with just your hard cock is sort of a pro-level move."

He chuckled. "Noted. So what can I do?"

I nipped at his chin. "Someday, with practice, we can probably get there. I believe in us. But for now, I'm gonna help you out." I reached down and put a finger on my clit. Surprisingly, I didn't have to do much. Thanks to Leo's size and sheer enthusiasm, I was already close. "Just keep stroking your big hard cock inside me."

"Damn."

"You like the dirty talk?"

"I didn't know until just this minute, but yeah. It's sexy as hell."

"I'll make a list. We have a lot of fun ahead of us, figuring stuff out."

"Looking forward to that."

"Me too."

He stopped talking and began pumping his hips in earnest. Fifteen seconds later, I came hard, shuddering with pleasure.

"Oh fuck!" He cried out as my muscles contracted around him, loudly enough that I put my hand over his mouth, glancing at the bedroom door. "Oh fuck." This time, he whisper-shouted, squeezing his eyes shut. I felt the pulsing of his cock, four distinct shots as he unloaded before collapsing onto my torso.

As much as I liked his weight on me, he was twice my size. I tapped his biceps, and he rolled off. Stretching my arm out to grab his discarded white T-shirt from the floor, I put it under my butt. At his quizzical look, I laughed. "I don't come with a plug, Bear. The minute your dick came out, so did about half of your *deposit*." I winked. "Sex is a messy business sometimes. In a perfect world, we'd have quicker access to hand towels, but sometimes you have to improvise."

"You can joke about it being messy, or awkward, or whatever, but what we just did—it was perfect. I never knew it could be like that."

"It was perfect," I murmured, meaning it. "It's never been like that for me either."

"Really?"

The vulnerability in his voice tugged at me. My heart clenched for early twentysomething Leo trying to figure himself out, being told he was less than. I'd show him that his lack of experience was a chance for us to explore and be playful. Not something bad.

Leaning over and kissing his chest, I snuggled into his side. "Really. You were wrong on Halloween when you implied that I had a lot of options. When it comes to being the best version of myself, there's only one. Only you. Anything else would be playacting."

Chapter Twenty-Five

Leo

NOW

We'd had great weather all week while putting together the booths and preparing Main Street for the Holiday Hoopla. Saturday dawned clear and cool, promising an event where folks could soak up the atmosphere while warding off the chill with hot chocolate and apple cider.

Maureen and Will had come to dinner at the house last night. She told me about a Hoopla during her teen years when it rained so hard that the rides shut down, but people still gathered around the city tree to sing carols and mingle with neighbors.

"It was basically Whoville. Teenage me thought it was so embarrassing," she said. "But I see the charm now."

"A few years ago, my students would have said it was *cringe,*" Marley added.

"They don't say that anymore?" I asked.

"It's acceptable, but not the current word of choice," James answered ridiculously.

"What is?"

In unison, Marley and James responded, "Corny."

"I like that." Miranda grinned. "It's a classic."

"You're a classic," I said, leaning down to kiss the juncture of her neck and shoulder. She giggled. Under usual circumstances, I was as skeptical of *corny* things as teenaged Maureen, but since I'd spent the past few days being openly in love with Miranda—and the nights making love with her—I was in the mood to be charmed.

Like James and Will, who had been dedicated city-dwellers before moving here, I'd succumbed to Coleman Creek's Christmas magic. That was in addition to the fact that, also like them, I was firmly under the spell of one of the Davis sisters.

Being with Miranda physically was a revelation. She never let me get in my head, never indicated that having my bedroom skills be a work in progress was anything other than an adventure.

I felt in tune with my body in a way I'd never been before and was gaining a new understanding of myself.

Last night, after I told her I doubted I'd ever have a high sex drive, that I loved making her come, but wasn't sure my dick would cooperate every night, she scoffed at the notion that I was confessing something terrible.

"I don't care if *sexual congress*"—she curled her fingers—"is a big part of our routine or not, Bear. No one can convince me we haven't been as intimate as any lovers, that you haven't been the other half of me since we met. I honestly could not care less about how often tab A goes into slot B or whatever."

"You're sure?"

"Completely. You are everything I've ever wanted. Exactly as you are."

I believed her. A few more days and I'd stop asking. Maybe.

As soon as we arrived at the Hoopla, Maureen and Will ventured off to film for her channel while James and Marley meandered toward the high school's booth. I saw Daniel there with his guitar. He blushed and nodded at Nan, sitting next to him and speaking animatedly to the group. With the love hearts beaming from his eyeballs, he belonged in the dictionary under the word "yearning." Ah, well. Good luck. He was a senior this year. Maybe he'd finally shoot his shot once he and Nan were both in college. James and Marley had a rooting interest in this, and I realized that I did too, since my brother and sister-in-law spent a fair amount of time gushing about their students. Plus, it was tough not to cheer for an underdog. Especially at Christmas.

"What?" Miranda asked.

I pointed at the booth. "Daniel."

She grinned. "I'm pretty sure Nan knows. Probably the whole town too."

"More power to them. With how I'm feeling, I want everyone to be as happy as I am."

Miranda pulled my coat open, slipping inside and snuggling against my torso. "I love you so much. I'm glad we found our way to each other."

I kissed the top of her head just as Kasen approached, carrying Katy's kids in his arms. Even though Rosie was nearly five, she still fit comfortably in his bent elbow.

"Knock it off, you two," Kasen teased us in a fake-gruff voice. "There are children present."

I reached out to shake his hand, settling for an awkward grab underneath where three-year-old Braxton perched on his forearm. "Everything turned out great, man. Thanks so much for helping me set up."

Kasen squatted to put the kids on the ground. "Hey, I just did what you told me to. The whole town is grateful you stepped in to pick up the slack. Safe to say you're an honorary Coleman Creeker now."

"He's already a Coleman Creeker by marriage," Miranda chirped. "Don't forget his brother is married to Marley."

Kasen flinched but washed it quickly. We'd been talking over the past few days while we worked, and I'd gotten a bit of his history, including some about the eight years during high school and college when he dated Marley. I knew he'd once tried to get her back, but she'd already fallen head over heels for James. They'd all managed to become friends, but I got the impression there was a scab there. At least for Kasen.

Thankfully, most of our discussions had focused on the work. I'd been pleased to discover that he possessed natural carpentry skills. His eye for detail made sense, since he worked as a graphic designer. While I made sure the booths were stable and the lighting and PA systems worked properly, he'd touched up the paint, set up the craft vendors' tables in neat rows with eye-catching displays, and printed fun new menus for the food stalls.

Because we'd had extra time, he also strung up more lights than the event usually had. I'd heard multiple people remark on how magical it was to have the twinkling colors twined around every lamppost, storefront sign, and tree on Main Street.

Braxton tugged on Kasen's leg and pointed at a family nearby. I recognized Travis and Vivienne Bloxham and their children.

"Sen, can we go see Scarlett and Connor?" Braxton asked.

Kasen made eye contact with Travis and hitched his neck toward Katy's kids. Travis nodded. "Sure, Brax. Make sure to hold your sister's hand."

The little boy nodded solemnly. "I will."

"You're good with them," Miranda said. "Katy's lucky to have your help."

Kasen shoved his hands in his pockets. "Like I said before, it's not a thing. They're great kids."

"They are," Miranda mused. She glanced over Kasen's shoulders. "But where is Katy? I know The Landslide closed for the Hoopla."

Kasen frowned. "She had to step away because *he* called." His voice remained level, but his expression thundered.

"Ah," Miranda responded unartfully. What could she say? Even I knew that Katy's ex was a jerk.

"I don't want to gossip," Kasen said, "but since Marley and I already know, I don't think Katy's keeping it a secret that Mike backed out of coming to visit for the holidays. He told the kids he would come for Thanksgiving, then begged off, and a few days ago, he canceled on Christmas." Kasen shook his head and pinched the bridge of his nose. "Then just now, he had the nerve to call and tell Katy he was having a 'little snafu with money.' He asked her to put his name on a few of the gifts she bought."

"That's pretty low." I grimaced.

Miranda huffed. "Also, stupid. Everyone knows kids get all their gifts from Santa."

Kasen's jaw ticked. "That's what she told him. But when it started veering off into a longer discussion about how he also wouldn't be able to produce his support payment—again—I grabbed Rosie and Brax to give her some privacy."

"Good call," Miranda said.

"Literally the least I can do," Kasen said gruffly. Under his breath, he added, "Tough to get her to let me help with anything."

I exchanged glances with Miranda, clearly on the same page that we'd ventured well past the line of what was and was not our business. I pivoted to a topic I hoped was more neutral, complimenting Kasen on the new signage he'd produced for the event. Our conversation turned benign—the Seahawks win streak, the weather, the number of times he'd had to read *Frog and Toad* to Rosie—and Kasen relaxed. Ten minutes later, Katy joined us, waving over to Travis and Vivienne.

"Everything okay?" Kasen asked.

She patted his forearm. "It'll be fine. Nothing to ruin our night over." None of us missed the stress in her voice, but I admired her fortitude. "The kids have been asking to ride the merry-go-round and get hot chocolate."

Kasen nodded. "Great. I'd love some cider."

Katy looked at Miranda and me. "Want to join?"

"Thanks," I said. "But we were headed to the park to listen to the carolers."

Katy smiled, shaking her head. "Brax won't go near them. Especially the ones dressed in Victorian garb. He says their big hats are scary."

I chuckled as she and Kasen drifted away.

Miranda and I walked toward the park, which had small groups of carolers stationed about every fifty yards. "I didn't realize we had a plan to listen to the singing." She quirked an eyebrow.

"I had to think fast." I defended myself. "Not to be rude, but I really want to be alone with you."

"Me too."

I kissed her on the nose. "Panda, I have to tell you something, and it might seem like it's coming out of left field."

My tone was light, so she knew nothing was truly wrong.

She smiled. "Good thing I'm in the mood for a curveball. What's up?"

"When we were talking to Kasen, a thought popped into my head. It's not fully formulated, obviously, but I guess I realized that I consider him a friend now. We got along really well this past week while setting things up. And I don't think James would mind that I'm friends with Marley's ex."

Miranda tilted her chin up. "He won't mind. Marley and Kasen are on great terms now, and I know she wants the best for him."

"That sounds like Marley."

"Is that what you wanted to say?"

"Not exactly. More like, I thought about how I consider Kasen a friend now, and I care about Katy and other people I've met here. I'm even crossing my fingers for Daniel and Nan. It's like the Coleman Creek vibe has taken a serious hold of me."

"O-kay?" she drawled slowly. "It's great that you're making connections, but I'm not following where you're going with this."

"Like I said," I spoke quickly. "It's not fully formed yet, but I think maybe I could be happy in Coleman Creek. James and Marley are here, and they'll have kids eventually, plus the only thing grounding me to Tacoma is my job and a few friends."

"What about your parents?"

I released a long sigh. "Honestly, years ago, before I concluded—very, very wrongly—that I'd never be in love with anyone, I hadn't envisioned staying near Seattle. But once I started thinking that my life would be spent solo, and I was struggling to make meaningful friendships because I didn't want anyone to figure out about me—"

"I hate that you ever felt like you needed to be ashamed or embarrassed." Miranda frowned.

"It's okay. Truly. The point is that I thought it might be a good idea to stay by my parents to maintain that sense of family. Plus, James was still in Seattle at that time. Now, I feel like I wouldn't mind starting over. My parents would understand. In fact, I bet they'd encourage it."

"So you want to move to Coleman Creek?"

"No. I'm just saying it's something I'd support if you ever wanted to. Obviously, my home is with you. If you want to stay in Los Angeles, then I'll start planning to move there. But I kind of get the feeling that you don't?"

She sucked in her bottom lip. "A part of me would love to come home. But I also feel like I want to prove myself at my job first. I know I can be good at it, that I can earn my coworkers' respect and Walt's trust. It's nice to know Coleman Creek is on the table, but we just did this big, huge thing—making the leap into a relationship. We don't need to change everything all at once."

"As long as we're committed to being together, we can keep talking." I lowered my voice, holding her tightly. "But just so you're clear, nothing about this leap feels too big to me. I'm not scared or worried or overwhelmed. I was all those things without you, but with you... With you, I can do anything. You might be @theadventurousmiranda, but I'm the one starting the most exciting journey of my life. All because of you."

"I love you," she hushed out. "We're going to be together forever, aren't we?"

"Yes, my beautiful, precious love. We're going to be together forever."

In the background, chaos reigned as Victorian carolers belting out "God Rest Ye Merry Gentlemen" competed with an a cappella rendition of Ariana Grande's "Santa Tell Me." I heard none of it, fully focused on the woman in my arms.

Miranda kissed me, and it was as much of a revelation as the dozens of kisses we'd shared since we declared our love. It was the promise of a future and a memory of the past.

The kiss was late nights laughing and video chatting, lamenting terrible hiking trails and wealthy clients demanding perfection. It was confessions of grief and shame, worries about the future, fears of being stuck in the present. It was power walking past toddlers at Disneyland and shaking a vending machine on the side of the road to get the Three Musketeers stuck on the ring. The kiss was the way she pretended to faint whenever she saw my dystopian paintings, and the secret smile we exchanged when someone mentioned Barbie or Thor. It was shared history, built-up trust, and so much more than just pressing our mouths together.

It was everything. She was everything.

And now we belonged to each other.

For real.

Epilogue

Leo

CHRISTMAS

My parents shook their heads at me and Miranda while exchanging glances with James, Marley, Maureen, and even Will.

The eight of us sat across various seats in the living room. Marley had talked us into putting on the footie pajamas from last year. As ridiculous as I looked in the gingerbread men onesie, I appreciated the do-over as Miranda snapped about five thousand happy selfies of us.

"Pay up," Maureen said to Marley, sticking out her hand.

"Nuh-uh." Marley swatted it away. "You just said there was no way they'd been dating since summer. You didn't guess the part about dating Stone."

"If Maureen's getting paid, I want to get paid," James said.

"No one's getting paid," our mom said. "Besides, you only guessed they weren't really dating at all."

"And you kind of had an unfair advantage there since you knew about Leo being demi-ace," Will reasoned.

"Well, I still can't believe the whole thing," Marley declared. Glaring at Miranda, she said, "Seriously, Stone Caseman?"

Miranda shrugged.

"What were the bets exactly?" I asked.

"They weren't bets. More like conversations you weren't a part of. We knew you guys were hiding something about this whole situation," my dad replied. "We disagreed about what it could be."

"Well, we're not hiding anything now," Miranda said.

"We're aware," Maureen said dryly. "When Will and I decided to stay at the house last night, we forgot the walls were so thin."

I leaned around Miranda to grin at her.

Miranda and I had just told our family the whole story. Even Bambi and Oscar were in the room. There had been a lot to tell—everything with Stone, my reasons for not dating, and some of what had happened between us. We kept the more private details to ourselves but had agreed that our family deserved the truth. They could be trusted to keep it to themselves and not harm Stone.

We had, however, ended the truth-telling with our families. As far as our coworkers and others were concerned, we were sticking to the story we'd given the public.

The interest in Miranda as a potential home-wrecker had dissipated almost immediately after the photos from the arcade. People seemed to prefer the narrative that she and Stone were just good pals. Reaction to pictures of us at the Holiday Hoopla solidified the general lack of interest in the matter.

Miranda told me she still planned to be friends with Stone and possibly even Naomi. I was surprised at how little that concerned me, but I figured if James could be okay with Kasen, I could be okay with Stone.

As though thinking of him had summoned it, Miranda's phone buzzed with a text.

"Stone wants to know if it's okay if he calls me in a few minutes," she said, concern in her voice. "That's pretty unusual for him."

We'd already opened gifts and had no plans for the day other than watching football, so she went into our bedroom to take the call.

I hoped whatever he had to say wouldn't derail what had been a wonderful couple of weeks.

Miranda had received some welcome news on a Zoom call with her supervisors five days ago. Apparently, several of her coworkers had pointed out the mastery of the @theadventurousmiranda persona she'd created, and Walt wanted her to be part of a team focused on expanding the company's business to include younger clientele and new media companies.

She was excited to return in January, eager to continue proving herself. I'd be staying in Tacoma for the time being, burning up I-5 until we figured out a long-term living situation.

Ten minutes later, Miranda poked her head into the hallway, motioning for me to join her.

I followed her into the bedroom, closing the door behind me.

"You'll never guess..." she said.

"He called to tell you about a big sale on surfboard wax? Or give you an update on the weed gummy situation in Vancouver?"

She rolled her eyes. "He called to let me know he's dating someone, and he didn't want to risk my finding out some other way."

"He's giving it a go with Naomi for real?"

Miranda laughed. "Um, no. As much as the public wishes that were true, they barely have anything to say to each other. They're sticking with the plan to break up publicly around Valentine's Day."

"Then who?"

"Shoshanna! When he let her know about our breakup, she admitted her feelings for him. Then I guess she insisted he make it clear to me that she never would have made a move while we were dating."

"You believe her?"

"Uh-huh. Shoshanna is a true boss. She'd respect girl code."

I smiled. "And Stone feels the same way about her?"

"Honestly, it sounded more like he was just sort of fine with it, like he hadn't thought about it, but once she proposed the idea, it made sense. At any rate, he wants to give it a try."

"Leave it to Stone to start a relationship with a proverbial shoulder shrug. I mean, he's a grown man and can do what he wants, but that just seems *odd*," I said.

"But on-brand," Miranda countered. "Besides Stone himself, no one cares as much about his career as Shoshanna. If they're both on the same page there, it might work."

"Still, it sounds so businesslike. Joyless."

Miranda raised her palms. "Stone just isn't in a place right now to put someone else's needs ahead of his own. Businesslike is probably the most he can handle."

"Welp, not our sink, not our dishes," I said. "As long as it doesn't bother you, I don't care who Stone dates."

"It doesn't bother me. I hope someone comes along someday to knock him off his feet, but he's happy focusing on his career right now."

"Just like I'm happy focusing on you." I toyed with the zipper at the top of her onesie.

"Ditto, Bear."

"You know I loved you every minute you were with him. So even if he wasn't doing it the right way, you were always loved."

"I knew that. Deep down. That's what made it *bearable*."

"*Bearable*. I see what you did there."

"I'm dork Barbie now." She twined her fingers with mine. "Cheeseball Barbie? Bad pun Barbie?"

I brought her hand to my lips and kissed her knuckles. "Not Barbie. Just my Miranda."

The End

Acknowledgements

The first people I have to thank are the folks who shared their personal experiences with me. It was important to me to get Leo's journey right. I learned a lot about the spectrum of asexuality and how different people navigate it. As with the other books in the Coleman Creek series, the concept of characters as complicated people striving to be their authentic selves remained at the top of my mind during the writing process. I hope I did them justice.

I want to shout out my author groups who provided excellent tips about pivoting between projects. This year has been a true learning experience in terms of what the "job" of indie author is, including the DIY nature of basically everything.

To my GLA comrades, Aviva, Chun, Erin, Leann, Madison, and Woody—I am so appreciative of your thoughtful embrace of these characters. Your careful beta reads helped with so many things, from plot development to fluency. Thank you!

To the Monday stalwarts, Alexander, Alicia, Dustin, Lila, Marc, Veronica—thanks for your fellowship and great conversation. Looking forward to the next year of talking through projects.

To Jenny at Editing 4 Indies—I can't thank you enough for your work. You have my deepest gratitude. This book would have a lot more "mixed singles" and a lot fewer "mixed signals" if not for you.

To Melissa at Alt 19 Creative—thank you so much for the beautiful cover. The look of this series keeps getting better and better. Sorry about all the back and forth emails about Leo. Beard, no beard, light blond, dark blond, streaks, length, bun, no bun, off-brand Robert Plant. I think we finally got there.

To my real-life friends and colleagues who continue to be my biggest supporters, and who do me the honor of treating this as seriously as I do.

To my readers and the Bookstagram community—I couldn't do it without you. Special thanks to Jaci (@currently_reading101) and Amanda (@booksand_biscuits) for always being lovely and supportive.

Last but not least, to my main man and my not-so-little director. You bring all the main character energy.

About the Author

Rory London is a contemporary romance writer who lives in the delightfully gray Pacific Northwest. She would spend a lot more time writing if there weren't so many books to read. When not engaged in something book-related, Rory is likely drinking large quantities of Dr. Pepper Zero, watching football or baseball (Go Seahawks! Go Mariners!) and using music and podcasts to make it through a gnarly commute.

Rory lives with two other humans who bring laughter, joy, and sarcastic commentary into each day, as well as the world's most lovable dog and three cats who are secretly plotting their revenge.

<u>Connect with Me:</u>
Website: www.rorylondonauthor.com
Instagram: @rory_london_author
Facebook: Rory London, Author
Goodreads: Rory London
Bookbub: Rory London
Book Playlists: Rory London on Apple Music

Also by Rory London

<u>Standalones</u>
The Outline

<u>Coleman Creek Christmas</u>
Christmas Chemistry
Christmas Comeback
Christmas Crisis
Christmas Crossroads (Fall 2026)

<u>The Hope Center Trilogy</u>
Our Last Night

www.ingramcontent.com/pod-product-compliance
Lightning Source LLC
Chambersburg PA
CBHW032348310726
48973CB00007B/1914